Louise Allen has been immersing herself in history for as long as she can remember, finding landscapes and places evoke powerful images of the past. Venice, Burgundy and the Greek islands are favourites. Louise lives on the Norfolk coast and spends her spare time gardening, researching family history or travelling. Please visit Louise's website, www.louiseallenregency.com, her blog, www.janeaustenslondon.com, or find her on Twitter @LouiseRegency and Facebook.

Also by Louise Allen

Snowbound Surrender
'Snowed in with the Rake'
Contracted as His Countess
The Duke's Counterfeit Wife
The Earl's Mysterious Lady
His Convenient Duchess

Liberated Ladies miniseries

Least Likely to Marry a Duke
The Earl's Marriage Bargain
A Marquis in Want of a Wife
The Earl's Reluctant Proposal
A Proposal to Risk Their Friendship

Discover more at millsandboon.co.uk.

A ROGUE FOR THE DUTIFUL DUCHESS

LOUISE ALLEN

MILLS & BOON

First published in Great Britain 2023
by Mills & Boon, an imprint of HarperCollins*Publishers* Ltd,
1 London Bridge Street, London, SE1 9GF

www.harpercollins.co.uk

HarperCollins*Publishers*, Macken House, 39/40 Mayor Street Upper, Dublin 1, D01 C9W8, Ireland

A Rogue for the Dutiful Duchess © 2023 Melanie Hilton

ISBN: 978-0-263-30505-0

03/23

This book is produced from independently certified FSC™ paper to ensure responsible forest management.
For more information visit: www.harpercollins.co.uk/green.

Printed and Bound in the UK using 100% Renewable Electricity at CPI Group (UK) Ltd, Croydon, CR0 4YY

For the Quayistas and our Friday evenings.

Thanks for getting me through again.

Chapter One

October 1st 1816, Vine Mount House, Norfolk

Her Grace Sophia Louisa Andrea Delavigne, Duchess of St Edmunds, sat on the great carved chair that her dignity required, took a deep breath and glanced down to make certain that her hands lay still and betrayed nothing but calm assurance. The sight of the lilac silk of her gown gave her a thrill of pleasure which made her lose focus for a moment.

Colour. After a year of solid black, she knew it would take more than a week before she stopped feeling delight at wearing colours again…even the muted shades of half-mourning. Little Freddie seemed to be finding it difficult to adjust to the sight of her, but then, he was only a year old and had never seen his mother wearing anything but gowns that resembled a crow's plumage.

Sophie felt a little pang when she remembered his face that morning seven days ago, when he'd reached out to touch her skirts and raised wondering eyes to her face. 'Mama?'

'Yes, it really is Mama,' she had told him. 'Look what a pretty gown I have for your first birthday.'

He had smiled up at her, the blue eyes so like his father's wide as he surveyed her. Then he had given that naughty chuckle—the one he had most definitely not inherited from the late Duke.

'Ahem...'

She looked up to see her steward, Duncan Grant, waiting just inside the door.

'Mr Grant.'

'Your Grace,' said her childhood friend, with all the formality he used towards her in public. 'He has arrived.'

'Then please show him in.'

She told herself that she must have confidence, that anyone whom Duncan trusted and recommended would deal, somehow, with the situation.

'He makes problems go away,' Duncan had said when she had gone to him six days ago, white and shaking with shock and anger at what she had discovered. 'He is exceedingly good at that.'

That had been reassuring—but then Duncan had always been stolidly comforting, from the time when he, the Vicar's eight-year-old son, had fished Lady Sophia Masterton, aged five, out of the village duck pond and managed to smuggle her back into the castle without anyone seeing her—not even Nanny.

If he had found her someone with experience of making problems go away, then the man was no doubt a fatherly ex-Bow Street Runner, or perhaps a large, efficient military man. Duncan had known him in the army, after all, although he had been strangely reluctant to go into details.

'Nicholas Pascoe, Your Grace.'

So, a Cornishman, Sophie thought, and then ceased to think for one disconcerting moment as a figure stepped past Duncan and into the room.

This was not a middle-aged Runner with a red face and a paunch. Nor was this a broad-shouldered, sabre-wielding army officer. This man did not make her think of sabres at all.

Tall, dark, elegant and very dangerous.

A human rapier stood before her, his eyes steady on her face. Why, then, did she have the impression that he might have described the room and everything in it in perfect detail—herself included?

But she was the Duchess of St Edmunds. She had been trained for twenty years to fill a position of the highest rank and had lived it for four, and that experience had taught her never to betray her true feelings. Perhaps that had been the most important lesson of them all.

'Mr Pascoe. Good morning.'

'Good morning, Duchess. And it is simply Pascoe.'

Only an acquaintance of rank might address her as Duchess, rather than Your Grace. By doing so, this... this *adventurer* was implying that he was not just a gentleman but an aristocrat. It was part of her duty to know the contents of the *Peerage* inside out and to have a good grasp of that even fatter volume the *Landed Gentry*. There were quite a few Pascoes in both, but this one she could not place.

Sophie allowed faint surprise and displeasure to show. He looked back steadily, quite unabashed. A Duchess did not blush when a man looked at her, and this one's gaze held nothing lascivious...nothing even mildly impertinent...yet she could feel the warmth gathering in her cheeks. Somehow she knew he was very aware of her as a woman. And she was certainly exceedingly aware of him as a man.

'Please, take a seat. Pascoe.'

'I prefer to stand, ma'am.'

Curse him. That meant she had to continue looking at his long-legged, slim-hipped, black-clad elegance in its entirety. His shoulders were quite adequately broad, she realised. It was simply that he felt no need to swagger and display them.

'I believe Mr Grant has explained to you that I have a situation that needs resolution,' she began.

'He told me that you have a problem, Duchess. My occupation is the removal of problems.'

'And how do you achieve that?'

'The means need not worry you, Duchess. But discreetly and permanently, I can assure you.'

'And legally, I trust?' she interjected, suddenly imagining him disposing of bodies with cool efficiency.

'Certainly—if you insist,' Pascoe said, his expression unchanging.

'Of course I insist,' Sophie said, before she realised that he was teasing her. Quite how she knew that she was not certain, but it was unsettling. People did not tease duchesses—even that rare creature a young, widowed duchess.

'Perhaps you would explain the nature of the problem that requires resolution?' he said.

The calm tone was the one used by her doctor when enquiring about the symptoms of a mild stomach upset. She had steeled herself for this—the necessity of describing details of her marriage that she would very much rather never speak of to anyone.

'I was the late Duke's second wife,' she said steadily. 'The first Duchess was, sadly, childless.' That was common knowledge, of course. The rest, less so. 'The late Duke had maintained a mistress for many years. The same…person throughout that time. She had her own separate suite in all the Duke's homes, including this one.'

That did produce a reaction. One dark brow rose

slightly. That a nobleman had maintained a mistress would come as no surprise to anyone—that she had occupied the same household as his wife was something else altogether.

'A situation that you tolerated?' Pascoe asked.

'A situation that I inherited. My husband was thirty years my senior.' It was her turn now to raise an eyebrow. 'I am sure you will appreciate that ours was hardly a love match of the kind in which His Grace would totally change his way of life for me.'

She had been raised to know her duty and to do it. And that was to be the perfect wife of a man of high rank, to bear his children—sons, of course, and as soon as possible—and to ensure that his life and his household ran exactly as he wished. That did not include attempting to remove his mistress of more than fifteen years—a woman he would have wed if she had been a lady of rank as opposed to a ravishingly pretty opera dancer.

The Duke had known his duty too, and that meant marriage to a lady of impeccable breeding. The fact that his first wife had been both barren and sickly had been a blow to him. Not, Sophie suspected, because of any great affection between them, but because he desired an heir above all things. Within six months of her death, in defiance of the rules of mourning, he had married her, Lady Sophia Masterton, eldest daughter of the Marquess of Radley, aged twenty to his fifty.

'My husband, as I am sure you are aware, was very active politically—a man of great influence within the government and a confidant of the Prince Regent. He knew everyone and, what is more to the point, he knew their secrets and their weaknesses.' She took a deep breath. 'My husband kept diaries all his adult life. Very full, very detailed, very frank journals. I think I had best show you the extent of the problem.'

She stood and Duncan Grant, who had been standing unobtrusively in the shadows at the back of the room, opened a door in the panelling for her to pass though.

'If you will come with me, Pascoe, I will show you the late Duke's study.'

Nick followed the upright figure. Her lilac skirts swished as she walked with a slight provocative sway that was surely unintentional. This woman appeared quite unaware of her own allure.

Grant hadn't told him what to expect, although Nick had done his research and knew the Duchess's age. Grant had not warned him about her beauty, though. Perhaps if you'd known a woman since she was five years old you didn't notice her looks. It was the only explanation. His old army colleague had never shown any signs of poor eyesight or a lack of interest in the opposite sex before.

She was tall for a woman, slender but not lacking in

curves, with dark honey-blonde hair and eyes of a subtle hazel-green shaded by long, dark lashes. Pale skin, slender, elegant hands with only two simple rings. A lady of taste and elegance—and also of considerable restraint, judging by what she had said so far.

The Duchess paused outside a heavily panelled door. 'Has Grant explained to you the nature of the problem?'

'No. Only that something is missing. He told me that you would prefer to explain the issue yourself.'

Something to do with those diaries, he guessed. Already he knew she was not the kind of woman to introduce irrelevances into the conversation.

She opened the door and he followed her into a room that might have served as an illustration of a nobleman's study in the first style of elegance in *Ackermann's Repository*. There was a massive desk, heavy velvet curtains at the window, open bookshelves that had the appearance of holding a day-to-day working library—doubtless there would be a much larger collection downstairs—and a few upright leather armchairs.

One tall bookcase with several keyholes had double glass doors. The shelves were filled with volumes bound in red leather with gilt stamps on the spine.

'My husband's diaries,' the Duchess said. She pulled a chain from around her neck and revealed a key.

Nick suppressed the thought that it would be warm

from her skin and watched as she unlocked the doors. As they swung open, and as he drew nearer he saw the gilt lettering was a series of dates.

'At a glance, there appear to be at least fifty volumes,' he observed.

'The Duke began his diaries when he attended Oxford University at the age of eighteen. He frequently filled more than one book a year, especially in recent years. He had a dozen blank volumes bound at a time and would add the date stamps to the spines himself.' She stood, one long-fingered hand on the edge of the door. 'I did not realise that there was anything wrong at first. Naturally, I supervise the housekeeping, including in these rooms which are, at present, unused. It was not until I realised that *she* had gone that it occurred to me to ensure that nothing had been...removed.'

She gestured to the lowest shelf and Nick saw that the last four volumes had nothing on their spines.

'Those are unused. They have been removed from the cupboard over there to make up the numbers.'

'When you say *"she"*, I assume you mean your late husband's mistress?' The Duchess gave a tight nod. 'But I had understood that you discovered the loss only a few days ago. Has she re-entered the house by some means?'

The lips he had thought full and soft hardened into a thin line. 'Under the terms of the late Duke's will she retained the use of her suite in this house for one year after his death. He also left her a town house in London. I took pains not to encounter her for that year. It was easy enough in a house of this size, because her rooms have their own ground-floor entrance. Then, after one year and one day, I went to tell her she must leave. I did not want her in the same house as my son any longer than his father had decreed.'

'And she had gone?'

'Yes. The apartment appeared to have been stripped of anything portable and of value. Her entrance is at the side of the house, and she had her own stables, her own servants. It would have been perfectly possible to accomplish all of that without my staff being aware of it, provided it had been done in the early hours and efficiently. I have every reason to believe she is very efficient.'

'What is her name?' Nick asked. He should have established that at the beginning. This woman was putting him off his stride.

'She calls herself Estella Doucette. I have no reason to suppose that was the name she was born with.'

'Sweet star? A poetic choice.'

The Duchess shrugged—an elegant movement that was more genuinely French than Estella's false name.

'She was an opera dancer when he met her, and not yet twenty. She will be about thirty-five now, I suppose. It occurred to me that if she had stripped her suite then I would be wise to check the safe in my husband's study, where the jewellery is kept. That was intact. I do not know what made me look at the diaries. Under the terms of the Duke's will they should have been locked away for seventy-five years, and I thought I had the only key. But when I checked I found there were no volumes for this year, or for last year, and those four blank ones were in their place.'

She relocked the doors.

'I suggest we return to the drawing room.'

'I will need to look at her suite and examine this room.'

'Later. Duncan Grant can show you whatever you wish to see—although not the remaining diaries.'

She led the way out without looking back to see whether he followed, and Nick reminded himself that duchesses must become used to absolute obedience from those they employed. This might become interesting. He had had quite enough of obeying orders in the army, let alone before that.

The Duchess rang for tea. 'Please sit, Pascoe.'

She indicated a chair on the other side of the low table. From her tone it was not a suggestion and, because he wanted her to relax—as far as she was able— he obeyed. He sat back comfortably, crossed his legs, and studied her whilst apparently admiring the Gainsborough portrait over her shoulder.

'Can you describe Estella Doucette?'

'I have never seen her face to face—only from a

distance. Of my height, slim...dark hair. She will be beautiful still, of course,' she added, with that slight shrug again. 'My husband was a connoisseur of all things beautiful.'

'You tolerated her presence under your roof for an entire year after the death of your husband, her protector.'

Her expression remained unchanged, but he saw a flare of something in those large green eyes. Anger?

'Duncan Grant tells me that he would trust you with his life. As I would trust him with mine—and, more importantly, with my son's—then I will be completely frank with you.'

That, Nick reflected, would make a pleasant change from many of his clients, who appeared to think he could work miracles without being in possession of half the facts—usually those they considered embarrassing.

The Duchess folded her hands in her lap. The emerald set in the ring on her left hand shimmered in the light from the window. She was not quite as calm as she wished to appear.

'I was raised to be the wife of a man of high rank and the mother of his heir. I am very clear on what my duty entails. Firstly, the instructions in my husband's will must be carried out exactly as he wished, and that includes allowing that woman to remain under this roof for one year from his death. I had no intention of allowing it for a day more than that. Secondly, I must ensure that my son is raised to fill the position he has held virtually since his birth. That does not include allowing the family name to be mired in scandal. Should the contents of the late Duke's diaries become public knowledge, or be used in any underhand manner, then that name will be dragged into the mud.'

She smiled faintly.

'It is my intention that my son grows up a happy and healthy boy, with an understanding of his duty, but not in such a way that he is crushed by it.'

'The late Duke died as soon as your son was born?'

'That night. He had been celebrating the birth with friends and seems to have lost his balance at the top of the main staircase.'

Nick had seen the stairs—a long, straight flight of marble steps down to a marble floor. Yes, he could well believe that a middle-aged man, full of celebratory wine, would have had little chance of surviving a fall down those.

'A tragedy.'

'Yes,' she agreed. 'But I wish my son to enjoy his childhood. It is my intention that he will do so as far as possible.'

He doubted that she had intended to reveal just how little she grieved for her husband. She must have been looking forward to the end of her year of mourning, the relief of having her own home free from the unseen, never forgotten presence of her late husband's mistress. Looking forward to her life without a man old enough to be her father, come to that.

Was this a woman of passionate feelings under that controlled exterior? Or had passion been trained out of her, crushed by such a marriage?

'You believe that Estella Doucette has taken the diaries and intends to sell them to a publisher who will promote them to create a positive storm of interest? I can imagine that they would eclipse Lady Caroline Lamb's exploits. Or Harriette Wilson's memoirs.'

'Quite. Or she intends to use the threat of publication to extort money from those mentioned in them. Or both. When I saw some were missing I read the remaining volumes for the most recent years, and I can imagine the scandal and furore that would be created by their publication. My husband had an entrée into the heart of government. He was well acquainted with everyone who was anyone—and he knew a great deal about the Prince Regent. I believe the expression is "He knew where the bodies were buried". I am opposed to theft, naturally. And I am equally opposed to extortion and to the creation of scandal.'

The Duchess leaned forward, and Nick found himself unable to look away from the green depths of her gaze.

'But most of all I am opposed to having my son's name embroiled in this.'

She sat back a little and took a deep breath. This was not a woman who allowed herself to give way to her anger easily, he guessed, but she would defend her son like a tigress.

'Frederick will not grow up to be known as the son of a man who brought down governments, disgraced public figures, brought the royal family into disrepute.'

The Prince Regent was more than capable of doing that single-handedly, Nick almost retorted, then bit his tongue. Did the Duchess possess a sense of humour? He had seen no signs of one yet, but these were hardly laughing matters.

'Are you prepared to buy them back? In effect, to outbid either the publishers who make a living from this kind of thing or the victims of her threats?'

'No.' The retort was instant. Fierce. 'I will not give that woman one penny piece of Frederick's money.'

'You want me to steal them?'

'I want you to retrieve stolen property. There is a difference.'

'Very well. I shall need her town house address, and then I will leave for London immediately.'

'Not quite immediately, Pascoe. I must have a day to pack and organise my household.'

'You intend on coming too? But—'

'And I shall be bringing my son with me.'

Nick could not recall the last time anyone had rendered him speechless. The Duchess was not only expecting him to escort her to London, but to bring her one-year-old child with her. He had very little experience of young children. None, in fact. But he did know they required endless attention, a great deal of luggage and, for a little duke, probably a small army of attendants.

She did not appear to think she was expecting anything out of the ordinary.

'As you wish, Duchess.'

The employer always got what they were paying for. Nick mentally adjusted his daily rates.

Chapter Two

Sophie closed the door of her sitting room firmly and walked to the window, but for once the verdure of the sweeping lawns, the shimmer of the lake, the framing of the artfully placed trees failed to soothe her. She had a problem, and she was not at all certain that the cure would not prove to be another one.

Nicholas Pascoe was respectful, even though he did not address her appropriately. He was clearly intelligent. He did not argue with her, although Sophie suspected that her insistence on bringing Frederick with her had taken him aback, and he behaved like a perfect gentleman.

So why did the man leave her in absolutely no doubt of how aware he was of her as a woman? It was a disturbing novelty. She had known that Augustus, whilst always punctiliously polite, even in bed, had regarded her as a vessel to bear his heir, as a hostess and as a necessary ornament. If a piece of furniture had been able to fulfil those roles, then he would have been equally courteous to a chest of drawers.

Her lips twitched and, alone for once, she chuckled at the mental image. Then the smile faded. That was something else she must take into account now: men. A young widowed duchess was a valuable commodity. She would be courted by men of rank. And, although giving Frederick a father figure in his young life might be desirable, she was very much aware that control over his fortune would be a major temptation to those men. She would lose all rights and everything would be in her new husband's power. It was a risk she dared not take.

Sophie gave a mental shrug. She would deal with suitors when they arose. What she had to cope with now was the close proximity of a man who made her… restless.

It was natural, she told herself. She had been in strict mourning for a year, her only occupation wrestling with estate papers. The lawyers—all of them— had not blood but paper dust in their veins, she was certain.

There, she was calm again.

She reached for the bell-pull and when a footman answered said, 'My compliments to Mr Grant, and I would be obliged if he would attend me.'

Then she drew some paper towards her and began to make lists. Duncan had once remarked that moving

His Grace's household was akin to moving a small army. With a baby involved she imagined they'd need to add another regiment.

Duncan Grant, as always, had performed miracles, and they set out from Vine Mount House at nine in the morning, two days later. Servants had left the day before, in the tracks of the rider who was to alert the staff at St Edmund's House in Bedford Square so that all could be prepared for their arrival.

A considerable cavalcade set out in a fine drizzle. First came the Duchess's travelling carriage, bearing her, Frederick, Nanny Green and Foskett, her maid, who kept a firm hold on her dressing case. A second carriage contained the nursery maids and the luggage that Nanny thought necessary for His Grace. The third vehicle contained Her Grace's clothes, and all the paperwork she and Duncan felt it prudent to have to hand.

Duncan and Pascoe were riding, followed by two grooms, each leading their spare mounts. Duncan, as always, sat his leggy bay gelding with the ease of an ex-cavalryman. Pascoe rode a black mare that Sophie recognised as part-Arab, as elegant and as subtly efficient as her rider.

She wondered whether black was an affectation with him. Or was the horse's colour merely coincidental?

She had been delighted to shed her black garments, although she had to admit the colour suited him...

At this point she realised that her gaze was lingering on the man who looked even more at home in the saddle than Duncan did. She dropped the window glass down in its grooves and leaned out a little.

'Mr Grant, are we ready to leave?'

'At your word, Your Grace.'

'Then let us go.' She took Freddie from Nanny and held him up with one hand while she took his chubby fist in the other to wave farewell to the staff lined up in the front steps. 'Wave goodbye, Freddie.'

It was never too early to teach him to show respect to those who laboured on his behalf.

They bowed or curtseyed in response and the carriages moved off. It would take them two days from Vine Mount House to Bedford Square, and they would stop overnight at Long Melford, at the home of Sophie's godmother, Lady Prestwick. Eighty-three miles the first day, seventy-three the day after.

It was a familiar journey, although one that she had never attempted with Freddie. It would be his first time away from home, and she could only hope that the motion of the carriage lulled him to sleep rather than made him ill. There would be six changes of horses that day, with opportunities to take him out into the fresh air. For now, however, he seemed happy enough on her lap, pointing at things through the glass.

* * *

Four hours later they drew into the market square in Diss and stopped outside the ancient Dolphin Inn. The nursery maids ran to take the squirming, very much awake young Duke from Nanny, and she and Sophie exchanged looks that spoke of relief, a wish for their luncheon, and a strong desire to lie down in a very quiet, darkened room for at least an hour.

Duncan Grant had sent ahead as usual, so that Sophie was ushered to a sitting room and Nanny, Freddie and the maids were accommodated in another private room.

'Do you wish to partake of luncheon alone, Your Grace?' Duncan enquired, with the careful formality he always used to her in public. Usually when they were travelling he would eat with her, but clearly he was wondering just how she would regard Pascoe.

'I would be glad of your company, Mr Grant. And Mr Pascoe's, of course.'

Pascoe, it rapidly became clear, was quite used to dining in society, and more than comfortable eating at a duchess's table. He was, however, silent.

'Does your work involve much travel, Pascoe?' Sophie enquired when the chicken soup had been served.

'Most commissions do. Some are confined to London.' He passed her the bread rolls.

'Thank you. The war must have restricted your activities?'

'I did not find it an impediment. My French passes muster. Butter?'

'No, thank you. Your military experiences have not left you with a dislike of the Continent, then?'

Duncan Grant had sold out of the army when a piece of shrapnel had sliced through his left thigh. Although there was only a barely noticeable hesitation in his gait, and he could still ride all day, he had accepted that the rigours of cavalry service were beyond him and had sold out. He had not told her why Pascoe had left.

'Not at all.' He applied admirable white teeth to his bread roll. 'I have to admit I prefer the scenery when I am not engaged in forced marches through blizzards. The food is better, too.'

And you are as slippery as the contents of that butter dish.

'And what manner of people are your clients, Pascoe?'

'People like yourself, who expect total discretion about their identity and their problems, Duchess.'

The appearance of a waiter with a platter of cold meats, salads and cheese retrieved that awkward moment. It was reassuring that he was so secretive, although she should have known better than to lay herself open to a polite snub.

The maid who was clearing the soup bowls seemed to be working very slowly. Sophie realised that the young woman was doing her best to flirt with Pascoe, peeping at him from under her lashes and then dimpling when she caught his eye. As Sophie watched, she saw the corner of his mouth quirk up, but he gave a slight shake of his head even as he smiled at the girl, who blushed, gathered up her laden tray, and left.

That had been tactfully done, Sophie thought. He hadn't encouraged the maid, but he hadn't humiliated her either—just sent an acknowledgment of her interest and an almost regretful refusal.

He must have no trouble in attracting the female attention that he *did* desire, she supposed, allowing her gaze to settle fleetingly on the dark hooded eyes, the sensual mouth.

'Do help yourselves to the ham, gentlemen.'

'It is always excellent here,' Duncan remarked, taking several slices and passing the platter to Pascoe. He knew she would take just a little of the cold chicken. 'One day when we are returning this way I will purchase an entire ham. Monsieur Guiscard may wish to set up a regular order.'

'You have a French chef, Duchess?'

'My husband would have nothing else. He lured him away from a *marquis* who had fled the Terror. He has gone on ahead to the London house, of course.'

'Of course,' Pascoe said gravely, and she narrowed her eyes at him. Was he mocking her? It was impossible to tell.

Sophie shifted her gaze to the bowl of salad and herbs. She was as bad as that maid, exchanging looks with the man. But those dark eyes had a disconcerting ability to attract her attention. They seemed capable of holding an entire conversation in a language she was unable to speak, but which she had an uneasy feeling she understood only too well.

Duncan steered the conversation to some colourful anecdotes about conflicts between members of staff. He made Pascoe laugh out loud at his vivid description of Monsieur Guiscard confronted by Nanny Green with her firm ideas of what constituted 'suitable English food' for herself, the nursemaids and, most importantly, for weaning His Grace.

'He listened calmly to her ranting about "that dreadful garlic", and her warning to him not to poison His Grace with "them snails", and then assured her with perfect courtesy that he would, of course, serve the nursery with nothing but the very blandest food, with any dangerous vegetables boiled to a consistent grey colour without a hint of seasoning. She was so furious at not making him lose his temper that she flounced out herself. And, of course, he sends up the most delicious and appropriate food to the nursery wing. The nursery maids adore him and Nanny Green has to pretend to force herself to eat it so as not to lose face.'

It sometimes seemed to Sophie that it would be easier to run a large business concern than manage a ducal household with its numerous departments, all of them more than ready to fight to maintain their position. In practice it should be a rigid hierarchy, with Duncan, as steward, at the top, and below him the butler, the housekeeper, the chef and Nanny, each in control of their own domain and staff. But then there were the people who didn't quite fit—the ones who were, like Duncan, gentlemen and not servants: her secretary, the chaplain and the archivist and librarian. Beyond that were the outside staff—gardeners, stable staff, maintenance men...

But someone was always jockeying for position, encroaching upon another department's privileges. These minor wars were always fought with the most extreme politeness—in fact, Sophie could usually tell when something was amiss only by how perfectly everyone was behaving. One of the most useful pieces of advice her mother had given her was to ignore such upsets entirely.

'You do not notice unless violence actually breaks out in front of you,' the Marchioness had said. 'Leave it all to your steward.'

So she did, and thanked goodness for Duncan daily, but now, as she watched the amusement fade from Pascoe's expression, to be replaced with his usual cool watchfulness, she wondered just how grateful she was that her old friend had found this remedy for her problem. She could believe that Pascoe was intelligent, daring, resourceful and competent, and that she could trust his discretion, and yet...

If she could have put a finger on the source of her

uneasiness it would, strangely, have helped, but all she could describe was an awareness, a consciousness of his presence, and a strange restless feeling which she refused to believe had anything to do with his looks.

'I shall take the air for a few minutes before we continue,' she said, pushing back her chair abruptly.

Both men jumped to assist her, but she waved them away. 'I will find Foskett. Please do not disturb yourselves.'

But when she reached the door of the parlour where the staff were eating she saw her abigail had not finished her meal, and stepped back quietly before she disturbed her. Diss was a peaceful and familiar little market town, so surely she did not need an escort within a few steps of the inn? The milliner's shop she had glimpsed on the other side of the market square had looked rather tempting...

It was strangely deserted when she stepped out into the square, although in the distance she could hear raised voices and shouts. A hue and cry after a thief, perhaps, she thought absently, her gaze on the splash of rich raspberry-red in the milliner's window. Not a suitable colour for someone in half-mourning, of course, she thought wistfully, but there was nothing to stop her buying the hat now and wearing it later, or at least making a note of the style.

The distant noise was suddenly closer, as she reached the middle of the square, and Sophie glanced around, then down, as something thudded at her feet.

It was a hard globe, about the size of a cricket ball, and she looked up, wondering where the child who had thrown it was.

It was not a child. What looked to her startled eyes like most of the male population of the town between the ages of fourteen and sixty was running towards her, and the ball at her feet, yelling and screaming, pushing, shoving and trading blows.

Sophie whirled around to run back, but her heel caught on a cobblestone and she went down hard and painfully on her hands and knees. The mob was almost upon her, like a tidal wave or a herd of stampeding cattle, blind with excitement and the red haze of fighting.

It was too late to move. Sophie began to curl up defensively, feeling almost blank with the certainty that it was pointless...that she was going to be trampled to death.

Freddie! She was going to die, and her baby was going to grow up forgetting her...

Then someone seized her by the arms, dragged her to her feet and slammed her back against the tall post that supported the inn's sign, which had been set in the middle of the square to be easily visible to oncoming travellers.

A long body pressed against hers, arms caged her on either side, and then the throng was on them, in a wave of heat and sweat and noise and dust. Her rescuer was thrust hard into her, and she sensed him grasping the post and bracing his feet against the onslaught at his back. He said something harsh and abrupt under his breath.

Sophie buried her face in his shirt-front, aware of the sharp scent of citrus and spice, the smell of clean linen, of male skin. She breathed it in as though finding air when she was drowning. She knew who it was who shielded her.

How long they stood there locked together, buffeted and deafened, she had no idea, but suddenly all was quiet except for the sound of their breathing, the thud of his heart, the rush of blood in her head. The arms bracketing her did not move.

When was the last time someone had held her? Never as an adult, she realised. Her husband's embraces had been purely sexual. The thought of gathering her into his arms protectively, or out of affection, seemed never to have occurred to him. Her parents had never been demonstrative, either. A cool kiss on the cheek was the extent of their displays of emotion.

But Pascoe had held her to protect her, and now she could only guess that he was keeping her in his arms for reassurance and support. She received those in plenty from Duncan, but he would never presume to touch her, let alone put his arms around her. Not since she was a small child, she thought. Whereas Pascoe, it would appear, had no problem with presumption.

Sophie found she was holding back a gasp of amusement and stiffened. The last thing she needed was to give way to hysteria—because surely that was what was filling her with the reckless urge to press her mouth against his chest to stifle her laughter.

Slowly he moved back a few inches, his right hand moving from the post to her waist as he stood, still braced to steady her. Sophie peeled her bruised back away from the rough wood and struggled to focus.

'Pascoe?'

What was she asking? She realised she had no idea.

'You are safe now.'

She knew that—had known it from the moment she had felt his heart beat against her cheek.

The dark elegance was gone, but the dust-covered figure in front of her, with its hair in its eyes and a trickle of blood down one temple, was rock-steady, the hand supporting her firm, the dark eyes as coolly assessing as ever.

'What *was* that?' she managed.

'A game of camping,' he said. 'Why the devil they were in the street and not on the common or the camping ground, I have no idea.'

'*Camping?*' Sophie looked around her at what looked like a battlefield. There were tumbled bodies, men sitting clutching their heads and groaning, barking dogs and wailing women.

'It's a ball game,' Pascoe said. 'Usually it is a grudge match, between one parish and a neighbour, or one end of a town against the other. They throw the ball and score points for hitting the target—there will be a goal at each end.' He glanced around. 'And work for the surgeon, if not the undertaker.'

'Is it legal?' Sophie demanded, getting her breath back, and with it her sense of priorities. They might have been killed. 'That *cannot* be legal.'

'It is when it is played in a field and no one dies,' Pascoe said drily. 'This was more like a riot—although how the magistrates are going to apportion blame for the mayhem, I cannot imagine.'

'Oh, Your Grace!' Foskett hurried across the square, Duncan Grant at her side. 'Are you hurt?'

'No,' Sophie said, ignoring the pain in her back. She would be black and blue by morning, she was sure, but it was nothing that a soak in a hot bath would not cure. 'Thanks to Mr Pascoe I am quite unharmed... merely shaken a little.'

More than a little. And that was not all due to the stampede that had rushed past them. The warm pressure of Pascoe's hand pressed just below her ribcage was not helping her composure either.

'But, sir...' Foskett was staring at Pascoe. 'Your left hand.'

Sophie turned to look where Foskett was staring. Pascoe released her, and moved to one side, but not before she saw the steady drip of blood onto the dusty cobbles at his feet.

Chapter Three

'You are wounded. Let me see.'

Sophie held out her hand. One thing she had learned very early was that, however exalted her position, the mistress of a household was responsible for the welfare of everyone in it. She supervised the stillroom, she paid for the dentist when the kitchen maids had toothache, and she retained the services of a doctor, a surgeon and an apothecary to deal with everything from sniffles to broken limbs.

'It is nothing. A splinter, merely.' Pascoe dragged a handkerchief from his pocket and wrapped it around his left hand.

'Mr Grant?' Sophie did not have to raise her voice, nor explain what she wanted Duncan to do.

'Come with me,' he said.

The two men exchanged a look which said, as loud as words, that no female was going to be fussing over Pascoe's hand.

He nodded abruptly. 'Very well. Once the Duchess is safely inside.'

Pascoe offered her his arm and she laid her fingertips on it, making it clear that she had no need to lean on him, but nor was she going to treat him like an invalid.

Once they were inside the inn she removed her hand and swept off to the private parlour, surrendering Pascoe to Duncan's ministrations. After all, a splinter was hardly serious…although it was strange that it had bled so.

'A tisane, Your Grace? Or a soothing powder? Perhaps you should lie down with a handkerchief soaked in vinegar on your forehead.' Foskett, a serious woman of thirty, hurried after her.

'Foskett, that was an unpleasant and surprising experience, but I am quite well, thank you.' Sophie looked down at her hands. They were shaking. 'However, I will take a glass of brandy. The noise did not disturb His Grace, I trust?'

Foskett tugged at the bell-pull. 'He was sound asleep, ma'am. Nanny has him in the little sitting room at the back, where it is quietest, and he's sleeping like a baby.' She gave a little titter at her own feeble joke.

A waiter came in, received the order for brandy and hesitated on the threshold. 'Should I take a decanter in to the gentlemen, Your Grace? Only that hand looks right painful.'

'A splinter, surely?'

The man pulled a face, as though he disagreed but couldn't bring himself to say so.

'I see. Yes, certainly take them brandy. Foskett, kindly find me the valise holding the salves and lotions.'

The maid hurried out and Sophie stood biting her lip. Just a splinter... But men did hate to make a fuss, and there had been rather a lot of blood.

When Foskett brought the valise Sophie took out a jar of the soothing ointment she made up to her grandmother's recipe. Honey, garlic and the herb arnica were just some of the ingredients. It smelt unpleasant, but it seemed to stop infection and made wounds heal better. Duncan doubtless carried bandages, but she found a roll of soft lint, took a sustaining mouthful of brandy, and then went in search of the men, wincing as she straightened her bruised back.

'How the devil did you do that?' Grant demanded, taking Nick's wrist in a tight grip.

They both looked down at the wedge of wood that impaled the flesh at the base of his thumb. The blood had stopped, except for a trickle, but Nick didn't deceive himself that pulling it out wouldn't start the bleeding all over again.

'I had to grab hold of the post to stop myself crushing the Duchess against it,' he said, lifting his hand to study the end of the splinter. 'You'll need to cut to get a grip on it.'

Grant muttered something and unrolled the canvas that held his medical equipment. Nick had a suspicion that he used it to patch up livestock and staff equally, but the array of unpleasant-looking tools was clean and the edges gleamed sharp.

'That looks army issue to me.'

'Aye, given me by a surgeon when he found me digging a bullet out of one of my sergeants with a penknife. You'd best get your coat and shirt off.'

Gingerly, Nick extricated himself from his coat, regretting, for once, his taste for well-tailored clothes. Grant, himself wearing a looser and more comfortable riding coat, looked unsympathetic, but he helped him drag off his shirt and keep the worst of the blood from the sleeve.

'Hell's teeth. Look at your back, man!'

'I can't,' Nick pointed out, wondering if it looked as bad as it felt.

The camping players, frustrated by the obstacle in their path, had punched and struck at him wildly as they passed.

'Looks as though they missed your kidneys,' Grant said, peering. 'But it wouldn't surprise me if you'd cracked a rib or two. Take a deep breath.'

Nick did—and cursed. 'Might have. Nothing's broken, though.' He sat down and laid his hand palm-up on the table. 'Get this out, will you?'

His old friend poured hot water from a jug into a basin and stirred in salt. 'Put it in that first. And have a swig or two of the brandy.'

Nick did as he was told, hissing with pain, but he knew it was best to get it clean or there'd be worse trouble ahead.

Eventually Grant moved the basin away, took hold of his wrist and drew a scalpel down half the length of the splinter, then pushed the hand under water again and reached for a large pair of tweezers.

'Keep still.'

'What the hell do you think I'm doing?' Nick demanded. 'Bloody hell, man, I hope you carve a roast joint more elegantly than that.'

'There. Stop fussing.' Grant brandished the large, splintered piece of wood. 'Let it bleed for a second or two...make sure it's all out.'

He dropped the tweezers and reached for the needle that lay to one side, already threaded. 'I'll just sew it up.'

Behind them the door opened and there was a sharp intake of breath. 'Duncan, what are you *doing*? You said a splinter—this looks like a butcher's shop!'

'I am doing fine needlepoint here, Sophie,' Grant said, startling Nick, who hadn't realised just how close the two of them must be. 'Go away. Don't distract me.'

'I have brought balm and lint,' the Duchess said, ignoring him, and put them down on the table, moving into Nick's sight as she did so. She kept her gaze on his hand, and he saw that her cheek was pale. 'There should be enough for Pascoe's back as well.'

Just don't offer to apply it yourself, he thought, distracted from the discomfort of Grant's 'fine needlepoint' by the vivid imagining of what her hands would feel like on him. *Very, very, good.*

He had been trying to banish the memory of her body against his as that mob had raged around them... the scent and softness of her, the courage that had kept her still and silent. It hadn't been paralysed fear, it had been disciplined self-control. And trust.

'Is there anything else you need?' she asked, still addressing Grant.

The Duchess had backbone, Nick thought. He must present a lurid picture if the state of his back was enough to startle Grant, and he would have expected the sight of his hand to cause any gently bred lady to swoon.

'Nothing, thank you, Your Grace,' Grant said, clearly having recovered his poise, and with it his formality. 'We will not be long.'

The door closed behind her with a sharp click and Nick reached for the brandy glass. 'Sophie and Duncan...?'

'I've known Her Grace since she was five,' Grant said shortly. 'I forgot myself.'

He applied ointment from the jar the Duchess had left on the table. It stank. Perhaps it worked on the same basis as foul-tasting medicine—it had to be doing you good if it smelt so unpleasant.

'There.' He finished bandaging, then smeared more of the ointment on Nick's back. 'Leave it a few minutes to soak in before you put your shirt back.'

Nick sniffed at the pungent jar. 'This will ruin my love-life.'

Grant snorted. 'Do you want a sling?'

'I do not.'

The bulky wrapping was bad enough, although he had more sense than to try and make do with a lesser dressing. He needed the full use of his hands, and ignoring a wound was foolish. And so was entertaining erotic thoughts about his employer—foolish, unprofessional and distracting, he told himself.

'There's no room inside the carriages,' Grant said as he washed his instruments and returned everything to its place. 'But you could sit on the box of one of them.'

'I'll ride. I'll seize up if I sit still.'

And he was not going to be treated like an invalid. It was bad for his image, and that was something Nick cultivated carefully.

'What are you grinning about?' Grant stuffed his

medical roll and the salve into a battered old leather valise.

'Oh, just a whimsical thought,' Nick lied.

He had been smiling at himself for not wanting to appear weak in front of the Duchess—that was the truth of it.

Idiot, he thought repressively. *You are just another useful professional in her eyes. You could have one ear, the dress sense of a hod carrier and be ninety-nine years of age and she would not care, provided you get those diaries back for her.*

He is simply an employee. A professional gentleman, to be sure, but that is all. He was a soldier— that is why he reacted as he did to that mob, and why he is stoical in the face of pain. Duncan would have done just the same for me if he had been out there when I fell.

Having given herself a firm talking-to, Sophie adjusted the set of her bonnet and drew on her gloves. 'Is everyone ready to leave?'

'I believe so, Your Grace.' Foskett peered out of the window. 'Yes, Mr Grant and Mr Pascoe are mounting up just this moment, and everyone else except Nanny and His Grace are outside.'

'Then let us be gone,' Sophie said. 'We are at least an hour behind time, and Lady Prestwick will be wondering what has become of us if we are late for our dinner.'

Staying one night at her godmother's charming house in Long Melford would certainly allow them to recover from the effects of their unfortunate stop at Diss. She made herself look forward to the evening and not brood about that unsettling incident.

'My cottage' her godmother called the dower house, with complete disregard for how that must sound to anyone who actually *did* live in a cottage, and not a house containing at least eight bedchambers and four reception rooms.

It made Sophie think of Marie Antoinette, living a rural fantasy at Versailles whilst the peasantry were sharpening their scythes at the gate. She hoped she would be able to raise Freddie with more awareness of the lives of the hundreds of people who depended on him both as an employer and customer.

Her father would tut at such radical ideas, of course. To him, the poor had been placed in their position by God, and disturbing the natural order of things led to dissatisfaction, unrest and violence. 'Look at the French,' he would say.

There, the upper classes knew their duty to those lower than themselves, he'd assure her, and then Mama would use the opportunity to list the numerous acts of benevolence that the lady of a great house was expected to perform.

Sophie most certainly did not want to think of her son as the target of a mob accompanied by a guillotine on a cart, and nor did she want to be characterised as a dangerous radical, but she couldn't help but feel that people who were well-fed, gainfully employed and suitably educated would be likely to think less of revolution and more how best to build a better society for their children. And what about the dwellers in those newly expanding towns where the manufactories had swallowed up their labour? Who carried out acts of benevolence for them?

Perhaps Pascoe knew about conditions in places like Birmingham and Manchester, she mused, and finally allowed herself to focus on the black-clad figure on the black mare. He was riding one-handed, his bandaged hand resting on his thigh, his battered back as upright as before. Her own bruises gave a twinge in sympathy—and she had a well-upholstered seat to lean back against.

She had no idea of his background. She knew nothing other than that he had held an officer's rank in the army, was well-spoken, and Duncan considered him suitable to associate with her. A gentleman, then, but a self-made one? Whatever his background, it would be interesting to hear what he thought about those industrial towns. Her financial advisor was recommending investments in coal and cotton, and she felt abysmally ignorant about such matters.

'Mama?' a sleepy voice said, and she turned from the window to smile at her son, who was wriggling free of Madge the nursemaid's arms, where he had been sound asleep ever since they'd left Diss.

'Come to me.' She held out her arms and winced as they took the weight of his solid little body. 'What can we see from the window?'

He waved his fists at the two horses riding just ahead of them.

'Horses,' Sophie said. 'A black horse with Mr Pascoe and a bay horse with Mr Grant.'

'Ga!'

'That's right—Mr Grant.' Duncan was a familiar figure to Freddie.

'Pas?'

Goodness, that was unexpected... 'Mr Pascoe, yes. Now, what animals can we see? Two horses and cows in the field and some sheep. What do the sheep say?'

Freddie stood up in the circle of her arms and bounced. 'Baa!'

'That's right. And what does the cow say?'

'Moo.'

The game lasted for several miles, past some conveniently barking dogs, a pig being led on a rope by a young lad, several goats and a flock of geese.

At last Freddie plonked himself down in her lap, worn out with the excitement.

He pointed again. 'Pas?'

'What does Mr Pascoe say? Not very much, really.'

'Damn!' Freddie said clearly.

Sophie almost dropped him. *'What?'*

'I'm sorry, Your Grace,' said Madge. 'I opened the wrong door when I was looking for a room where I could change His Grace, and I walked in on Mr Grant and Mr Pascoe. Mr Grant was doing something to Mr Pascoe's hand, and he said… Mr Pascoe, that is…he said—'

'Yes, well, we will not repeat it, Madge. We will just hope His Grace forgets it soon.'

Perfect. First of all he sets me in a fluster and now he is teaching my son bad language.

'Yes, ma'am.'

They stopped to change horses and also, as Madge declared, a small boy, and were soon on the road again. Freddie slept, and Madge nodded off, despite Nanny's eagle eye on her. Foskett began to snore gently, and finally Nanny succumbed to the heat of the afternoon and the swaying of the well-sprung carriage.

Sophie lowered the window glass to halfway. The water carts had been out to lay the dust on the road, and the scent of greenery, agricultural odours and the occasional drift of woodsmoke floated into the carriage.

The two men were riding side by side now, heads inclined together, talking. Sophie strained to hear, but they were keeping their voices down. What was it they were so earnest about? Reminiscences of the war? Or were they planning how to retrieve the diaries?

They probably intended to keep her out of whatever scheme was afoot, but she would not allow that. She'd had over a year of independence now, and experience of the authority a wealthy, well-connected widow could wield, and she was not going to be kept out of things that men thought her too fragile to cope with or too innocent to comprehend.

A small niggle that she identified as her conscience enquired sarcastically if that was because she wanted to spend more time with Pascoe. Sophie told her conscience to hold its tongue.

How would she go about it if she were a man? Stealing the diaries back was one option—if *stealing* was the right word when Estella had purloined them in the first place. But that would involve an act of burglary...a serious offence. There was persuasion, she supposed. An appeal to the woman's better nature. But did Estella possess such a thing? Surely not, or she wouldn't have stolen the journals in the first place— and to make such an approach would warn her that the theft had been discovered.

Threats? Again, that would alert her, and there was no actual proof that she had taken them. An appeal to the authorities from a duchess would provoke action, that was certain, but if nothing were found then their whereabouts would be a constant source of anxiety and Sophie might provoke the very scandal she was so anxious to avoid. It was, after all, the reason she had employed Pascoe.

So what did that leave? Some form of trickery, she supposed, although she could not imagine what. *Which is why you called upon an expert,* she reminded herself, her gaze resting on that dark figure on the black horse. That evening she would ask him what he proposed to do. It made her uneasy to leave something so sensitive in another's hands and have no inkling of how he was going to proceed.

As she watched Pascoe shifted slightly in the saddle, moving his shoulders as though to ease them, and she remembered the reddened skin, the beginning of bruises flowering across his muscled back. Had she been right to leave him to Duncan? She wondered if he been insistent enough in dosing him with willow bark infusion and applying the salve. Pascoe was in her employ, and therefore her responsibility, but how could she lay hands on a man who was a virtual stranger to her if there was someone else to do it with far greater propriety?

That elegant coat and the fine linen of his shirt must have been damaged. Those, at least, she could deal with, even if she was beginning to have grave doubts that she could deal with the man.

Pascoe was dangerous. Dangerous to whoever his

opponent might be at any given time and dangerous to foolish females who were beginning to discover, rather late in the day, that duty was a cold bedfellow and that having a child to love did not mean that other forms of...*affection* were not a temptation.

Duchesses and widows were just as susceptible to daydreams as the next woman, it seemed.

Someone had told her once that frogs could survive all winter, frozen in the mud at the bottom of a pond, and come back to life with the thaw. Sophie winced at the thought of herself as a frog, but she began to suspect that her thaw was just beginning.

Chapter Four

'Sophia, my dear, how late you are! I was beginning to fear an accident had befallen you on the road.' Lady Prestwick held out her hands as Sophie entered the drawing room. 'I have told Pierre to hold back dinner, so you will have time to refresh yourself—but do not think of changing. There are just the two of us. And Maria, of course,' she said, with a vague gesture at her youngest daughter, who had risen and was now hovering uncertainly in the background.

'I am so sorry, Godmama, but there was a near-riot at Diss—some sporting event that ran out of control—and it held us up. Maria, it is so good to see you. I hope you are well?'

Maria, a pale and put-upon spinster, smiled wanly. 'As well as might be expected,' she whispered.

It was never clear to Sophie what ailed Maria, who was an honorary cousin to her. Probably it was simply her existence as The Disappointment—the one daughter out of four who had failed to make a good match and who was now doomed to be A Comfort to her mama, as Sophie thought her.

'I will go up and tidy myself,' she said. 'I would hate Pierre's wonderful dinner to be spoiled.'

'He has a new French recipe for lamb,' her god-mother called after her. 'Quite divine!'

Sophie found Duncan and Pascoe in the hall. 'Are you both taken care of?'

'I am in my usual room and Daunt has given Pascoe the adjoining bedchamber. We're dining with Brodding.'

That was Lady Prestwick's steward, so they would be suitably entertained, she was sure. 'Do you need anything from my medical supplies?'

'Thank you, but no. I have everything we will need,' Duncan said.

Pascoe stood at his ease, surveying the hall. As she had sensed when he had first entered her drawing room, Sophie knew that he was assessing the place, studying its security, its valuables, the points of entry and egress, its possibilities and its dangers. He might almost have been studying a battlefield. It was curiously exciting.

'Please do not omit to include the replacement of your damaged garments on your expenses, Pascoe,' she said, recalled to her responsibilities now she could see the burst seam on one coat sleeve and the blood on his shirt cuff.

He turned his cool gaze on her. 'You do not employ me as a bodyguard, Duchess. If my clothing is disarrayed in the course of assisting a lady, that is simply a matter of mischance.'

'As you please,' she said, nettled, and turned to climb the stairs, head up, lips tight on a retort.

That had been a snub—a reminder that he was a gentleman and that picking her up, shielding her from a mob and being battered in the process, was simply an act of chivalry to be expected of any man with a grain of honour in him.

Really, what an adventurer thought he was doing administering a snub to a duchess, she could not imagine…

Intolerable arrogance.

Then Sophie caught herself on the thought. It was she who was being arrogant. What reason had he to offer her more than politeness? She had done nothing to deserve his regard other than fall over her feet into the path of a mob and require rescuing.

'I will not change, Foskett,' she said, walking into the familiar bedchamber. 'But I must wash the dust off and you may redress my hair.'

'Yes, Your Grace. There is hot water ready in the dressing room.'

It was not until five minutes later, as she sat at the dressing table watching the maid skilfully restoring her coiffure to order, that she allowed herself to think about Pascoe again. Just who was he? Or, more importantly, *what* was he? Not a man of dubious character, or Duncan would not have recommended him. And Duncan did not lie to her, so Pascoe *had* been an army comrade of his, at least for a time.

Duchess, he always said when speaking to her. Not, *Your Grace*, which was the correct form of address from anyone not of the aristocracy. From anyone, come to that, who was not a near-equal or a close acquaintance. But he did not say it with veiled insolence, nor as though he was simply ignorant of protocol. Duncan would have rapidly corrected him if that was the case. He said it because it came naturally to him. He needed to establish a close working relationship with her, one in which she trusted him enough to confide in him, so he used that mode of address. Pascoe was not simply a gentleman; he was from an aristocratic family.

Did that make a difference?

Sophie picked up the pearl ear drops that Foskett offered and slipped one into her right lobe while she pondered. She hoped that it would not affect how she judged his character, or his work for her. Her best and dearest friend was the son of a country clergyman and her own steward.

The other ear drop was in place before she realised that it did matter, and that was because she was uncertain of who he was. He was hiding his true identity from her. And so was Duncan.

At this point her inconvenient conscience decided that now, just before dinner, it would give her a dose of indigestion-provoking reality.

You are concerned because you are attracted to him. As a man. Physically. Carnally, it added, just in case she had missed the point. *And you are uneasy because you cannot fit him neatly into a box labelled, 'Suitable' or 'Unsuitable'.*

Which was true, Sophie acknowledged.

And she could add a third box to that. One labelled, *Have You Lost Your Senses?*

'Thank you, Foskett. I hope you have a pleasant evening meal.'

At least she still sounded like a rational, calm, emotionless duchess, and not a confused, unsettled woman.

'Stop fuming. Pour yourself a glass of something.' Grant gestured towards an array of decanters on the sideboard in the steward's dining room.

'I am not fuming. I do not fume,' Nick said coldly.

But he poured a glass of what looked like an old, dry Madeira and tossed it back, then lifted another glass in Grant's direction.

'No, thank you. And don't lie to me. I can almost hear your teeth grinding from here. You rescue the damsel in distress and then you are annoyed because she doesn't gasp, "Oh, Sir Galahad!" and cast herself on your manly chest, but instead offers to pay for your damaged clothing.'

'Don't be ridiculous.'

The wine sent warmth down his throat but did nothing to thaw his irritation. Which, if he was honest, was mainly at himself. Although the Duchess *had* been clasped to his chest, and very stimulating that had been. He only wished he'd had more leisure to appreciate it at the time.

'Look, either tell her who you are or accept being treated as a sword for hire with all the consequences that entails.'

'She did not employ me as a bodyguard. She employed me to retrieve certain articles.'

'You are splitting hairs.' Grant leaned one hip against the sideboard and flexed the leg stiffened by his old wound. 'You chose this way of making a living. You can always swallow your pride and go back. Oh, no, I forgot: the one thing you'll never swallow is your pride.'

'Damn it, Grant—'

'Good evening, Mr Grant, Mr Pascoe. I hope you find your rooms comfortable?' Paul Brodding, second son of a baronet and Lady Prestwick's exceedingly efficient steward, came in and closed the door behind him. 'Delighted to have your company this evening. A glass of wine—or shall I ring for the soup at once?'

Nick smiled and responded, and shot Grant a look intended to reveal nothing except delight at the prospect of an excellent dinner.

His old friend merely stared back, a slight frown between his brows.

'You sent for me, Duchess?'

Pascoe stood inside the door of the morning room, just where a shaft of early-morning sunlight fell on black hair with the gloss of a crow's wing. His disconcertingly dark gaze rested on her with no discernible emotion and Sophie felt a flicker of heat run through her, then an unsettling dizziness.

She had hardly slept, she was bruised, battered and shocked, but she must not show it. A duchess did not show weakness Mama had instructed her, because she is always in control of any situation.

'I wished to assure myself that you have taken no lasting harm from yesterday's injuries. Does your hand show any signs of infection?'

To her surprise—she had expected a prickly refusal to co-operate—he held out his left hand to reveal a new, much smaller bandage that protected the base of his thumb but otherwise left his hand free.

'No sinister red streaks…no unpleasant throbbing,' he said, his deep voice generating a throbbing in her that was not at all unpleasant, if unsettling.

And humiliating, Sophie told herself sharply. She was a lady, and ladies did not lust.

Unfortunately.

She knew better than to enquire about his back— a part of his anatomy she should never have set eyes upon in the first place.

'Have you formulated a plan for when we reach London?'

'I intend to meet the lady as soon as possible. Until I have done that, speculation is pointless.'

'Why do you need to meet her?' Sophie asked. 'Surely the less contact the better?'

He smiled slightly—a mere twitch of the lips—and came further forward, to within touching distance. The air in the little room was stuffy and warm, and cutting through that she could smell the sharp, clean citrus she recalled from when he had held her. His soap, perhaps.

'Women of her sort respond to masculine attention, to closeness. To a touch on the hand, a kiss on the fingers. She is alone now, and looking for a protector. She will reveal more than she intends as she assesses potential lovers.' His smile became deeper, more cynical now. 'If she was faithful to your husband then she is out of practice in the game.'

'The game?'

Don't ask, you idiot...

'Seduction. Her profession.'

His voice took on a deeper tone and Sophie's hand

curled into the velvet of the chair-back against which she stood.

'The commerce of the bedchamber.'

Common sense was clamouring at her to ask no more. But, throwing aside a lifetime of training to obey that inner voice, she said, shocking herself, 'You intend to seduce her?'

'I was rather hoping that she might attempt to seduce me. She will be less wary of me then.' When she stared at him, puzzled, he added, 'When you resist something someone is offering, they are far less likely to suspect you of wanting something else from them.'

'There are two objections to that,' Sophie said, making her voice crisp and firm. The effort steadied her. 'Firstly, the late Duke left her well provided for. She has no reason to seek another protector. And secondly, I will not be responsible for you…prostituting yourself.'

The infuriating man choked back a laugh. 'I can assure you, Duchess, she is going to expect any exchange of money to go in quite the opposite direction.'

'But—' Sophie sat down and then wished she hadn't. Pascoe loomed. 'Please, sit down.' She waved one hand at the chair opposite—a nice, safe distance away. 'As I said, the late Duke left her a house, money, jewellery… I do not understand why she has taken the diaries, except out of greed, and I certainly do not understand why she would want to find a new protector.'

Pascoe crossed his legs and sat back. Sophie felt as though he was sizing her up, assessing not her looks but her intelligence, her comprehension.

'Can you imagine what must start a young woman on that path?' he asked. 'An opera dancer—which is generally understood to be a woman who sells herself. And yet, according to Grant, she was well-spoken and behaved like a person raised in polite society. You seem incredulous?' he asked, when a slight snort escaped her.

'She was no doubt quick to learn to mimic her betters,' she snapped, and immediately regretted how harsh that sounded.

Pascoe shrugged. 'Either she clawed her way upwards or she fell downwards. Whichever it was, her position must have felt utterly perilous. Because if she came from nothing, then there was only one way to go. And if she was gently born and fell because she was seduced, or perhaps left penniless after losing her family, then she had nowhere to go either—except down to the gutter. Can you imagine having literally nothing?' he asked. 'Having to beg in the streets or sell yourself to survive? Even if all the ducal investments failed, even if the lands were infested with a murrain and the buildings crumbled, you would still have enough to live respectably, to raise your son decently.'

He was right, of course. She could not imagine such poverty. Of all the terrors that woke her at three in the morning and kept her awake and worrying, utter destitution was not one of them.

'No,' Sophie admitted.

'Have you ever been hungry?' the cool voice asked.

There was no emotion in the tone, no accusation, just polite enquiry. Pascoe might have been asking her what she thought of a theatre performance, or whether she had enjoyed a stay at Brighton.

'Not the hunger of missing a meal or two, but hunger so bad that you would contemplate eating anything you could beg borrow or steal, however foul? Once you have fallen so low the memory of it never leaves you. However much money Estella Doucette has now, however many jewels, she will never feel safe, never believe it will be enough.'

'Grant says she is still beautiful.'

Sophie had once asked Duncan whether her husband's mistress was prettier than she. And had regretted the question almost the moment it had left her lips.

'Pretty?' Duncan had said. 'Neither of you are *pretty*. You are both beautiful, in your own way.'

And he had gone to her escritoire, where she had set an arrangement that she had picked on her morning walk. It had been a charming arrangement of random flowers and leaves from hedgerows and borders, with feathery grasses and sweet-smelling herbs, in a crystal vase. He'd moved it to the table.

'Is that beautiful?' he'd asked, and she had nodded.

Then he had gone out to the hall, returning with an arrangement the gardener had made with hothouse lilies in a marble urn. Every bloom perfect, exotic, manicured and primped. The arrangement had been balanced, the colours and forms selected with great skill.

'And that?' he had asked, setting it down with a grunt that betrayed its weight.

Yes, she had agreed, that too was beautiful.

'Yet they are different, and they serve different purposes. She makes him comfortable,' Duncan had added. 'She looks like that—' he'd pointed to the lilies '—but she makes him feel like that.' He'd nodded towards the softly informal arrangement. 'You are the reverse.'

Sophie had felt ruffled and indignant, but she'd thought she understood after a few days spent brooding. Her role was to perfect the Duke's public face, but with Estella he wanted to be comfortable, and she knew how to let him relax.

'Beautiful?' Pascoe said now. 'That is immaterial. The great courtesans do not need beauty.' He smiled. 'Cleopatra had the most enormous nose, by all accounts, and yet she almost brought down empires. They have a glamour, a style, a confidence in themselves as women that bewitches and makes you realise, when you become dizzy, that you have been holding your breath.'

'You have clearly encountered a number of them,' Sophie observed tartly.

'One or two...and I find I prefer to be able to breathe,' Pascoe said. 'But to return to Estella. She will be feeling insecure...she will be counting and re-counting her resources, planning and plotting. She is not so young any more, although she has all the experience of maturity and that is also a powerful weapon. But she will know all too well the fate of other women who have been careless with what seemed like boundless wealth. All too many courtesans end their lives in poverty and disease, and the terror of that will always be with her.'

'Can you imagine having literally nothing?' Pascoe had asked her.

Had she ever been so hungry that she would have contemplated eating anything she could beg or steal? The memory of it would never leave her, he'd said, and she realised that he was speaking from experience—that he had been starving once, had been without anything.

When and how could that be? Because even if she was wrong, and he was not of an aristocratic family, she was certain he was at least gentry-born. What on earth could he have done to be cast out to the gutter?

'So, you will allow La Doucette to assess you as a potential protector?'

He nodded.

'As yourself?'

'As myself, Nicholas Pascoe—which will tell her nothing, of course. But I will appear to be a wealthy, if mysterious gentleman. Possibly I will hint at secrets. I need to get into her home and I need to discover how her mind works, and to do that I must intrigue her.'

Something must have shown in her expression, because he lost his smile.

'It does not do to underestimate her, you know. Your husband was a man of considerable intellect, and I do not think he would have suffered fools around him— certainly not for so long and so intimately.'

'You sympathise with her,' Sophie said, suddenly angry. *One rogue feeling pity for another...* 'I am employing you; I expect you to have my interests entirely at heart. Mine and no one else's.'

She found she was on her feet, confronting him almost toe to toe, because he had stood too. Her husband had been intelligent... Estella Doucette was to be pitied—and she was supposed to be *understanding* about this?

It began to dawn on Sophie that the man she was confronting was angry, although he said nothing, made no move. It also dawned on her that she was feeling something more than indignation herself. Her pulse was thudding, and not only in her throat. Another insidious feminine rhythm was making itself felt...a sensation that appeared to be running from her breasts to her belly. She recalled the feel of his arms lashing her to him, keeping her safe, the scent of male skin, the warmth of him…

'Well?' she demanded, because fuelling her own irritation seemed a better choice than simply melting at his feet in a puddle of desire. 'Say *something.*'

Pascoe's eyes looked so dark that for a moment she thought he had no pupils. But then she saw that they were wide, the black swallowing the brown irises. Was that answering anger, or something else?

'I understand her,' he said. 'But I do not condone her actions. She has broken the law, and at the expense of a small child and the woman who was her lover's wife and who deserved his loyalty. Does that answer your doubts about me? Because if not then there is no point in my continuing, is there?'

Something seemed to snap inside her—some tether that was keeping her upright and fixed on her duty, on the submergence of who she was in the role of Duchess of St Edmunds. Her back ached intolerably, her ears seemed to be full of the howling of the mob, a wave of the terror she had felt when she'd thought she was about to die was sweeping through her again, and now Pascoe might leave her.

'I don't… Yes. I mean, yes… I am answered. Of course I am.'

Strange…it was not only his eyes that were black.

The whole room seemed to be growing darker and darker…

'Duchess?'

'Impossible,' Sophie said. And fainted.

Chapter Five

'Breathe,' a voice said. 'I have you safe.'

She knew who it was, of course, although quite why she was in his arms this time Sophie had no idea. She found she had no objection to it, which was puzzling.

Cautiously she opened her eyes.

No screaming mob, no dusty market square. Simply the plush, comfortable morning room of her godmother's house. Pascoe appeared to be sitting on the sofa and she was in his arms. It should have felt comforting. Or perhaps shocking. Instead it felt...*agitating* in a strangely pleasant manner.

'What...?' she managed.

'You fainted.'

She tried to sit up and flinched at the pain in her back. 'Nonsense.'

'You are bruised, you had a severe shock yesterday, very little sleep last night, if I am any judge, and you have been bottling up your feelings and fears for far too long. Sooner or later something has to give way. You should stay here for a few days and recover.'

'I cannot. You know I cannot.' Sophie twisted around to look him in the face and winced—but not at the pain.

'And I had thought you an intelligent woman, Duchess. What can you hope to do in London? There was no need for you to come in the first place. Grant and I can manage perfectly well.'

'I am sick to death of sitting with my hands folded while men do everything,' she said fiercely. 'I want... I want to *do* something. Hit something.'

'But duchesses do not go around hitting things with no provocation, do they?'

'No,' she agreed wistfully, her gaze fixed on the knot of his neckcloth, which seemed a fairly safe thing to be looking at. Her heartbeat felt oddly unsteady, yet his hands were respectfully still around her waist and shoulders. There was nothing to get agitated about, no reason to feel so heated. In a moment she would stand up and go upstairs to organise their departure. No doubt she would sleep in the carriage...

Pascoe shifted her, freeing an arm. She felt one finger under her chin, tipping up her face. He was very close.

'Duchess?'

'Yes...' she breathed, without any conscious thought

at all, only in instinctive response to the question in his voice.

The kiss lasted seconds. A fleeting pressure of his lips on hers. Long enough for her to register warmth and the taste of coffee and man. Long enough to send quivering arrows of sensation from her lips to her nipples to secret places far lower.

Quite long enough to realise that she must have taken leave of her senses.

'How dare you?' She found she was on her feet, that Pascoe had risen and set her there as though she was as light as a doll. Furious, Sophie slapped him across the left cheek, then stepped back, appalled. It was herself she was angry with.

'As always, at your service, Duchess.' He rubbed his fingers over the red marks.

'You…you…'

'You wanted something to hit. I gave you a reason and a target,' he said, with a reasonableness that almost had her lifting her hand again.

How could he? How could *she*? That was more to the point. A lady never committed an act of violence unless her life or her virtue was in danger, and the only risk to her virtue was her own wicked curiosity about this man.

And I said yes. Because I wanted him. What is happening to me?

She turned with all the poise she could summon

and stalked to the door. The confounded man was before her, opening it without a word. Sophie swept through and was halfway up the stairs before she realised something else—Pascoe appeared completely unmoved by the entire episode. Not by her anger, not by the slap and, most infuriating of all, not by the kiss.

Not that it had been much of a kiss, she told herself. The merest brush of his lips…a moment's exchange of breath. Not that she had any experience of such caresses. The Duke had performed his marital duties regularly, briskly and without any display of affection. In public he'd kissed her hand or her cheek. And before her betrothal she had behaved with the utmost decorum—no young buck had ever caught Lady Sophia alone on a terrace or in a convenient alcove at a ball, where he could snatch an improper embrace.

Really, for a first kiss it had been entirely unsatisfactory. The reason that her knees felt wobbly and her pulse was racing was simply anger. That was all.

Nick turned from the door and caught sight of his own reflection in the glass hanging above the fireplace.

'The portrait of a perfect idiot,' he said out loud. 'Have you completely lost your senses?'

A question to which the answer was, quite clearly, *Yes*.

That kiss had been unprofessional, ungentlemanly

and unwise. But he had done it without being aware of any intention whatsoever. The excuse that he had offered her—that he had wanted to provide a target for her anger—had been very much an afterthought.

But they had both wanted it.

He made himself examine those few hectic seconds coldly. No, he had not been mistaken. Sophie had wanted that kiss as much as he had, and she had known what he was asking when he had spoken that single word. The fact that she had reacted so angrily afterwards simply proved that she had come to her senses just as fast as he had.

Several times he had been employed by women who had made it subtly obvious that they would welcome an advance, and every time he had behaved as though those little hints had gone completely over his head. He had worked for ladies he found both attractive and arousing and had never had the slightest difficulty in not kissing them.

The fact was, he wanted Sophie—had done so from the moment he'd set eyes on her. She was stiff, starched, dutiful and entirely virtuous. And that, rogue that he was, only made her more desirable. Now he knew what that pale and lovely face looked like when it was blushed pink by emotion. When those faintly smiling lips were parted and panting. When she ceased to be a duchess and was purely a woman.

Purely—that was the word. She was utterly respectable. It would never have occurred to her to imagine the things that his mind presented to him when he thought of them together.

Nick thumped his clenched fist on the mantel shelf and then swore when he realised he'd used the bandaged one.

He had thrown away her trust in him, he feared, and he needed that back if he was to retrieve those diaries for her.

Resigning the commission crossed his mind for a fleeting moment and was dismissed. He finished what he started. Always. Whatever it cost.

The cavalcade of carriages, riders and led horses finally drew up before the front steps of St Edmunds House in Bedford Square at seven that evening, by which time Sophie was feeling like a well-wrung dishcloth.

Freddie had decided that another day in a jolting carriage was too much, and had howled himself into exhausted sleep—only to wake at every change of horses and reject food or cuddles or entertainment.

Her back hurt, her mind refused to confront what had passed between Pascoe and herself before breakfast, and she was strongly tempted to join Freddie in a display of extravagant weeping.

But duchesses did not allow themselves such weaknesses. Mama had drilled into her the fact that a lady of high rank must always overcome the discomforts of the body and mind in order to do her duty.

So now Sophie descended, thanked the driver and the grooms and outriders, greeted her household staff with every degree of gracious attention, made decisions about dinner and the requirements for an exhausted little duke's bedtime, and finally collapsed into an armchair in her suite.

Foskett bustled about, apparently revived from her own travel weariness by the prospect of ordering about the housemaids and footmen. Hot water for Her Grace's bath, a reviving cup of tea, this trunk and that valise to be brought to the dressing room at once for her Grace's evening clothes…

Sophie closed her eyes and let it all wash over her. Until the nursery maid came in to report that His Grace had revived miraculously at the prospect of his bath and that both he and Nanny were about to sit down to a light nursery tea before bedtime.

'Call me when it is time for his bedtime kiss.'

'Yes, Your Grace.'

Which meant that she must rouse herself, bathe and change, put on some jewellery and be a calm and reassuring presence in the nursery before appearing downstairs to eat in solitary splendour.

Or not so solitary, it transpired.

As Sophie descended to the ground floor she was met by Duncan in the hall.

'Might we join you for dinner, Your Grace? A jackdaw's nest has just come down the chimney in my eating room and the place is full of soot.'

Duncan occupied a suite of two bedchambers, a dressing room, an eating room-cum-study and a sitting room on the top floor, below the attic rooms for the servants. It gave him privacy and space to accommodate single male visitors—such as her man of law, when he visited.

'We can go out to a chop house if we would be disturbing you, of course.'

'Not at all. Please tell Padwick to have extra places laid.'

Pascoe was in the drawing room when she entered. 'Duchess…' He bowed, immaculate in the severest evening black and white.

'Pascoe.' She inclined her head graciously. There, they might only just have been introduced. 'Do pour yourself a glass of Madeira. I will take one also.'

Sophie settled in her favourite chair with a view out to the square. 'I trust you are comfortably housed and that the soot has not reached your room?'

'Most comfortable, Duchess, thank you,' he said from the sideboard, where he was investigating the silver labels on the decanters. 'The problem is entirely confined to the eating room. I shall, in any case, be moving on tomorrow.'

How very formal they were. Sophie found herself

relaxing a little—and then his actual words struck home.

'Moving on?'

'Of course. It would hardly do for Estella Doucette to associate me with this house. And I am sure, if I manage to arouse the slightest interest in her, she will investigate me very thoroughly.'

'She will?'

He handed her a glass and took the seat opposite. 'Would you not look into a potential investment with great care? If she is going to spend any time with me then she will want to be certain it is worth her while.'

'But will you not be known in London? How can you keep your identity secret?'

'I will not even attempt it. I am known, of course, but mostly by people who have absolutely no desire to provoke questions about how we come to be acquainted. They are not likely to gossip. She will discover in me a gentleman of some means, prepared to pay well for her company. I shall make it clear I will not remain in London above a few months, and that should attract her. She will want to dip her toe into society waters again. I will do for that, whilst she looks around for a more promising, more permanent attachment.'

'And *you* move in society?' Sophie asked sceptically. 'I can hardly imagine you at Almack's.'

'Believe me, the lady is hardly likely to be seeking a voucher for the Marriage Mart.'

The thought appeared to amuse him. It amused Sophie too, to picture Pascoe drinking tepid lemonade and flirting in an unexceptional manner with youthful debutantes.

'I will have no problem in attending the kind of function where La Doucette will be seeking her new protector. Those will be the sophisticated parties that careful mamas steer their innocent charges away from.'

There was laughter lurking in his dark eyes, she realised, fighting the instinct to sway towards them.

'I belong to London clubs, and I have a wide circle of acquaintance. I realise that you regard me as some sort of adventurer, lurking in the shadows, but I can assure you that I am perfectly acceptable in society—even if you are unlikely to find me at a duchess's tea party.'

Sophie, who had been taking a sip of Madeira, almost choked.

'You appear to think me one step up from a Bow Street Runner,' Pascoe said.

'I think you a rogue!' Sophie countered, provoked.

'Oh, well, that I hold my hand up to,' Pascoe said. 'But I am a socially acceptable rogue, at a clearly defined level of society.'

Sophie set down her glass sharply on the little table

by her chair and got to her feet. Pascoe, of course, being a gentleman as well as a rogue, promptly got to his.

'I am at your disposal if you wish to hit something again, Duchess. Ah, no… I see you prefer to swish back and forth. Decidedly less painful for me.'

She had just reached the end of the room and now turned with, it was true, a loud swish of silk as the demi-train of her evening gown swept over the carpet.

'Has anyone ever told you how very provoking you are, Pascoe?' she enquired, rather pleased with the cool tone she achieved.

'Frequently. They do, however, find me very effective,' he said, equally cool.

Defiantly Sophie stalked down the length of the room again, turning with an ever more dramatic swish at the end. She was not used to this. She employed a wide range of professionals and she had friends and close acquaintances of her own rank, or close to it. She had never experienced someone from the first group who behaved to her as though they were of the second.

She frowned at him. Pascoe met her gaze and, quite perceptibly, the corners of his mouth twitched into a smile.

'Pax?' He held up his hand in the fencer's formal sign of surrender.

Damn the man.

Duchesses did not swear, of course, so provoking

her even to think such a word was a black mark against him. She ought to be severely displeased at his familiarity, and show it. But, treacherously, Sophie's mouth curved into an answering smile.

'Pax,' she agreed as he lowered his hand and held it out to her.

It would be businesslike to shake hands, even though it was not something ladies did, she thought as she took a few steps towards him. A nice, firm handshake would establish the nature of their contract.

Pascoe's fingers closed over hers and she let their joined hands curl together, braced for a brisk, masculine shake. Nothing happened. They stood, hand-fast, looking at each other, it seemed, without being capable of either words or actions. His pulse beat under her fingertips, as hers must under his. There was that subtle hint of citrus again, and that smile in those unfathomable eyes, and she really ought to let go. *Now.*

'I do apologise for keeping you waiting, Your Grace,' Duncan said from the doorway behind her.

Sophie froze, but Pascoe's fingers had already released hers and he was offering, with the other hand, a glass of nut-brown liquid.

'Madeira, I think you said, Duchess?'

It was his own glass, of course, she realised, after a second of confusion during which she wondered if he was a conjuror as well as everything else.

'Thank you. Do not forget your own.' She made a

vague gesture towards the glass on the side table. 'You have not kept me waiting at all, Duncan. Pascoe and I have been discussing his tactics. Do take some wine.'

'Thank you.' Her old friend, who did not appear to have noticed anything out of the way, went to the sideboard. 'Strategy before tactics, I think, Pascoe.'

'Oh, I have the strategy clear enough…' As Sophie sat down Pascoe subsided with long-limbed grace into his own chair. 'Now I have to come up to the enemy and engage.'

'No scouting and skirmishing?' Duncan sat on the arm of the sofa, one leg swinging, glass in hand.

'Skirmishing comes later.'

Her steward snorted.

Sophie decided that this military banter was, in fact, masculine bawdy teasing. Well, three could play at that game. Anything rather than try and work out what had just happened between Pascoe and herself.

'Oh, do explain skirmishing to me, Duncan,' she said, all wide-eyed innocence, with a look she knew perfectly well he would recognise as false.

'Pascoe is the expert at that,' he riposted.

'It involves engaging the enemy in light attacks—flea bites—to distract and weaken them. It also helps to establish their strengths and vulnerabilities.'

'Preceded by scouting, I assume?'

'Exactly. I need to establish where La Doucette is, where she goes, what she plans, and then intercept her.'

'And if you see her marching into a publisher's office with four red-bound books under her arm…?'

'I throw a sack over her head, bundle her into a hackney carriage and remove the books,' he said promptly. 'Daylight abduction in a busy street does tend to cause a certain degree of uproar, but most hackney drivers will do anything for a sovereign or two.'

'Excellent,' Sophie said, and then had qualms. 'It would be very alarming for her…'

'A thief must expect some alarm in the course of a life of crime,' Duncan said grimly. 'And it isn't as though we'd dump her into the Thames.'

'We'd simply remove the diaries, deposit her in a respectable street and leave her to extract herself from the sack. She would never know who had snatched her,' Pascoe summarised tersely.

'Is that a likely scenario?' Sophie asked, fascinated by the depth of their planning.

'Shouldn't think so for a moment,' Duncan said with a grin. 'About as likely to occur as the lady walking into a publishing house in broad daylight.'

'Oh! You are teasing me!'

He hadn't done that since she had put up her hair and begun to wear long dresses. And Sophie found that she had missed it—although why her old friend was suddenly so much more relaxed, she didn't know. Unless, of course, it was Pascoe's influence.

She felt a kindling of warmth towards the man, almost enough to overcome the prickly reserve she was trying to erect between him and her own treacherously wanton reactions. Duncan worked hard for her, albeit in return for a very fair salary and excellent accommodation. But his consciousness of his position as her trusted right-hand man made it difficult for him to form close friendships. Pascoe, it seemed, was an exception.

There was a discreet cough from the doorway. 'The evening post has arrived, Your Grace. Do you wish to see it now or after dinner?' enquired Padwick, her butler. 'I believe Monsieur Guiscard expects to send up the first course in fifteen minutes.'

'In that case I will glance at it now—if you will excuse me, gentlemen.' Padwick proffered a silver salver. 'Goodness, so many…'

'Opening up the house has alerted the newssheets, Your Grace. I believe your arrival has been mentioned in the Court and Social columns of a number of the better publications.'

The butler took himself out with a bow, and Sophie sifted through the handful of post. 'Two advertisements for dressmakers, a programme of concerts of ancient music and four invitations. A musicale, a dinner party, a reception—and, of all things, a picnic. I had not expected any social engagements at this time of year.'

'The poor weather at the end of the summer has sent many people back from the seaside or the countryside, I suspect,' Duncan said. 'Now things have improved they are looking around for entertainment, and a picnic in early October probably struck one hostess as novel.'

'Lady Faversham. Her gardens are lovely, so I may well attend if this weather holds.'

Sophie glanced at the rest and set them aside. She would probably accept them all, even though butterflies began to stir in her stomach at the thought of crowds of people after so long. She had withdrawn to the country when she was four months pregnant with Freddie, as the Duke had forbidden any excitement or exertion that might harm his longed-for heir. Then a year of mourning immediately after the birth had left her feeling that London and its social whirl was a half-remembered dream.

All my clothes will be sadly out of the mode, and I have no idea about any of the gossip, she thought, rapidly making mental lists of modistes to visit and journals to purchase.

'Dinner is served, Your Grace,' Padwick intoned. 'And Mr Spencer arrived an hour ago.'

'Excellent, thank you.' Jeremy Spencer was her secretary, and he had followed them down once he had set all in order at his department at Vine Mount House. 'Ask Mr Spencer if he would care to join us.'

Sophie found a social smile and prepared to practise her somewhat rusty conversational skills upon the three gentlemen.

Safety in numbers, she thought.

Chapter Six

Pascoe had gone from the house by the time Sophie came down for breakfast the next morning. She found it made her unsettled—which was foolish, because he was out there doing something about Estella Doucette and the diaries. She was quite safe from stampeding mobs of villagers, or even fainting fits, and had no need of him in person. In fact, it was much better that he was somewhere else, so that she could recover from whatever reaction it was that he had provoked in her.

Jeremy Spencer joined her at ten o'clock, the large diary that he kept for her in his hand, and they went through the invitations from the night before which had now been joined by two more: an At Home and a Venetian Breakfast.

'The hour for that is four in the afternoon.' Jeremy frowned at the invitation card. 'Somewhat late for breakfast.'

'A silly term, I agree. But it has nothing to do with either breakfast or Venice, so far as I can tell, and there will be a great deal of gambling. Refuse that one, please, but accept everything else.'

'Then that is everything that requires your attention, Your Grace.' He gathered up his papers and got to his feet as she thanked him.

Sophie decided that she had earned an hour with Freddie and went upstairs. Time spent listening to his complicated and highly conversational attempts at language whilst they rolled a large ball back and forth or played pat-a-cake and peep-bo was possibly the best part of her day.

'Mama! Mama!'

She picked him up and hugged him. 'Clever boy. What shall we play this morning? Ball? Horse?'

The estate carpenter had made a wooden horse on wheels that caused great hilarity when pushed.

'Pas?'

'Mr Pascoe has gone, dear.' Sophie sank down in a swirl of skirts and rolled the ball.

Freddie's lower lip jutted out. 'Pas. Want.'

'No, Freddie.'

Why on earth had Freddie formed such a fascination with Pascoe? The man hadn't even spoken to him.

'I expect he liked Mr Pascoe's pretty horse, ma'am,' Nanny said comfortably. 'Now, then, my little dukeling…no sulks when Mama has come to see you.'

Exactly, Sophie thought. *No sulks.*

* * *

Three days later Sophie re-joined society.

'Her Grace the Duchess of St Edmunds!'

Close to the door where Lady Harper's major domo was making his announcements, the loud buzz of conversation hushed.

Sophie, a faint social smile firmly in place, stepped into the reception room. Her nerves were bolstered by an evening gown in the very height of fashion that Madame Felice had, she assured her, been keeping ready for the moment Her Grace returned to London, but even so she felt a faint qualm as she was immediately surrounded.

Old friends, many acquaintances, and not a few gentlemen with a predatory gleam in their eyes all clustered around. Sophie took the proffered arm of Admiral Bradford and gratefully allowed him to chase away the hopeful young gentlemen. With a glower from under beetling white eyebrows he steered her in the direction of a glass of champagne.

An hour later the stir caused by her appearance had died down and she was able to circulate in comfort. The ostensible reason for Lady Harper's reception was to launch her favourite nephew into society, now that he had graduated from university, but the Countess was never without an excuse for a party, so no one was very interested in young Humphrey's moderate academic triumphs.

After the Admiral's gruff company and the stimulus of the wine Sophie found her nerves had subsided. Her old social skills came back as though she hadn't been away from high society for almost eighteen months.

She was discussing the latest court gossip with Lady Gaydon when the Countess stared past her, eyebrows raised.

'Who is that very striking gentleman, I wonder? He looks familiar, but I cannot quite place him.'

Sophie turned a little so she could scan the crowd casually.

'All in black and white,' Lady Gaydon prompted. 'Standing beside the arrangement of roses and ferns.'

And there was Pascoe, a sleek magpie, severe and sinister, amidst colourful uniforms, fancy waistcoats and glittering gowns.

And looking around him with as much hidden mischief as that bird, I'll wager, Sophie thought.

'He is a Mr Pascoe,' she said out loud. 'I encountered him the other day.'

'Cornish family?' Lady Gaydon mused. 'Very decorative, if you like the Italian assassin type. I can just see him in *The Perilous Quest of Isabella de Ville*—have you read it yet? Too thrilling and spine-chilling for words! There's a sinister monk and a mysterious assassin, and Isabella and her true love Augustus are trapped in a castle haunted by hideous spectres.'

'I must put my name down for it at Lackington's circulating library,' Sophie said vaguely.

Who was the woman Pascoe was talking to? There was something about her...the turn of her head, the rich brown of her hair...that stirred memories.

'Who is he with?' she said out loud.

'I have no idea.' Lady Gaydon studied the woman. 'She is elegant—that is a gown by Cherisse, for all that it is so apparently simple. I do like that muted shade of rose. Another widow recently returned to society, do you think? She has an air of confidence about her. Older than him, of course, although she hides it well.'

Sophie, who was beginning to have a strong suspicion about just who this composed and stylish woman was, said lightly, 'Now I am definitely intrigued. I shall go and discover her identity.'

'Do let me know.' The Countess narrowed her eyes at the curvaceous figure so well displayed by the seemingly modest gown. 'The more I look at her, the more I think she is the sort of female one keeps one's husband well away from.'

I rather suspect you are all too right about that, Sophie thought as she began to drift across the crowded room, stopping here and there to exchange a few words with old acquaintances, but always making for the couple by the lavish flower arrangement.

She moved as though to pass them, a faint smile of acknowledgement on her lips. It took all her self-control to keep any hint of recognition from her face. If Pascoe wanted to make his companion known to her, he would say so.

And it seemed he did. 'Duchess.' The sketched bow was perfect. 'How very gratifying to see you in London society again.'

'Ah... Oh, yes, Mr Pascoe. Yes, it has been a while.'

'Indeed. May I present Mrs Sweeting, who has also been away from town for some time? Mrs Amanda Sweeting, Your Grace. Mrs Sweeting—Her Grace, the Duchess of St Edmunds.'

'Mrs Sweeting.' Sophie kept her expression blandly pleasant as she inclined her head.

The other woman dropped a slight curtsey. 'Your Grace...' She might have acknowledged Sophie's rank, but her manner was anything but obsequious.

Sophie caught Pascoe's glance. *Sweeting, indeed! A neat enough version of Doucette. And Amanda?* That meant love, or loveable, if she remembered rightly. One could not fault the creature's poise. *Of course,* Sophie mused, *she must have seen me from across the room and has had plenty of time to compose herself to meet her lover's widow. And she despises me because I could not hold my own husband's affections, I am sure.*

'Do you make a long stay in London, Mrs Sweeting?' she asked graciously, unable to resist making her tone slightly patronising.

'I am undecided. Some weeks, at least. I had a bereavement some time ago, and now I must decide how my future will develop.'

She was far too subtle to allow her gaze to do more than touch Pascoe, standing silently beside her. Sophie found herself admiring her adversary's style. It would not do to underestimate 'Mrs Sweeting' for one moment…

Nick watched the Duchess with a growing feeling of appreciation. She had clearly not expected to encounter Estella Doucette here at this reception, and it must have come as a shock to find her so subdued and ladylike in dress and manner. If he had not known any better he would have placed the courtesan as the highly respectable widow of some gentleman of means.

The evening before he had engineered an introduction to her at a select card party, and shown his own interest in her so subtly that he doubted any respectable lady would have noticed a thing. But La Doucette most certainly had. When she made eye contact her gaze lingered just a fraction too long, when she was close to him her pampered white hands fluttered, occasionally touching his sleeve, his hand, as if she was unaware of it.

And when Nick allowed his hand to linger at the small of her back, or on her arm, she did not give him a shocked or reproving look. Instead, he knew she was assessing him as closely as he was her. Those caressing fingers now knew the quality of his coat, and those heavy-lidded looks had valued his watch chain, the single heavy signet ring on his left hand, and the fineness of the linen handkerchief he had produced to flick away some drops of champagne that had fallen upon her skirts.

Money and taste, that assessment would have told her. *Sophistication,* she would have concluded from the way he treated her, the company he was at ease in. And she was sufficiently intrigued by this, and his vagueness about just where he had been and what his business was in London, to allow this chance-met acquaintanceship a few days and discover what might develop.

She had her eyes on a far bigger prize, of course. She would be seeking a protector with a title and with significant wealth. But when she had that gentleman in her sights she would want to devote her undivided attention to him. So first she needed to realise the asset she had acquired with the late Duke's diaries.

I will do very well, Nick thought with a wry inward smile. *I can squire her about, spend some money on her, allow her to get her feet firmly under the table in London society. She will take care not to alert the ladies that she is dangerous, even as she hunts their husbands.*

The Duchess now made some graciously sympathetic comment on La Doucette's bereavement—no, he must not think of her like that, but as Amanda Sweeting—and he felt the woman beside him bristle at being patronised by the younger lady…the one whose husband had been hers for so many years.

'So pleased to have met you, Mrs Sweeting,' the Duchess said. 'Mr Pascoe…'

She let her gaze lock with his for just a few seconds more than the conventional before she nodded graciously and strolled away. Nick could not decide whether she was deliberately flirting with him to annoy Mrs Sweeting or whether, like him, she was recalling that almost-kiss. The thought that she might be sent a stab of desire through him—one that he channelled instantly towards the woman beside him.

'So very young for a duchess and a widow…' he murmured, letting his right hand rest at the small of Amanda Sweeting's back, so that she would feel its warmth. 'But pretty enough. I suppose she will soon find a number of suitors for her hand.'

'You sound dismissive.'

'I would never be so disrespectful. But I find youth in combination with haughtiness unappealing. I prefer a little more maturity…a little more warmth.'

'Indeed?' Mrs Sweeting laid her hand on his arm and leaned subtly towards him. 'How discerning of you, Mr Pascoe.'

'Won't you call me Nick?'

'Nick,' she agreed, and the white fingers closed a little more tightly on the superfine of his coat.

'What happened?' Sophie asked, the moment Nick was shown into her small sitting room at ten the next morning. 'I mean…good morning, Pascoe. Will you take coffee?'

'Good morning, Duchess. And, yes, I will, thank you.'

'Black with no sugar, I assume?' she said, pouring from the delicate Wedgwood pot at her side.

'How ever did you guess?' he murmured, accepting the cup and saucer she passed him.

Sophie lifted one eyebrow but made no comment.

Nick told himself firmly that he must stop thinking of her as anything but *the Duchess*, and drank to give himself time to order his thoughts. The very fact that he needed to set them in order, given that they had been perfectly marshalled before he entered the room, was concerning.

He stayed on his feet, as he had been trained to do as a young officer, reporting intelligence to his commander. The formality felt more comfortable, somehow, and helped him order his scattered thoughts. He drained his coffee in one swallow and placed the delicate little cup and saucer back on the table.

'As you have no doubt guessed, Mrs Amanda Sweeting is Estella Doucette. We have established that

I am…interested in her, and that she is not averse to spending more time in my company. I was permitted to drive her home last night and invited in for a nightcap.'

That eyebrow rose again, and the lush lips thinned a trifle.

'A very excellent brandy was all that I partook of—very properly—in an elegant drawing room, with a footman in attendance in the hall.'

'I am glad to hear it,' the Duchess said crisply. 'I was concerned that you might have put yourself in a compromising position on my behalf.'

Nick was conscious of irritation. Did she think that he was some innocent who might fall into the claws of a predatory female? And then he realised that was not what was rubbing at him at all. He was not given to self-deception, and he had to admit to himself that he was piqued that Sophie—damn, there he went again—the *Duchess* was showing no signs of jealousy. Merely the responsible concern of an employer anxious that she might have placed someone in an invidious position.

Which meant that he was finding her attractive. He both desired her and found it hard to resist acting on that desire. That had never happened to him before.

The wisdom of not mixing business with pleasure was a cliché, but none the less valid for all that—and besides, he preferred his relationships uncomplicated.

An entanglement with a duchess was the very opposite of that. Not that it was going to happen. Not with this woman, who appeared to have duty and decorum engraved on her soul.

'What is it?' Sophie said sharply. 'There is something you are not telling me: I can see it in your face.'

'Nothing,' Nick snapped back, shaken that he had betrayed anything.

'I don't believe you.'

She was on her feet too quickly and she swayed, unsteady for a moment. Her hand reached out, seeking something to steady herself, and his was there, drawn to hers like a magnet to iron. He tugged and she was standing right in front of him, one hand still caught in his, the other palm flat against his chest.

For balance or to feel his heartbeat?

'This is what is wrong,' Nick said as she looked up into his face, her eyes wide, her lips parted.

She would pull away, or slap him now, he thought. Because he could see her awareness in those wide green eyes.

'You want me?' Sophie asked, and he could hear bewilderment instead of her usual calm and decisive tones.

'You noticed?' Nick spoke harshly. It was deliberate. She would step away now. Or slap him first. Yes, a slap would be best.

Sophie did neither. Instead, she gave a little sigh and

stepped closer. Hell. He should move back, release her hand. Leave the room. *Run.*

'I didn't think… My husband never desired me.'

'Then, with all due respect to the late Duke, the man was an idiot.'

She gave a little gasp of laughter. It transformed her face from its calm beauty to something enchanting and very young.

'And no one has ever tried to flirt with me.'

'Because you are a duchess, and a very proper one at that. And I am not flirting.'

'No?'

'No. I am entertaining thoughts that deserve another slap,' he admitted, even while his feet appeared to have taken root in the Aubusson carpet and his fingers, curled around her hand, had forgotten how to open.

'So am I,' the Duchess admitted. 'I am hoping you will kiss me again—properly this time. No one ever has, you see.'

If she had sought for a week to find something to surprise him she could not have done better.

'But… You were a married woman, Sophie. You have a son.'

Sophie was blushing now, a delicious rosy tint that aroused his thoughts of where else on her body the skin might be so soft and pink.

'My husband came to my bed to perform his marital duties until he had me with child. He behaved towards me with respect, not affection. My cheek and my fingers have been very thoroughly kissed, but not my lips. Never my lips.'

She would realise what she was doing in a moment and order him to go. Or she would turn and run.

Run, he thought as he bent towards her parted lips. *Run now, before it is too late.*

Sophie moved closer and their lips met.

She tasted of coffee and woman and roses. The part of his brain that still worked thought there must be some cream she put on her lips, because they were even softer than he recalled from that fleeting brush when she had slapped him. They had been parted when he bent his head, but now they were closed, and Nick realised that she was, indeed, quite unfamiliar with kissing.

He ran his tongue along the seam of her lips and could almost hear her puzzlement over what he was about. He nudged again, and this time she opened her mouth to him with a little gasp. It took a moment or two, but then she met him, shyly at first, and then more boldly.

Beneath that controlled and proper exterior was a sensual woman, Nick realised, gathering her close, feeling his body respond to the warm curves pressed against it. When the fingers of her free hand curled into the hair at his nape he felt his control crumbling, his hands flexing as they yearned to stray over her body, find laces and buttons, strip her bare and lay her on the chaise longue in front of the window.

Go on, then. Behave like a reckless idiot and debauch an innocent lady.

Chapter Seven

'Oh!' Sophie found herself standing a foot away from Pascoe, her right hand still in his, his other hand resting lightly at her waist. For once he was looking distinctly ruffled and his breath was coming hard. She found to her surprise that she glad to see what an effect that kiss had had on him.

'You tripped,' he said tightly.

'I did nothing of the kind,' she retorted, even while one part of her mind was demanding to know what on earth she was thinking of. She should have accepted the excuse he was offering her, the opportunity to regain her dignity and act as though that kiss had not happened. But it had, and it had been glorious, so why was he pretending now?

And then she realised.

She had been untutored and inept. Pascoe had not enjoyed the experience and now he was offering them both a way to ignore the whole thing.

Augustus had always discouraged her tentative attempts to reciprocate the things that he did to her body in their bed. Perhaps men did not want that. And her caressing his hair, his neck, touching her own tongue to his, had disgusted Pascoe. Augustus had not liked her to respond to him and Pascoe must be the same.

'I… Yes, of course. I tripped. How clumsy of me. Thank you for catching me.'

'It is forgotten,' he said. 'Everything is forgotten.'

'Thank you,' Sophie said again, wishing that Aubusson carpets came with trapdoors to swallow one up.

No miracle occurred to save her, so she returned to her chair and sat down with painstaking attention to her deportment. She had thought herself humiliated by her husband openly keeping a mistress under her roof, but she had never realised how much greater humiliation could be if one brought it upon oneself.

She focused on her own hands, clasped in her lap, until she had outwardly regained her composure. 'What are your plans now, Pascoe?' she asked. 'In regard to Mrs Sweeting, that is?' she added, and felt herself blush again at how clumsy that had sounded. He would have no plans regarding *her*, that was certain.

'I shall call on her this afternoon, to discover her intentions for the evening. I shall ensure that she sees me at whatever gathering best suits my timing, and then go and search her house in her absence. After that I shall reappear, making certain that she sees me again.'

'You will have enough time?'

'Probably not. This may be the work of several evenings,' he said indifferently, as though repeated housebreaking was as trivial as visiting his tailor for a new top coat.

'And if you are caught?'

'Highly unlikely. But if I am then my intentions are entirely amorous, not larcenous. I will be awaiting the lady with a gift.' He dug in the fob pocket of his waistcoat and pulled out a black velvet pouch. 'Your hand, Duchess?'

When she extended it, Pascoe tipped the contents into her palm. There was the tickling caress of a gold chain warmed by his body heat and then the solid weight of an emerald, its banked green fires glowing darkly in the morning light as though waiting for the night time to shine.

'This is a valuable piece,' she said.

He shrugged. 'If I have to give it to her I will regard it as a loan. She will not get to keep it.' His mouth that had been so warm and supple, so caressing on hers, curved into a thin smile.

Sophie shivered. 'Take it back.'

His fingers barely grazed her palm as he lifted the jewel, but she had to repress the desire to close her own around them, trap that sinister green gem between them until it was warmed by their blood. Instead she flattened her hand completely, as she would when offering a titbit to her horse, and watched the swaying gold chain slither into the pouch.

When he gave it to Estelle Doucette would he trail that fluid snake of golden links across her naked flesh? What would that feel like?

The image was so erotic that she stood up abruptly and turned to the door. 'Doubtless you can show yourself out, Pascoe. I must go to my son.'

'Of course, Duchess.'

Despite her sudden movement he was at the door before her. As he opened it, she passed so close that the frill at the hem of her muslin morning gown fluttered over his Hessian boots.

'All forgotten, Sophie,' he murmured. 'All forgotten.'

Sophie. Her name spoken in that deep voice felt like the pressure of a hand at the base of her spine...like the slide of rich chocolate over her tongue...the caress of the velvet collar of her evening cloak as it brushed against her throat.

If his words were meant to reassure her, they had the opposite effect. He was reminding her, surely, of his power and her indiscretion, and her own body was betraying her. She should feel shamed and afraid— and she did—but she knew too that she wanted more...that Pascoe's kiss had woken something that should have stayed buried and sleeping for her own safety.

* * *

'Are you sure, Your Grace?' Foskett stood back and bit her lip.

Sophie studied herself in the long glass. Madame Celine had excelled herself. 'It is a beautiful ball gown...'

'But you are in half-mourning, Your Grace.'

'It is grey,' Sophie pointed out. 'And white. And purple.'

That was all perfectly accurate. A cloud of pale grey gauze floated over an underskirt of the matte white satin that had also been used in the intricately pleated bodice and the tiny puff sleeves ornamented with seed pearls. Thin silk ribbons in shades of purple and lilac were plaited through the edge of the neckline, in amongst the pleats of the sleeves and around the hem.

With the gown Sophie wore the fabled Delavigne moonstone parure. In themselves, moonstones were not particularly valuable, but a century before a skilled Mughal craftsman had wrought a set of the perfectly matched stones that held a mysterious milky glow into an intricate set of tiara, earrings, necklace and bracelet. Presented to a member of the Delavigne family who had been an ambassador to the Agra court, they were now treasured, but rarely worn, because of the difficulty of finding the right gown to set them off.

'And moonstones are like pearls and jet—perfectly suitable for half-mourning,' Sophie added, a little uncertain herself now.

It was not just because of the gown. Although it was exquisite, highly flattering, and within the rules of mourning—even if it stretched them to the limit. It was not even the swooping neckline and the amount of décolletage that displayed the moonstone necklace that was making her uneasy.

Attendance at the Marchioness of Hallington's ball, wearing a gown like this, was a declaration that the Duchess of St Edmunds was once more back in society in a way that her earlier appearance at a relatively insignificant reception had not been.

She could expect a great deal of interest—gentlemen beginning to make discreet advances, mentions in the gossip columns as well as the court and social reports. She would be deluged with invitations and must pick her way through the minefield of encounters with great care. It was not only military men who had to employ strategy and tactics. Everything she said and did, every friend she made, every old acquaintance she renewed, must be calculated to preserve and enhance the family's name and standing.

At least concentrating on all that would stop her thinking about that reckless kiss four days ago and the man she had shared it with…

Lady Hallington's ball was, as one lady declared as Sophie entered the great panelled room, 'The most frightful squeeze, darling!' In other words, a resounding success even before the first set of dances had drawn to a close.

Her entrance created a stir, as she had expected, but she kept her composure, and her smile, and was relieved to find that at this more formal function she was not mobbed by too many slight acquaintances. Instead she found old friends to talk to, and eventually settled on a small sofa in an embrasure close to the chaperons' corner as partners took their places for the next dance.

She was congratulating herself on finding somewhere to catch her breath and survey the throng when a very familiar voice said, 'May I join you, Duchess?'

No, was the answer that sprang to her lips, but years of training won and Sophie found herself saying, 'Of course.'

Pascoe subsided elegantly onto the seat next to her and Sophie shifted a little, so that she was half facing him, as was only polite.

'What on earth are you doing here?' she demanded, most impolitely, keeping her voice low and her social smile fixed.

'Hunting, naturally. Our quarry is present—although how she obtained an invitation I am unsure.'

'How did *you*?' Sophie managed not to scan the throng in search of Mrs Sweeting.

'I know Lord Jon. We were at university together.'

Lord Jonathon Brough was the Marchioness's second son.

This was another tiny insight into Pascoe's background. Sophie was just being seized with the sudden thought that she could consult the printed registers of the universities—it had to be Cambridge or Oxford, and not one of the Scottish ones—when he said, 'Dance with me, Duchess.'

'Wha—? I mean, certainly not. I am in mourning. I am not dancing.'

'Then why come to a ball? And wear that gown?'

'To see and be seen. I must begin to re-enter society for Frederick's sake.'

'And the approval of society is essential?' Pascoe gestured to the crowded ballroom.

'Of course.'

'May I speak frankly?'

It seemed he was going to, whether she wanted it or not. Sophie gave a tight nod.

'You were brought up to be the wife of an important man. A duke, as it turned out. Your role was to provide an heir and be an impeccable hostess to this powerful man. Now he is dead. And the power has passed into your hands—if you choose to wield it.'

'I have the power to manage Frederick's affairs while he is a minor, yes, but—'

'No. You are still thinking like a young wife. But you are no longer that girl. You are a duchess. You are rich, intelligent, and in a position inferior only to the royal family. You will have control of the young Duke and his vast estates for the next twenty years. No one controls you. You have *power*, Sophie. Influence. You do not have to do what society expects of you. Society will be waiting to see what you do, where you lead, who gains your patronage and approval.'

It was as though someone had drawn back a curtain in a darkened room and let reality flood in. This past year she had found lawyers and bankers and estate managers eager to obey her, but that was only because, she had assumed, they were serving the new little Duke through her. It had not occurred to her that now nobody controlled her, nobody told her how she must behave, how she must be. Not her father, not her brothers, not her husband. She could make decisions for herself, and on her own behalf, not only on Freddie's.

'I had not thought of it like that...' she said slowly. *Power? No, it is freedom.*

'And if you want to dance, then you dance. You are out of your blacks and you have behaved impeccably for over a year in memory of your late husband. Now do what you want, Sophie.'

'Very well.' It would be a tragedy to waste this gown, and the world would not come to an end if she took part in a quadrille. She opened her unused dance card. 'Oh. But it is a waltz next.'

'I assume that you received the blessing of the Patronesses of Almack's to waltz quite some time ago?'

'There is no call to be sarcastic,' Sophie said, feeling the colour come up in her cheeks. 'And what do you know about Almack's, anyway? I cannot imagine you eating dry seed cake and sipping indifferent ratafia there.'

'I know that young ladies require an introduction to a suitable partner by the set of dragons there. Presumably that is to ensure that their virgin sensibilities are not overset by too much vigorous whirling? Or perhaps you find that the dance makes you dizzy?'

'No, it does not.' She refused to rise to his teasing.

'Excellent timing, then.'

Pascoe stood up and she realised that the couples were coming off the dance floor.

He held out his hand. 'Duchess?'

She caught sight of Lady Larchmount, a contemporary of her grandmother, who had been a constant source of moralising strictures and lectures on proper behaviour when Sophie had made her come-out. She had her eyeglass raised and was regarding Sophie with pursed lips.

'Certainly,' she said, putting her hand in Pascoe's.

I outrank her now. And anyway, who was she to judge my behaviour?

It was a liberating thought and she felt pleasantly naughty—which was a novel sensation. She dared not allow herself to think about that kiss, nor about why Pascoe had sought her out and pressed her for this dance, because she must appear cool and calm and quite as though this was the accepted thing.

But thinking about Pascoe was enough to put her in a flutter, she realised rather too late as they took their places and his hand came to rest at her waist. Actually standing this close and touching him was causing sensations that she was hardly able to admit to, let alone try to understand.

It is only a dance, Sophie told herself. *You have waltzed too many times to recall. This is no different.*

The music began, and she made her fingers relax and followed Pascoe's lead. As they swirled down the length of the room she caught sight of people watching them. There were some raised eyebrows, but her friends were smiling, and nobody called out, *Scarlet woman!* Or, *Shocking!*

Conversation, she told herself. *You are not a tongue-tied miss dancing at your first ball.*

'How is your hand now?'

'Quite healed, thank you.'

'You said you were hunting?' She found she was addressing the top of his neckcloth and tipped her head back a little to meet his gaze. 'Shouldn't you be dancing with your quarry?'

'My quarry is watching us now and is quietly seething,' Pascoe said, executing a tricky turn to avoid a blundering major and his over-excited partner. 'That I should not immediately ask her for a dance is bad enough, I imagine. That I should be waltzing with you will not be well-received—not that she will show it.'

'Why risk alienating her?' Sophie asked, forgetting in her puzzlement to watch her steps.

Pascoe almost twirled her off her feet as she stumbled, then set her down again safely. 'Nobody values what comes easily, and she hates you.'

'What cause has she to do so?' Sophie demanded, rather too loudly, and hastily fixed a smile on her lips. 'I am the one who should feel anger towards her: she was committing adultery with my husband!'

'She has done you wrong and she knows it. It is a common human failing to feel resentment and anger towards those we have wounded, because that is less painful than reproaching ourselves. I will dance with you and she will be determined that I shall dance with her—and find her a superior dancer and better company. She will be set on having her small victory in, as she will see it, luring me away from you.'

'How clever of you,' Sophie said with a brittle smile. 'I do admire your tactics. No wonder you've risked offending convention by asking me to dance.'

And risked my reputation, she thought resentfully.

And there she had been, feeling delightfully flustered by Pascoe's attentions, when this dance was nothing more than a ruse.

She should not feel resentful—he was working on her behalf and it was entirely her own fault that she had allowed herself to read something into the mildest of flirtations. She was as green as one of those white-clad girls, blushing and giggling their way through their first grand ball, she thought. She would have to acquire a harder protective shell before any gentlemen intent on matrimony started to cast their lures in her direction.

She found further conversation beyond her, but soon the music was reaching a crescendo. A few final turns and it came to an end. Sophie curtseyed, Pascoe bowed, and offered his arm to escort her back to her seat.

'Oh, no. Over there, if you please. I see Lady Trent is sitting out. I will join her.'

Her friend, who was disguising the early signs of her pregnancy in flowing skirts, obligingly moved to one side of the padded bench to allow Sophie to sit next to her.

'Dorothea, please allow me to present Mr Pascoe. Pascoe—the Countess of Trent.'

There was a polite exchange of bows and then Pascoe turned away into the thick of the crowd. Sophie did not watch him go.

'My dear, such an age since I have seen you!' said Dorothea. 'And what a very handsome man you have chosen to set society upon its ear with.'

'Nonsense. I am a widow—not a young girl. I may dance with whom I choose,' Sophie said, making play with her fan. 'Although he *is* rather decorative in a sinister kind of way, is he not?' she added lightly. 'He is carrying out a small commission for me, that is all. Now, tell me how you are keeping. Is the heir to the earldom behaving himself?'

'If it *is* an heir.' Dorothea wrinkled her pretty nose. 'With my five brothers, everyone expects me to have a boy, but who can tell? As it is, Trent insists I do not dance. Otherwise I would be casting lures to your Mr Pascoe!' She frowned. 'I am sure I have heard his name before, but I cannot recall… Oh, yes! It was last Season, when young Wilbraham got in such a pickle with that dreadful group of card sharps. Trent said that Pascoe pulled the irons out of the fire again. Apparently he considers him an expert in untangling delicate problems.'

'Then you know all about him,' Sophie said, careful not to make it a question.

'Not a thing, dear. Trent was rather mysterious. If you ask me…' the Countess lowered her voice '… Pascoe is not even his name.'

Sophie shrugged. 'Grant vouches for him.'

Then she was cross with herself as she found herself looking at his immaculately tailored back as he bowed over the hand of a lady who was unmistakably Mrs Sweeting.

Chapter Eight

That was clumsy, Nick told himself as he walked away from the Duchess. *Clumsy and thoughtless.* And he had thought himself neither.

He should either have told Sophie from the beginning what he was about, and asked her to dance with him as part of that manoeuvre, or he should have kept his mouth shut about having any other motive than a desire to take to the floor with her.

As it was, he had been at best tactless, at worst hurtful. And then there was that kiss… He should regret that, but he could not, despite the fact that Sophie's feelings about him were probably now deeply confused.

He was attracted to her. There was no denying that. But was she feeling the same? Because if she was, that made everything infinitely more complicated. Although now, as he had just been so clumsy, Sophie was probably regarding him as somewhat lower than the stable yard's tom cat, which would solve that problem.

But what had come over him?

'I beg your pardon, ma'am.' He found himself almost treading on the hem of a ball gown in deep crimson trimmed with a cascade of black lace. 'Ah. Mrs Sweeting... Please forgive me. I was distracted.'

'Indeed?' Amelia Sweeting was too clever to allow her annoyance to show in her voice, but her fingers, tight on the sticks of her fan, betrayed her. 'You were on your way to the card room, perhaps?'

'I was on my way to ask you to dance,' Nick said, taking a savage grip on himself and smiling. 'I suspect I was dazzled.'

The twist of her lips was part pout, part reluctant amusement at the ludicrous flattery. 'I do not intend to dance,' she said, languidly swaying the fan in the space between them.

'Not even when you are wearing such an exquisite gown?'

Not that *exquisite* was quite the word. Provocative, subtly dangerous, darkly feminine... Some lethal animals wore warning signs in their colouration, and he found he was thinking of the hot shadows of a jungle.

'Not even then. Although I am happy to take your arm and promenade, Nicholas.' She used his first name with the hint of a caress.

'An honour, ma'am.'

She was too subtle to lean, or to apply pressure. Instead she strolled with her hand on his forearm, close enough for the scent of warm female skin and musky perfume to fill his nostrils, as she murmured small talk softly enough that he had to bend his head close to listen.

She was steering him, Nick realised. Steering him in a winding route towards where Sophie sat with her friend.

Nick had no intention of ignoring the Duchess. 'Your Grace... Lady Trent.' He paused, bowed and walked on.

'You are on friendly terms with the Duchess?' Mrs Sweeting observed.

'Oh, she is a mere acquaintance. We have mutual friends. It does not do to ignore duchesses,' he added.

'I suppose not... A dear creature. Very young, of course, and really quite out of her depth without the support of her husband. Ah, there is Colonel McCaffery. He has promised me a match at the card tables and I am looking forward to quite a duel.'

The Colonel was sixty if he was a day, a widower, and by all accounts a very wealthy man. Of course this lady would want to flutter those long lashes at him over the card table.

'I will reluctantly surrender you,' Nick said. 'But you will allow me the pleasure of escorting you home, I hope?'

For a moment he wondered whether he was moving too fast, but then she cast him a roguish look from under those lashes. 'How very gallant, Nicholas. I would welcome being in such safe…hands.' Her voice was like a warm finger being trailed slowly down his spine. 'At two of the clock, then?'

He inclined his head and she flitted off to the Colonel—whose chest, Nick could have sworn, expanded by several inches at her approach.

So far so good… Although now he had to pass several hours until the lady was ready to leave, and had to stay stone-cold sober into the bargain. He was going to be able to gain entry to her boudoir, it seemed. Getting out again might be another matter.

At which point the Earl of Chalfont was announced. 'What the devil—?'

Nick realised he had spoken out loud when a man standing near him remarked, 'Indeed, sir. I cannot recall the last time Chalfont attended anything as frivolous as a ball. I'll be amazed if he has not come with bell, book and candle to exorcise the lot of us for our sinful ways.' He chuckled, clearly amused by the sight of the notorious Puritan Earl in the midst of such a social whirl.

Nick was far from diverted. He had made a fine art out of avoiding the man, and this was just about the worst time to find himself in the same room as the Earl. At least he could take refuge in the card room— unless, of course, Chalfont intended to stride about overthrowing tables and lecturing the players on the evils of gambling.

It was not so much running away as beating a strategic retreat, he told himself, as he found an unoccupied table in a corner and began to deal himself a hand of patience.

'What are you up to, Pascoe?' Lord Jon Brough, his hostess's son, slid into the seat opposite him.

'Lurking,' Nick admitted. Jon was one of the very few people who knew who he really was. 'You saw who just came in?'

'Your esteemed sire. What the devil is he doing here?'

'My thought exactly. Play?' He scooped up the cards and began to shuffle.

'Why not? Shilling points, mind. I am on an economy drive.'

The day that happened pigs would fly, in Nick's opinion. He dealt and studied his cards.

'Do you think Chalfont is seeking a new wife?' Brough asked.

Nick made a play. 'Not much point, I'd have thought. Unless he intends to have me disposed of in order to supplant me with a more satisfactory heir, of course. I suppose a fresh young wife might provide him with another son, and then he could consider how to remove me.'

'You are mighty cool about it.' Jon discarded two cards.

'I lost all my heat when I walked out of Cambridge after one week, spent the inheritance from my mother on a commission and went to war. My only regret is that I wasn't there to see how he took the news.'

'That would have been worth buying tickets for,' his friend agreed. 'But he must have been all about in his head...thinking you'd ever make a clergyman.'

'No, he just identified what it was I would most hate and ordered me to do it. Where he was wrong was in assuming I would do as I was told. Are you going to play, or just sit there staring at that hand?'

Jon glanced up. 'Play. I can take a hint. Talking about Chalfont is enough to give *anyone* the blue devils.'

Nick told himself to concentrate on winning this hand, keeping an eye on Mrs Sweeting and trying to work out how to mend fences with the Duchess. He needed to stay focused to achieve all that. Thinking about the man he hated...the man who had driven his mother to an early grave and bullied his gentle older brother into his...would only cloud his mind.

He relieved his friend of several guineas and then sauntered after him to the door of the card room, when Jon announced that he had a partner for the supper set of dances.

'I need a favour,' Nick said abruptly. 'If you feel up to causing a breach of the peace, that is?'

'Sounds amusing.' Jon grinned. 'Tell me what you need.'

With all safely arranged, Nick studied the crowded ballroom. There was no sign of the Earl at first sight… And then he saw him promenading down the length of the room with his partner in the quadrille. The Duchess of St Edmunds.

'A delightful house,' Nick remarked several hours later, as he stood in the front hall of Mrs Sweeting's house, just to the east of Cavendish Square.

'I like it,' she said. 'It will do very well for the present. Would you care for a glass of wine?'

She was going to take him into one of the reception rooms, he thought, irritated. 'That would be very pleasant,' he said.

'This way.'

Then he saw that the footman who had opened the door to them had gone. Amanda Sweeting led him up the sweep of the staircase, trailing her gauze scarf behind her as though making a trail for him to follow.

This was better. A lady kept the things most precious to her in her most private, intimate space—her boudoir. The trick now would be to gain as much intelligence as possible about the layout of her suite of rooms while not finding himself in bed with her. Nick had no objection to amorous encounters, but he disliked deception. And besides, he found the idea of feigning passion for a woman who made the hair on the back of his neck stand up—not in a good way—distasteful. But he could rely on Jon.

He followed Amanda Sweeting through a small sitting room into what seemed to be both boudoir and dressing room. She shed clothing and accessories as she went. Her scarf drifted on to a chair, her reticule and fan were tossed on to a side table, her gloves, peeled off with seductive slowness, were dropped on a small sofa.

'The decanters are there.' She waved a languid hand towards an array of cut crystal and sank down on to the pink satin of the sofa.

Nick took his time pretending to make a choice while he covertly surveyed the room. There were enough items of dainty French furniture scattered about to conceal any number of diaries—most of it with cupboards, drawers and keyholes. There were also some small pictures set quite low above the chair rail, light enough for her to lift down easily. They might conceal safes in the wall. He'd need a good selection of lock picks when he returned.

He took two glasses of wine across and sat down on the sofa.

'Thank you. Would you unclasp my necklace? I told my maid not to wait up for me.'

A likely tale, Nick thought, brushing aside the curls of hair at the white nape being so provocatively offered to him. He unclasped the necklace and she caught it just as it slithered towards her cleavage, then let it trail across the swell of her breasts before she placed it on the table next to her wine glass.

He knew what was expected next, and shifted to take her in his arms.

Come on, Jon.

The racket from downstairs was prodigious. By the sound of it his friend had hired a dozen link boys or several pairs of chairmen to hammer on the door and shout obscenities.

Mrs Sweeting gasped and jumped to her feet. 'What is that?'

'Drunks.' Nick went to the window and looked out. 'A fight of some sort. I will go down and see what I can do to move them along before they damage your front door or railings. Will your footmen help?'

'Yes… Yes, of course.' She jerked on the bell-pull as Nick opened the door. 'Do be careful.'

'I had best not come back inside afterwards,' he said. 'This will have roused your neighbours and I might be seen…which would be indiscreet.'

'Very well.'

A maid came in, fully dressed and wide awake. The tale of having sent the girl to bed was, as Nick had suspected, untrue.

'Oh, Milly, hurry down and close all the shutters on the ground-floor rooms. Then tell the men to help Mr Pascoe move those wretches away.'

As he ran downstairs, the maid at his heels, Nick reflected that now not only had the maid seen him, she knew his name. Mrs Sweeting was making sure that anything he said to her…anything that might be taken as a promise…was witnessed.

He met the two footmen in the hall. 'Just a drunken brawl, I think. But they are alarming the lady.'

As he opened the door half a dozen men were revealed, pushing and shoving each other and shouting. As the light from the hall spilled out they took to their heels, although they kept up the cursing and abuse as they went.

Nick suppressed a smile. Jon had briefed his actors well, and likely parted with some guineas to help their enthusiasm.

'I think they have gone for good,' he said to the men behind him. 'I'll see when I get to the end of the street. You should stay downstairs for a while, to be on the safe side.'

'Yes, sir,' they chodrused. Then, 'Thank *you*, sir,' when he tipped them.

'So what happened? What have you discovered?' Sophie asked.

She was in the drawing room and had asked Duncan to join them when Pascoe arrived. With his stolid presence in the room there was no chance of trips or kisses—accidental or otherwise.

'I escaped with my virtue intact,' Pascoe said, which made Duncan snort with laughter and earned him a frosty look from Sophie. 'My friend Jon Brough or-chestrated a small riot in the street, which I dealt with and then departed.'

'And?' She was not going to gratify him by enquir-ing about his ingenious scheme.

'I now have some idea of the layout of the house. I know where the footmen sleep and I am aware that Mrs Sweeting keeps her maid up, waiting for her. Which makes me think that entering the house to search early rather than late might be sensible. The abigail is more likely to be with the other staff below stairs when she expects her mistress to be absent for several more hours, I would guess.'

'It still seems very risky…' Sophie found she was worrying at her lower lip with her teeth and stopped instantly. She'd be biting her fingernails next.

'We need to act soon. Amanda Sweeting has es-tablished herself in London now. She'll be feeling confident enough to start making enquiries about publishers, or whatever her plan is to profit from the diaries. Lady Fellingham is holding a grand masquer-ade ball next Tuesday. Mrs Sweeting has secured an invitation and so shall I. I will wear something distinctive, make myself known to Mrs Sweeting early on, and then leave to go housebreaking. Meanwhile, someone else wearing the identical costume will be very much in evidence.'

'But who? No one would ever mistake Grant for you, however concealing the mask—you are quite different in height and build.'

'Jon Brough again. I am perhaps an inch taller, and our eyes are different colours, but from across the room it will not be noticeable.'

'Can we trust his discretion?' Grant asked.

'I'll not tell him what this is about, of course. He'll enjoy the deception.'

'I have received an invitation,' Sophie said. 'I had intended to decline, but under the circumstances I will definitely attend. If something goes amiss I may be able to intervene in support of Lord Jon.'

There was a tap on the door and one of the footmen came in. 'Excuse me, Your Grace, but Mr Spencer has received a letter about a legal matter and is most concerned to speak to Mr Grant without delay. A court case, he said.'

'That must be the suit over the right of way in the west park,' Duncan said, getting to his feet. 'There is a very tight timescale for us to present our evidence. Will you excuse me, Your Grace?'

'Of course.'

Duncan strode out, closing the door behind him and

leaving Sophie alone with Pascoe. She tried to think of some neutral, practical thing to say, and failed.

'I should apologise for last night,' he said abruptly. 'I should have explained my tactics in asking you to dance. Clearly the suggestion was unwelcome, and yet you were kind enough to indulge me.'

'I… No. Yes. That is…' She scrabbled to order her thoughts. 'I was taken aback because I had not considered dancing. But I enjoyed it—although it was disconcerting having to think about that woman suddenly.' There, that sounded less like pique and rather more rational.

'It must have been. And again I apologise. But you decided that you would fully enjoy the ball and continued to dance, I believe?'

'Yes. Several gentlemen asked to partner me.'

'Including the Earl of Chalfont?'

She wrinkled her nose at the memory. 'I found him a rather strange man. He did not appear to enjoy dancing, although he did partner several ladies…'

'He considers dancing and music as frivolous at best and sinful at worst. They call him the Puritan Earl,' Pascoe said, with what sounded like distaste.

'Oh, yes! I recall the Duke remarking upon him on one occasion. I suppose he is looking for a new wife.' She gave a little shiver. 'I do not envy the lady his choice falls upon.'

'She can always say no.'

'Not if it is her parents' wish that she marry him. He is highly eligible.'

'Was that your experience? Your parents told you to marry the Duke, so you obeyed?'

'Of course. Although I did not feel uneasy in his presence. The Earl makes me feel nervous, which is foolish. He reminds me of someone…but I cannot think who.'

'I am sure whoever it is would not feel flattered by that,' Pascoe said, his voice clipped. He stood up and went to look out of the window onto the street. 'You would not be tempted to accept a proposal, should he offer?' he asked over his shoulder.

'No, indeed. Not from him—not from anyone. That is one of the strengths of my position—I am entirely free to marry or stay single, as I wish. And as I cannot see any reason why I might wish to wed again that is a very good thing,' she added, with some feeling.

'Not ever?' He turned around, regarding her through narrowed eyes. 'Surely there would be benefits to having a husband?'

'And twice as many dangers,' Sophie retorted. 'I would lose control of everything—including my son. If I made the wrong decision…married someone who had poor judgement or who was bent on milking the estates… I would have no defence. And no escape.'

'You trust your judgement so little?'

Pascoe walked back and sat at the other end of the

sofa. He was barely within arm's length of her, and yet she felt an almost irresistible desire to move. But not away. It was a shock to realise she had almost edged closer to him.

'It is impossible to be certain about the character of someone until you live with them,' she said, smoothing her skirts to cover up that involuntary movement.

'Or find yourself in a situation of danger or stress. That is true, I suppose. In the army I saw men's true natures very clearly. Not just their degree of courage, but their meanness or generosity, arrogance or intelligence. I understand the dangers that you speak of, but surely there are still benefits to marriage for a lady? Companionship? Intimacy?'

Sophie could feel her cheeks heating. Intimacy? Did he mean physical intimacy, or the closeness of two people who understood and trusted each other? Of course he would not understand—would not guess at the aching loneliness that had filled her life.

'I would not know. I mean, that is something I give no thought to.'

'No?' Pascoe said, his gaze intent on her face.

The fire in her cheeks seemed to blaze through her body.

He means physical intimacy.

Chapter Nine

I want him. I desire him. The shock of that explicit thought, of the images it brought with it, almost took her breath. What was happening to her? Why was this man doing this to her?

Somehow she found her voice, and with it words that were not *Yes...now...with you...here.*

'Of course not. That is something that belongs in marriage and I have explained to you why I do not consider it. To marry for...for carnal reasons would be utterly irresponsible.'

'Many ladies in your position would take a lover.'

'Indeed?' She stood up, sweeping her skirts around her as though saving them from his contaminating closeness. 'And that is a responsible course of action? I do not think so.'

Pascoe was on his feet too. 'So you will be a martyr?'

'That supposes that I might be interested in taking

a lover,' she flashed back. 'That I would be suppressing my own needs. I think you should leave, Pascoe.'

'Of course.' He paused, his hand on the door. 'But at least be honest with yourself, Sophie.'

As the door closed behind him she picked up a book from a side table and threw it. It hit the panels with a satisfying thump and fell to the floor.

Of course she had to pick it up, and reassure herself that she had not broken the spine or torn a page. Then Francis, one of the under-footmen, came hurrying in, convinced he had heard her fall, so he had to be reassured. By the time she was alone again Sophie could have quite happily heaped the entire contents of the library on Pascoe's head.

Why was he having this effect on her? Or perhaps this ache inside her would have happened anyway and he had simply coincided with it? Whatever it was— lust, suppressed desire, or the after-effects of all the strains of the past year—she was not herself. Not a self she recognised.

She thought again about those frogs encased in the mud at the bottom of the pond, coming to life as the water warmed. Or perhaps she was hatching out of a chrysalis. What would she be? A butterfly, she hoped. But they were fragile creatures, born for a short life of glamour. Better to be a frog.

She wrinkled her nose at her reflection in the over-mantel mirror, exasperated at her own foolish fantasies. There was no time for this. She had to find a suitable masquerade costume.

'Good evening, Duchess.' The Tudor executioner in black doublet and hose, with a black skull cap and mask and a sword strapped to his back, bowed. 'Or should I say, Maid Marian?'

'Indeed, that is who I am, sir. That is not a real sword, I hope?' she added.

The passage of several days had helped dull her embarrassment over their last encounter and Pascoe showed no awkwardness either—although behind that mask, who could tell?

'A blunted and ancient blade and as lethal as the miniature bow and arrows hanging from your belt. Come this way.'

Pascoe took her arm and steered her through a door, along a passage and up a narrow flight of stairs. Sophie found herself in a gallery overlooking the ballroom. Heat, perfume and the smell of crowded bodies rose up to meet them, along with the strains of the orchestra and the sound of several hundred people all talking at once.

'No one can hear us here,' Pascoe said, surveying the crowded room. 'As I thought, no other gentleman is dressed in plain black as I am. I will stand out by my sheer lack of colour. Now, where…? Yes, look. There is Brough. See? The pirate.'

'Oh, yes, by the door.'

The tall, slim figure wore a flamboyant scarlet and gold sleeveless jerkin over a black doublet and hose. A heavy gold chain hung about his neck and an earring glinted in one lobe. A red bandana covered his hair and his mask was very like Pascoe's. A cutlass in a red velvet scabbard hung from a baldric across his chest.

'When I am ready to leave I will pass Brough my sword. He will hide his jerkin and bandana, take off the jewellery and cutlass and put on the black skull cap he has in his pocket. He will become the executioner.'

'How can we tell what Doucette is—I mean Mrs Sweeting?'

'The Fairy Queen over there.' Pascoe pointed to a woman dressed in iridescent robes, surrounded by a press of gentlemen. 'I shall go and ask her to dance, make certain she knows who I am, and then appear to be much engaged with partners on the far side of the room. She will have plenty of requests for her hand and will not expect another dance from me. Then Brough and I will effect our exchange, I will go and search her house, and then reappear and talk to her before the evening is done.'

'I suppose that will work...' Sophie said, still dubious. 'Is there anything I can do?'

'Nothing except perhaps dance with Brough once our exchange is done. That will draw her eye to him.'

'Why should it? She will not know who I am.' Sophie stood up and twitched her skirts into order.

'Oh, she'll know. I did. That is a very fetching outfit, by the way. Most appropriate for Maid Marion.'

'Oh, this is simply an old summer riding habit. My maid shortened it and made the jacket into a waistcoat with lacing, and used the remains of the fabric to fashion the hat.'

They had both been rather pleased with the result. The leaf-green fabric was just right for a woodland outlaw, the jaunty little cap with a feather perched neatly to one side of her head, and her hair was in a long plait down her back. In keeping with the role Sophie was wearing ankle boots. But, with a cautious eye on the length of her skirt, she had put on the breeches she wore under her habits. The fabric was a lightweight cloth, for summer, so she did not think she would become too heated.

'Be careful—and do not pierce too many hearts with your arrows,' Pascoe said, and she could have sworn that in the shadow of the mask his eyes were smiling. 'I must go down.'

Suddenly serious, she caught at his arm. 'Do not get caught.'

'I won't. But wish me luck.'

Yes, he was definitely smiling.

The impulse came so quickly that she did not have time to think. Sophie stretched up and kissed him, full on the mouth, then gathered up her skirts and fled down the narrow staircase.

Whatever have I done? she thought distractedly as she stepped out into the ballroom. Then, *I don't care. It is done.*

The taste of him, familiar now, was on her lips as she accepted the offer of a harlequin for the next set of country dances. The executioner's black skull cap was just visible as he went down the line on the far side of the room, the Fairy Queen's draperies fluttering about him.

Oh, do be careful.

The clock had struck eleven when Sophie next saw the executioner. That was Lord Jon, she was certain. He did not move with Pascoe's grace and his sword was slung from the other shoulder.

How long would Pascoe need? She was sitting out an energetic set and wondering about that when there was a flurry of movement almost in front of her. Dancers scattered and one gentleman fell over as the Fairy Queen, spun by an over-enthusiastic partner, landed on top of him in an awkward sprawl.

'Madam! Madam, are you hurt?' Her partner, an improbable Eastern potentate, hurried to help her to her feet, but she gave a small shriek of pain when he caught her hand.

'My wrist! It is sprained. Oh, you careless creature!

Do not touch me!' The Fairy Queen got to her feet, then staggered. 'And my ankle…' She subsided again into the arms of the unfortunate gentleman—Henry VIII—onto whose well-padded frame she had crashed in the first place.

'Madam, I am a doctor. Allow me.' A knight in knitted chainmail pushed through the crowd. 'Give the lady some air. Fetch a chair. We must carry her to a quiet room and have her carriage sent for.'

Sophie, who had kept well clear, jumped to her feet and began to scan the disorganised throng of masqueraders. Where was the executioner? *There*.

Using her elbows ruthlessly, she wriggled through to Lord Jon's side. 'Lord Jon? I am the Duchess of St Edmunds. You know why Pascoe asked you to change costumes?'

He took her arm and pushed a way for them through to the hall. 'I know he had to get into that lady's house, but not why.'

'He is searching for something stolen from me. And now she will be taken home and he is not expecting her for hours yet.'

'I will go and warn him.' Lord Jon turned, then stopped. 'But I do not know where he has gone.'

'I do. We will both go. It will take an age to have our carriages called—we had best take a hackney.'

What the cab driver thought of being hailed by a sinister executioner and a lady in green, both masked, she couldn't think. But London hackney drivers must encounter many strange sights, because he merely leaned down to ask for their direction and set off at a brisk pace.

'He must think we are leaving the masquerade ball for a romantic assignation,' Sophie said, stifling an almost hysterical urge to giggle. This was too serious for that. 'We must plan.'

'This is very close,' Lord Jon said as they stopped after a few minutes. He paid the driver and they stood on the pavement as the cab drove off. 'I had best break in and warn Pascoe.'

'No, we need a distraction. I know! You will knock at the door, say you have come from the ball, and tell them Mrs Sweeting's maid is needed because she is injured. That will get the woman downstairs and keep the footmen occupied in finding her a cab and sending for a doctor. I will go in at the back and find Pascoe. Oh, and wait! You must not be identified as the executioner.'

She pulled him into the cover of the next house's gate. 'Take off your skull cap and mask and that sword and put on my hat and jerkin. It won't do up, but that doesn't matter.'

'I should be the one to go in,' he protested.

'No, you must get back to the masquerade as soon as possible and be seen there as the executioner. If everything goes wrong, and Pascoe is taken, then I will need your help, and you cannot be seen to have been involved. I expect I can just throw pebbles at the window to let him know I am here,' she added vaguely.

Lord Jon agreed, although she could tell he was reluctant, and they managed the transformation in moments. Then Sophie gathered up her skirts and ran along to the archway that marked the entrance to the mews behind the houses as his urgent knocking echoed down the street.

The mews were lit by lamps in the stables, but with their employers out for the evening the stable staff were inside and, judging from the snatches of laughter and cries of disgust, deeply into a game of chance.

She counted as she went and found the gate into the back garden of Mrs Sweeting's house. It was not much more than a patch of gravel bordered by shrubs, with a wall separating it from the steps down to a tiny sunken yard by the door into the kitchen.

There were no sounds coming from the kitchen, and the ground-floor windows at the rear were dark, but on the first floor she could see a subdued light from one room, and the lower sash of the window next door to it was open.

That must be how Pascoe had entered, but how could she get his attention? If Brough's knocking and dramatic tale of their injured mistress had drawn the servants to the front of the house she could try the kitchen door, she thought. But it only needed one kitchen maid left scrubbing pans to raise the alarm.

Or she could climb, as Pascoe would have done.

She peered into the gloom. That flower urn, then that trellis, then the top of the wall screening the yard, then the drainpipe and into the window… She could do it—but not dressed as she was. Sophie unfastened the skirt of the habit and hid it behind a bush, then climbed onto the urn, took a sideways step to the trellis, moved up several squares of that, and then she was on top of the wall.

Up there it seemed higher and narrower than it had looked from the ground, and the open window was further away. It was a pity that she had never climbed trees as a child, she thought, steadying herself with a firm grip on the downpipe.

On the other hand she could mount a large horse unaided after a fall, and that window was not snorting and stamping as she tried to get her foot in a stirrup. If she put her toe into that crack in a broken brick and pulled on the pipe with one hand she could reach the window ledge…

Yes, like that.

And then she was lying across the ledge, half in, half out. With a wriggle that tore at her shirt she tumbled to the floor and lay there catching her breath and listening. Silence.

She looked around but the room was dark, and the

faint line of light betraying the position of the door
she had seen as she lunged for the ledge had vanished.
On hands and knees she crawled to where it had been,
groping for a door handle. She was in a dressing room,
she guessed, as her hand found a drawer knob and then
another. She stood up cautiously and almost screamed
as a ghostly white shape floated towards her. A gown
hung from a rail—that was all.

Unless Pascoe was in a clothes press, he was not
in here. There was a door... She tried that and found
herself in a bedchamber with still no sign of—

'*Ough!*' she managed against the hand that covered
her mouth.

'What the hell?' a voice in her ear demanded in a
furious whisper. 'Sophie?'

The hand lifted.

'She's coming back. She had an accident at the ball
and hurt herself. Lord Jon is downstairs, creating a
huge fuss and making out that he's been sent to fetch
her maid and a carriage.'

'And you climbed? Give me strength...' Pascoe was
already moving away from her, and a thin stream of
light fell across the carpet from what she supposed
must be a dark lantern. 'In breeches?'

'You try it in skirts,' she retorted in a furious whisper.

'I've got the safe open and found the diaries.
Through here.' She followed him into a boudoir. Pas-

coe lifted a picture off the wall and opened a small square door behind it. Stacked there were three familiar red books.

'Take them quickly. We must go.'

'Those are blanks. I brought them with me from Vine Mount House.' He lifted a satchel from the floor by its strap. 'Here are the real ones.'

Pascoe closed the safe door and fiddled with the lock. It seemed to Sophie to take for ever.

'That's it.' He hung the picture back in place and then froze, one hand lifted in warning. 'Someone is coming.' He blew out the candle in the lantern, thrust it at her, grabbed the satchel with one hand and Sophie with the other, and dragged her into the narrow space behind a sofa. *'Down.'*

'But the window—'

'We don't have time for both of us to get out, and—'

He broke off as the door opened, light flooded in, and the sound of several agitated people filled the room. Sophie, flattened by Pascoe's hand between her shoulder blades, squinted from under the sofa at four pairs of buckled shoes and white stockings. They must belong to footmen in livery, and by the sound of her loud complaints they were carrying Mrs Sweeting. She must have left the ball almost immediately after Sophie and Jon.

'Gently! Do not jolt me so. Oh, my ankle!'

'Where to, ma'am?'

'My bedchamber of course, you idiot. Where is Milly?'

'Here, ma'am. And Dr Herbert has been sent for.'

'Thank goodness.' Amanda's voice was less strident now, as she was carried through to the bedchamber. 'That clumsy fool at the masquerade had no right to call himself a doctor. He had no idea how to treat a lady. Ouch!'

Sophie twisted enough to look up at Pascoe, who was half lying on top of her. She raised an eyebrow and jerked her head towards the door.

He shook his head.

The footmen came back into the room.

'Wait outside. I do not know what the doctor will want fetching, and I cannot leave my lady.'

That must be Milly, the abigail.

When there had been silence for several minutes they eased themselves into a better position in the narrow space, spooned together, with Pascoe's back to the wall and Sophie facing out with a view under the sofa.

'We may have a long wait,' he breathed in her ear. 'Can you keep very still?'

She nodded. One of the many things Mama had been very strict about was the need for a lady of high rank to be able to stand or sit without fidgeting for hours. Court occasions, she had warned, were particularly trying.

Lying behind a sofa in a courtesan's boudoir with

an attractive man curled tightly around her was not what Mama had had in mind, but Sophie was deeply grateful for the lessons now.

It was curiously restful, lying like that. The carpet was thick and soft under her, and Pascoe's body felt safe and warm. She should be both frightened and embarrassed—she knew that. But somehow she had total faith that he would extract them from this situation, and she could not find it in her to regret this intimate embrace. She would just have to come to terms with the fact that she was not a perfect duchess, with no feelings or emotions, and instead was a young woman with very natural desires.

Not that she would act on them, of course.

The door opened again and a footman ushered in a gentleman, by the look of his expensive footwear. There was a tap on the inner door. 'Dr Herbert is here, ma'am.'

'Show him in. Oh, Doctor, I am in such discomfort!'

'Dear lady, there is no need—'

Whatever it was that was unneedful was cut off. The door closed, and the footman crossed the room in front of them and went out.

Sophie felt her eyelids begin to close. She did not fight the sensation, but let her body relax into the carpet, into the sheltering arms wrapped around her. She could feel Pascoe's breathing, his heartbeat, as she drifted into sleep.

Chapter Ten

It took Nick a while to realise that he had his arms full of sleeping duchess and a further few minutes to work out that the emotion he was feeling, besides surprise, was pleasure. She was no fool, Sophie. She knew perfectly well that they were in a highly difficult situation. So if she could drift off to sleep it must be because she trusted him absolutely. That was absurdly flattering, and he found himself smiling into her hair.

He must be losing his touch, he told himself. He was working. There would be the devil to pay if they were discovered. Not so much for him—he could fight his way out of this—but for Sophie.

The doctor had left an hour ago, but Nick was only just beginning to hope that the household was settling for the night.

There were two ways to get out. They could creep through Amanda Sweeting's bedchamber, trusting that she was not a light sleeper or lying awake in discomfort. But what were the chances that the maid had closed the window in the dressing room? It had stood conveniently open—to freshen the gowns hung around the room, he supposed—but she would most likely close it against the night air. How noisy would it be to open?

Or they could go downstairs to the basement and out of either the front or rear doors. The rear would avoid a footman on duty dozing in the hall, but in many households the scullery maid or the boot boy slept in the kitchen area. Even so, he concluded, that would be the safest way out. His blood ran cold at the thought of Sophie climbing down from that window with the hard paved yard below her.

Somewhere in the house a clock chimed four. Now was the time to go. If he left it much longer the weary staff would be waking again to start the day's labours.

Nick curled one hand over Sophie's mouth and whispered in her ear, 'Time to wake up.'

'Mmm…?'

Her lips moved against the palm of his hand and he fought the urge to start kissing his way along exposed the skin of her neck and cheek.

'Sophie. Wake up.' He kept his hand in place and nipped gently at her earlobe.

'Mmph!'

Then he felt consciousness coming back to her, tensing her limbs. She nodded, and he took his hand away.

'Stay there.' He eased himself to his feet, wary of

treading on her, conscious that his muscles were stiff from lying still in one position for so long. When he had stretched and flexed arms and legs he bent down. 'Can you get up?'

Sophie pushed herself up to her knees, then stood, grasping the back of the sofa. As he had, she began to stretch out her limbs. Nick tried not to stare at her legs in the revealing breeches as she emerged, carrying the satchel.

It took them at least twenty minutes to reach the basement. A footman was snoring in the hall, audible even through closed doors, but nothing else stirred in the house except for all the usual, alarmingly unfamiliar sounds that a large house always made and which its inhabitants completely ignored.

A rat trap snapping closed as they stepped down into the basement from the back stairs had them both freezing in place, and then they heard breathing from a room off to the side of the passage. Nick drifted, soft-footed, along the paved floor and looked in. A lad was curled up on a pile of old blankets, fast asleep as only a healthy boy could be.

He beckoned to Sophie and she crept along to join him. There was no one in the kitchen, which was lit by a faint glow from the banked fire in the grate. Nick lit the dark lantern from the coals and studied the door.

'Bolts...' Sophie breathed, so close that he felt the hairs on his neck stir.

'I can pick the lock,' he whispered back. 'And lock it again from the other side. They will think they forgot to bolt it—that is all.'

The lock was large, but simple, and he had it open in less than five minutes. Drawing the bolts was trickier, and seemed to take for ever. Sophie knelt at Nick's feet and worked the lower one, while he reached up to the topmost, but at last they had them free, without waking anyone in the process.

When Nick stood up from relocking the door he saw Sophie had found her skirts and was once more respectably covered. The trouble was, he could not forget what he had seen, and he knew very well that the image of those slim, strong legs was going to haunt his dreams. If he ever managed to get to sleep in the first place, of course.

He blew out the lantern and looked up at the dressing room window. Yes, it was closed.

'Time to go home,' he said, and they shut the back gate behind them and stood in the mews. Nick found he needed a moment to breathe before they set off again. 'But take a moment to rest first.'

Sophie nodded. 'What an evening! When we realised that she was going to be taken home Lord Jon and I rushed over here, and he changed his costume so he no longer looked like an executioner. Then he knocked on the door and made a terrific fuss about how they needed to send her carriage and her maid. I went around to the back and climbed in to warn you.'

'Why the devil didn't *he* climb in?' Nick demanded.

'Because it wasn't believable that a lady would come to warn the staff, and I wanted him to return to the ball as the executioner again. Besides, I didn't tell him I might have to climb.' She turned and looked up into his face, trying to read his expression in the gloom as she said urgently, 'He did argue, Pascoe.'

'Nick,' he said. 'My name is Nick.'

'Nick…' she murmured, and his heart thudded as it had not, even when they had been most in danger.

His body was flooded with the familiar release of tension and waves of something else—something fierce and hot and demanding. *This woman.* This woman made him want and ache and…

He forced his muscles to obey him, to turn away and lead her out of here, back to the luxury and light that was where she belonged.

'Nick, kiss me?'

Which of them moved? He did not know. But they were in each other's arms, pressed tighter than they had been even behind that sofa, and they were kissing as though their lives depended upon it. Hungry, demanding kisses. And Sophie was as urgent as he.

His hands slid to her waist, then to cup the curves of her bottom, lifting her against the crude demand of his arousal. It was no way to treat a lady…a duchess…but this was something beyond rank and station. This was quite simply a man with a woman who was as hungry for him as he was for her.

Even so, his instincts had not entirely deserted him. Further down the mews he heard leather scuff against stone, and when he lifted his head he saw something shift in the shadows.

'Sophie!' he warned as he reached for the slim knife he wore in a sheath at his back. 'Behind me.'

She neither questioned nor argued, just slid around and away from him, giving his knife hand free movement.

'Pascoe?' a voice called softly.

'Jon?'

His friend emerged from the shadows.

'I couldn't leave it any longer. I've been waiting at your house, but when you didn't come—'

'All safe. And thank you.' Pascoe put away the knife and clasped his friend's arm, wondering what he had seen just now in the semi-darkness. 'Duchess, are you recovered? She felt faint with relief just now,' he explained.

Hopefully, if Brough had seen them clasped together, he would assume Pascoe had been supporting her.

Again, Sophie surprised him by catching his intention at once.

'I am better now,' she murmured. 'It was just the

relief. I felt light-headed for a moment. Thank you so much, Lord Jon.'

A horse whinnied in the stables and another answered it.

'We had best be gone,' Pascoe said. 'If we can find a hackney at this hour.'

'I have my carriage around the corner,' Brough said. 'Best get you home, Your Grace, before your people become agitated and start sending out a search party.'

That had not occurred to Sophie, it was clear from her expression. 'What is the time?'

She was answered by a nearby church clock chiming the three-quarters.

'Goodness, yes. We must be on our way before the mews begins to stir.' Her hand curled into his and she gave a little tug. 'Come on, Nicholas.'

He found he was grinning like a schoolboy as he followed her into Brough's smart town carriage, then felt the smile fade as he watched Sophie arranging her dusty skirts with unconscious grace.

She was a duchess. And he might be a viscount, and heir to an earldom—if his father did not make history and find a way to disinherit an acknowledged son—but Sophie would not contemplate taking a lover, surely? Her sense of duty was too strong, and her life revolved around little Frederick.

And as for marriage… She had made it abundantly

clear that she had no desire to marry again, which was…

'Here we are, Your Grace. Pascoe, old man, have you fallen asleep?'

'I would not blame him if he had,' Sophie said with a laugh. 'He has been awake all night, while I had a very comfortable doze on an expensive carpet.'

Nick jerked upright. He'd been asleep, right enough. And dreaming. Marriage? That was the last thing he wanted at the moment. He needed to be free. And besides, what kind of life could he offer a respectable lady? Attached to an adventurer who might go anywhere at any time…who might end up injured or dead, for that matter.

One day, perhaps, when he *did* walk into the parson's mousetrap, it would not be to entangle himself in all the complexities that Sophie brought with her. And besides—a duchess? She was used to the highest status, to great wealth. Even if he were not the man she thought him to be, the world would consider her to have stepped down in society. What was the matter with him? He'd be writing love poetry and going off his food next.

'Let me see you to the door—' he began, but the footman was already opening the carriage door. 'No, I suppose it would be more discreet if he knocks. Here,' he said to the man and handed him the satchel. 'Carry this for Her Grace.'

'You will come tomorrow?' she asked from the pavement.

'I will. It may be late afternoon.'

'Of course. You will need your sleep,' Sophie said with a twinkle in her eyes. 'Good day, Lord Jon, and thank you once again for your help.'

'You got what you went for?' Brough asked as the carriage started up again.

'Yes.'

All I went for and more.

Sophie ran upstairs, clutching the satchel, and let Foskett fuss over her as she undressed.

'So late, Your Grace! I was that worried. You hear such things about these London masquerades. And these skirts! What have you been doing? Oh, and the shirt is torn too.'

'I tripped and fell into a flowerbed,' Sophie said, too weary to think up any other excuse. 'I will just wash my face and hands. I am too tired for a bath now. Yes, thank you, Foskett, that will be all.'

She was bone-weary as she climbed into bed. Sleep should have been only a matter of closing her eyes, but instead Sophie's brain was in a whirl.

The diaries were safe. That was the main thing. Duncan would have secure storage built and she would lock them all away and forget them. Life would revert to normal.

Except there had been that kiss. Those kisses… And especially those heated, hectic, urgent moments in the mews. She had been shameless then and she could not find it in herself to feel shame now. Reliving that embrace filled her with hot, urgent need, not the cold shudder of repentance that she knew she should be feeling.

When she had protested her reasons for not wishing to marry again Nick had remarked that widows often took lovers, she recalled. Had that been more than an observation? Perhaps a thinly veiled suggestion?

If it had been, then it was one she was greatly tempted by, she thought, as exhaustion overcame even desire and she began to drift off to sleep.

Then she opened her eyes abruptly, shocked by her own thoughts. It would be so dangerous, surely? However did anyone manage to keep such a liaison secret? One heard of so many scandals, and she had a small son to raise and to protect. He must not grow up knowing that his mother's reputation was in question.

Somehow the knowledge that she was doing her duty was not the satisfaction it usually was.

That afternoon Nick purchased a large bouquet of pink roses and presented himself on Amanda Sweeting's doorstep.

The lady was resting in her boudoir, the footman

informed him, but he would take up Mr Pascoe's card if he would care to wait.

The man returned five minutes later to escort Nick upstairs. He had dark circles under his eyes, Nick noticed, presumably from being kept up half the night by Mrs Sweeting's demands for attention. He had Nick's sympathy.

Nick waited until the door had closed behind him before advancing across the carpet, the thickness of which he had reason to recall with gratitude. 'My poor Amanda! I had not even hoped to find you well enough to leave your bed and receive guests today. What an oaf that man was.'

'The one who knocked me down or that cow-handed excuse for a physician?' she enquired acidly. Then she seemed to recall that she had a gentleman to charm and produced a faint smile. 'Do forgive my short temper today. I had the most unsettled night, as you may imagine.'

Recalling her soft snores, Nick had trouble hiding a smile.

'I saw you fall, but by the time I was close there was such a gathering around you I felt there was little I could do to assist.'

Sophie and Brough had described the scene to him in as much detail as they could on the drive back through the early-morning streets.

'I have brought these in the hope they might cheer you a little.'

He proffered the flowers and Amanda cooed her delight and permitted him to kiss her hand and then her lips. Unless she was a consummate actress, she had no idea yet that a burglary had taken place.

'Does your doctor have any idea when you might be able to go out again? For a drive around the park, for example?'

He had absolutely no intention of taking this any further than a few innocuous meetings before he found himself called away on urgent business, but he wanted to allay any suspicions when she discovered that the diaries had gone.

There was a discreet tap on the door and the footman re-entered. 'The gentleman with the appointment has arrived, ma'am.'

'Ask him to wait in the drawing room for a few minutes, then show him up, Cecil. Oh, Nicholas. I am so sorry. A tiresome matter of trust funds, I fear. You must excuse me... But I would be delighted to drive with you in a few days.'

She held out her pampered hand for another kiss, but he could tell her attention was distracted.

'And the flowers are delightful.'

As he descended the stairs Nick could see a calling card on the silver salver on the hall chest, and another tall hat, gloves and stick beside his own. He unhooked the single fob hanging from his watch chain and as the footman handed him his hat fumbled, appeared to knock it against his waistcoat and dropped it. A nudge from his foot and it rolled under the chest.

'Damnation! No, do not trouble yourself. Mrs Sweeting is waiting for her visitor. I will find it.'

He dropped to his knees and the footman, with a hasty, 'Thank you, sir,' opened the drawing room door. 'Mrs Sweeting will see you now, sir.'

Nick stood and picked up the calling card.

Phineas Foster, Esq. Publisher
Lion Yard, Fleet Street

Trust funds indeed.

The door closed upstairs.

Nick knelt again, and reached one long arm under the chest.

'Not found it yet, sir?'

The footman had returned and crouched down beside him.

'I'll fetch a broom, sir. Mayhap I can reach it with that. Have a care for your breeches, sir.'

Nick stood up and made a show of dusting himself down, straining his ears to hear any sound from above. The footman hurried back with a spider-dusting brush on a long thin handle and began to sweep it back and forth under the chest. Suddenly the fob shot out and Nick picked it up.

'Thank you. Cecil, isn't it?' He pressed a coin into the man's hand just as a shriek of rage came from upstairs. 'You had best hurry upstairs. Your mistress seems to be in some distress,' he said. 'I will see myself out.'

'Pascoe is here,' Grant said, coming into the smaller of the two drawing rooms, where Sophie was making a tangle out of her embroidery silks in an effort to finish a cushion cover. 'Looking pleased with himself too.'

'At last. I was beginning to think he had left the country,' Sophie snapped, knowing as she did so that she was being impatient. 'Please stay, Duncan.'

'As you wish.' He opened the door. 'Come in.'

Nick entered on his heels. 'Duchess,' he said formally.

His eyes said something else.

'Pascoe,' she responded, equally formally, and did not look at him directly. 'Do please sit down, gentlemen.'

'Amanda Sweeting knows the diaries have gone,' Nick said. 'She discovered it an hour ago, just as I was leaving, having taken my good wishes and roses to her sick room.'

'That is not a good thing, is it?' Duncan said thoughtfully. 'She will be able to time their removal to last night.'

'I would rather a few more days had passed, but I

think our precautions will hold up,' Nick said. 'She found them missing because after my visit a publisher was being shown up. I made an excuse to linger in the hall just long enough to hear her cries of rage.'

'A publisher…' Sophie murmured. 'I was so sure she would try blackmail. There must be many men who would pay a great deal to have my late husband's tales about them kept very quiet.'

'This would have been the safer option. Her name need not appear. And consider some of the people who might have something to fear from those diaries. If I was a woman on my own, with no protection except what I could buy, I would be very afraid of what they might do to me.'

'And a publisher would not have the same fears?' Duncan queried.

'I would have been here earlier, but I was making a few enquiries about Mr Phineas Foster. He is the kind of man who has bodyguards as a matter of course. His usual output is of works that no decent man would have in his house, but two years ago he published the diaries of Lady Giddington.'

'Good G— Er…goodness me,' Duncan said. 'Those were very ripe indeed. Her Ladyship had to go into hiding, and I know of at least three marriages which have broken as a result. One even ended in divorce. There was an attempt to prosecute the publisher for obscenity, but it came to nothing.'

'And those were sexual scandals,' Nick said. 'Shocking and distressing for many people, but in most cases the gentlemen concerned were not overly concerned. Their virility was demonstrated in most cases. His Grace's diaries, however, will expose intellectual weakness at best and crime at worst, I imagine.'

Sophie nodded. 'I have read very little of them, but many high-ranking gentlemen are exposed as fools, or corrupt, over and over again. In one case there is even a suggestion of dealings with the French. Yes, I can see that if she approached the wrong person and attempted extortion they might react with violence.'

'Then it is as well that you managed to retrieve them, Pascoe,' Duncan said. 'Mrs Sweeting, or whatever her true name is, can have no idea how they were removed, and even if she knew you were behind this, Your Grace, she has no way of retaliating. They were stolen property. Now, if you will excuse me? I will make preparations to take them back to Vine Mount House first thing tomorrow morning. I have already sent instructions to the estate carpenter to create secure cupboards for the entire collection. I suggest we place them in that small chamber off the library. The one with the concealed door.'

'The secret cabinet of curiosities, where my late father-in-law kept the more lively pieces he brought back from the Grand Tour?' Sophie queried. 'That is an excellent idea. We can have the door screwed closed as an added precaution and forget about the wretched things until I suppose my grandson may finally view them, under the terms of the will. By that point they will simply be of historical interest.'

'You do not look relieved, Sophie.' Duncan turned back from the door, concern jolting him out of his usual careful formality. 'Is something else wrong?'

'Wrong? Goodness, no. Simply the effects of a late night and everything that happened yesterday. You go and make your preparations, Duncan.' She held out her hand and he came and bent over it, but she tugged, bringing him down for a kiss on the cheek. 'Thank you.'

'You lie most convincingly,' Nick said as the door closed behind her steward.

Chapter Eleven

'Whatever can you mean?' Sophie said with a laugh that even to her own ears sounded brittle and unconvincing.

'Last night.' Nick did not appear willing to help her.

'You refer, I collect, to the fact that there was a certain…intimacy between us?' Sophie said, with a shrug.

It would have looked more convincingly unconcerned if she had been able to meet his eyes, she knew. But if she did she would drown in those dark depths again.

'You lay in my arms as though that happened every night, and then we kissed with what can only be described, if you will excuse my bluntness, as uncontrolled passion. If that is not a matter of concern to you this afternoon, I can assure you it is to me. I kissed you in a mews as though you were a woman of easy virtue.'

Startled, Sophie turned to stare at him. She had not mistaken his tone: Nick was angry. But with whom?

'I wanted you to kiss me. It was the relief of all that tension, I expect.'

Why was he angry? She wanted him to want her as much as she wanted him—even though it was wrong, even though whatever this was must stop now.

'We must simply just for-forget it happened,' she stammered.

'Forget? How?' he demanded, on his feet now. 'Or are you in the habit of kissing men like that and then forgetting about it?'

'You know I am not.' She stood up, toe to toe with him. 'You make it sound as though I assaulted you!'

'No. You are right. We both wanted what happened. But it feels as though you have assaulted my soul,' Nick said, his quiet words at odds with the heat in the hard black gaze.

'You…you feel—?'

'I have no idea how I feel.' He spun around, took several strides down the length of the room away from her. 'I know that you are a duchess,' he said, his back still turned. 'I know that you are a woman of strict morals and high standards. I know that I want to lay you down on this carpet and make love to you until we are both sobbing with exhaustion.'

'Yes,' she said. 'Yes, that is how I feel.'

That brought him round as though she had tugged at his arm. 'You want to make love with me?'

'Yes,' Sophie said again. 'But I do not know what to do about it. I have never felt like this before, you see.'

From that distance she could not read his feelings in his face, but then, she was not certain she would have been able to even if they'd been close enough to exchange breath.

Her words brought him back close. Close enough to see that his eyes were not really black or dark brown but the deepest, darkest blue. That there was a pulse beating at his temple and that she was not the only one in the room who was holding on to control by a thread.

She held out her hand and he lifted his. Their fingertips touched and then pressed together, until their hands were joined as though in prayer, a barrier between them and a lock that joined them. They stood in silence, breathing together, reading each other's eyes, feeling their hearts beat through the pulses in their wrists.

I want this for myself, Sophie thought. *I have never wanted anything for myself except to be perfect, and that is impossible. To please Mama and Papa. To please Augustus. I have been good and dutiful and I have done my best all my life. And now here is the one thing that I want just for myself...this man. Standing in front of me. Touching me. Waiting. For me.*

Nick parted his fingers and she slid hers between

them as he pulled her gently towards him. He bent his head and she lifted her face for his kiss.

A kiss that stopped a finger's breadth from her lips.

A heartbeat—a second, a third—and then they spoke together.

'No,' Nick said, and released her hand.

'No,' Sophie echoed, and stepped back.

'I would not be able to leave you,' Nick said. 'Not once we had been one.'

'And it could only ever be once,' she said. *One taste of bliss, one teasing glimpse of passion*. 'Better not to—'

'I cannot risk—' he said at the same moment. Then, 'I will leave.'

She stood where she was and watched him cross the room, watched his long fingers curl around the door handle, watched the black-clad figure she had once found sinister vanish from the room...from her life.

Quite how she had come to be sitting on the window seat gazing blankly out into the street she had no idea. She must have walked there of her own volition because there was no one else in the room.

As one might probe a wound with a cautious finger, fearful of pain, Sophie searched her feelings. There was nothing. She felt blank...empty. Something splashed on to her hand and she touched her face. She was weeping. How could that be when she felt nothing except this numbness?

She touched her handkerchief carefully to her eyes and concentrated simply on breathing, on studying the street with all of her concentration.

Eventually she stood up and went to find Frederick. She needed the feel of his warm, sturdy little body, his smile. A reminder of why she had just done what she had.

'You must tell me everything,' Dorothea demanded as she settled beside Sophie in the barouche. 'I am out of town for a week and not a word of gossip have I heard. I swear Trent forbids news to reach me in case I am agitated.' She smoothed a hand over the barely visible swell of her stomach. 'I cannot persuade him that I am much calmer and happier when I am hearing all there is to hear.'

As the barouche moved off towards Hyde Park the Countess of Trent snuggled the lap rug more closely and fixed Sophie with a smile that clearly invited confidences.

'Well, let me see...' Sophie racked her brains. The last thing she had felt like doing over the past week had been reading the social pages, or listening to gossip, but there was one striking item that she would have to have been unconscious to miss. 'Edwina Brackhurst was found with the butler in the silver closet by her husband.'

'*No!* What happened?'

'She convinced him that the silver was inadequately polished and she was showing the butler the pieces that were particularly neglected. She must be powerfully persuasive, when you consider that the butler's coat was off and his shirt hanging out. *And* one of Mrs Brackhurst's earrings turned up in the soup tureen that evening, and was ladled out by a footman into Mr Brackhurst's bowl. Lady Imming's woman had this from Mrs Wright, whose maid is cousin to the Brackhursts' cook.'

'The man is an idiot!' Dorothea gasped, fanning herself with her hand. 'What else?'

'Oh, I don't know… I have been so busy with Frederick and getting the house to rights and so forth,' Sophie said vaguely.

Her friend pouted. 'You are keeping secrets, I swear. What about your deliciously sinister Mr Pascoe?'

'Pascoe? Oh, he finished the commission I had for him. I have no idea where he is now,' she added, trying to sound faintly bored by the topic.

She had spoken the truth. When Duncan Grant had informed her that he had settled with Pascoe for his work he had appeared ready to talk more of him. In fact, Sophie thought, he had seemed disconcerted when she had thanked him and immediately changed the subject.

Dorothea wrinkled her nose. 'Disappointing… I had a lovely fantasy about you having a scandalous *affaire* with him and telling me all the naughty details.'

'I thought you were in love with your Earl?' Sophie said, quick to turn the subject from herself. 'Never tell me you yearn after a lover?'

'Of course not. I dote upon Trent, and he is more than adequately naughty, if you take my meaning,' she added with a twinkle. 'Only he is treating me like spun glass at the moment, so even a second-hand account of wicked goings-on would be diverting.'

'I have not been having an *affaire*, so you must remain disappointed,' Sophie said as the barouche entered the park. 'Oh, do look at that enchanting hat. The pale pink with the feathers.'

'That is from Maison Griselda, I would swear.'

Diverted, Dorothea turned to stare, and then began to recount the distressing tale of her latest milliner's bill, which she rather thought she must hide from her husband on account of his reaction to the size of the bill for her new court dress.

'Goodness… Really…? Yes, I can understand…'

Sophie listened with half an ear and tried not to think about Pascoe.

There had been no passionate *affaire*, the memory of which she could hug to herself on long lonely nights. Just the memory of his arms and his strength, his kisses and the thrill of danger shared with him.

'Ghastly,' she said.

'Oh? Do you think so?' Dorothea's lower lip trembled just a little. 'I had thought it so pretty...'

'What? I am so sorry. I was wool-gathering and must have misheard you.'

'My new bonnet. Do you think Trent will forgive me the bill when he sees me wearing it?'

'It is enchanting. A man would have to be made of solid wood not to think how lovely you look in it,' Sophie said loyally.

They were approaching the southwestern quarter of the park, where Rotten Row was situated and where the fashionable and not quite so fashionable crowd gathered to see and be seen. Sophie had forgotten to tell her coachman that she wanted to stay in the quieter part of the park and now it was too late to turn without causing a nuisance and probably comment.

Several gentlemen on horseback drew alongside, raised their hats to the ladies and, after an exchange of greetings, rode on. Others kept pace with them.

On Dorothea's side a major in scarlet regimentals leaned down to engage her in light-hearted flirtation, which made her laugh, and Lord Abertarn, the cheerful red-headed son and heir of the Marquess of Gower, chatted easily to Sophie.

She rather thought he was working around to a serious approach—it would certainly be a very advantageous match for him and a suitable one for her. He was about her age, and his reputation was unmarked by scandal. She liked him well enough, and might even have given some thought to introducing him to Freddie, to see how he connected with a small child, but since Nick had begun to trouble both her thoughts and her sleep the idea of remarriage felt utterly alien.

She smiled and responded to Lord Abertarn's inconsequential conversation, then noticed another rider approaching. Her coachman drew up, clearly assuming she would want to converse with all her admirers.

The new arrival was the Earl of Chalfont, erect and sparely elegant on an iron-grey horse. 'Your Grace.' He raised his hat. 'Lady Trent. You are both ornaments to the company on this fine day. How fortunate that the weather is clement, despite the date, and carriages can be open.'

'Thank you, Lord Chalfont. Indeed, the weather is remarkable for late October.'

Sophie was not at all sure how to respond to him, or why he had troubled to stop and speak to her. He was old enough to be her father, and had been a widower for many years—surely he was not courting her? His unsmiling visage was not easy to read, and his manner was exceedingly reserved, and yet she felt something…a completely unexpected familiarity.

'What a very fine horse,' she said. 'Such beautiful dapple markings.'

It was the right thing to say, and it was clear she had pleased him. 'Trojan. One of my own breeding. His dam was a thoroughbred with a sire who was the best hunter I ever owned, which gives him his stature and his stamina.'

'You are obviously an authority on the subject. I wonder—' She broke off, realising she had been led into more familiarity than was justified by their brief acquaintance. It was most odd.

'You require some advice about horses, Your Grace?'

'Well, yes. My favourite hack—a mare—is getting old, and I would not like to subject her to the long journey to London for my use here. I should be finding a new riding horse, but I confess I am at a loss where to start here in town.'

'If we were to discuss what you are looking for in detail then I could have some horses brought to you on approval. Tattersalls, whilst the best source in London, is no place for a lady.'

'That would be most kind of you. Let me give you my card…' She began to open her reticule.

'No need, Your Grace. I am aware of your direction. May I call tomorrow afternoon?'

'Yes, thank you.'

A small voice was telling her that encouraging Lord

Chalfont might lead him to make assumptions—*He knew your address already*, it whispered—but she ignored it. She needed a riding horse and she felt he was trustworthy, although she had no idea why she should.

'Now, that is a very fine animal,' he observed, nodding towards a small group of horsemen crossing the Row. 'Part Arab I would—'

He broke off, staring fixedly, and Sophie followed his gaze.

Nicholas. Riding his lovely black mare.

She knew why her own heart was thumping erratically, but the expression on the Earl's face was a mixture of anger and...could it be yearning?

She could understand why anyone might be angered by Nicholas if he had outwitted them in the past, but that strange blend of emotions mystified her.

Almost as soon as she had seen it the Earl's face was once more bland. He touched his whip to his hat brim. 'Your Grace... Lady Trent.'

Sophie was so puzzled that she realised she had lost sight of Nicholas—although what good it would do her to know where he was she could not have said.

'Well, now, there's a surprise!' Dorothea turned to her with wide-eyed curiosity. 'Is the Earl of Chalfont courting you?'

'Certainly not. He is old enough to be my father, for one thing.'

'So was the late Duke,' Dorothea pointed out.

'I have no intention of marrying again, and if I did I would most certainly chose a younger husband.' It was an effort not to make her retort with betraying heat.

'But does he know that? It is puzzling… Unless he has fallen head over heels in love with you? Oh, don't pull that face. I was only teasing. One might think he wants a young wife to give him an heir, but there is nothing he can do about the one he has, so that would be pointless.'

'What is wrong with his heir?' Sophie realised she had no idea who that might be. 'Is he a rakehell or of unsound mind?'

'He has vanished,' Dorothea said, with ghoulish emphasis. 'Good day, Lady Trumpington!' she called as a matron in a passing barouche bowed to them 'Goodness, what a fright that daughter of hers looks in pink. Where was I…? Chalfont had two sons. The elder, by all accounts, was something of a milksop. No great intellect, no interest in sports—nor anything else, come to that. Perfectly pleasant, but ineffectual. George, I think he was called. The second son was quite the opposite, and very like his sire, by all accounts.'

She gave a little wriggle, like a hen settling on its nest and prepared to recount more gossip.

'Trent told me that the Earl and the second son— Perry? Gerald?—I can't recall. Anyway, they argued the whole time, and when he was eighteen the Earl packed him off to university to study theology, intending him to be a clergyman.'

'That sounds a most peculiar choice for the kind of young man you describe.'

'Indeed it was. And you will never guess what happened.'

'I have no idea.'

'He ran away within the month and joined the army.'

'The Earl must have been furious,' Sophie said, wide-eyed, imagining her father if one of her brothers had done such a thing. 'His son a common soldier!'

'He had money from an inheritance and he bought a commission as an ensign, so the story goes. But he changed his name and nobody seems to know what happened to him—at least us ladies do not. I expect if it is disreputable the gentlemen would not have told us. The Earl was apoplectic. Then his eldest son—the heir—caught the measles and succumbed to that, and his wife faded away with grief. So now, unless he has Jerry, or Perry, declared dead, he can do nothing about the inheritance.'

Ahead of them the Earl had been caught up in a jam of carriages as someone lost control of a Dennett gig and sent pedestrians and riders scattering. Sophie watched the upright back, the spare, elegant frame and his easy seat on the horse and felt a cold lump in her stomach.

Surely not?

'I wonder who that lady is staring at you so,' Dorothea remarked. 'Look over there. The one with the dark red parasol. She is older than us and very *soignée*. I do like her ensemble, but she does not like *you*! Or perhaps it is me she is glaring at. If looks could kill, I swear the carriage would catch fire.' She spread one hand instinctively over her stomach.

Sophie glanced across, guessing even as she did so who Dorothea had seen. 'Mrs Sweeting. She appears to have taken me in dislike for some reason. Just ignore her.'

The icy sensation was worse now. Not only was Nicholas still in London, but the man she guessed might be his estranged father was taking an interest in her. And, judging by Amanda Sweeting's expression, she had realised who was behind the removal of the diaries.

Not that Mrs Sweeting could do anything about it, Sophie reassured herself. She had no proof. And besides, she could not invoke the law without admitting her own theft.

'The confusion ahead seems to be getting worse. Shall we return home, do you think?' she said.

'I suppose so,' Dorothea agreed. 'I will please Trent by allowing him to find me with my feet up, reclining restfully on the sofa and reading an improving book of sermons.'

'Sermons? Truly?'

'No, of course not. All the latest ladies' journals, naturally.'

* * *

Sophie positively ran up the steps when she reached home, passed Padwick with a word of greeting and went straight to the library.

The *Peerage* sat self-importantly on its shelf in a prominent position, fat, scarlet and covered in gilded lettering. She pulled it out and flipped through the pages to *Chalfont*.

Edwin Montague Prior Taversham, Third Earl of Chalfont

She ran her finger impatiently along the tiny print.

Viscount Denham, Baron Fordingbridge

She skipped past his parents to his wife.

Millicent Rose Pascoe Tremain

Then his sons.

George Arnold Tremain Prior Taversham

He had died aged only twenty-one.

Jerrard Nicholas Pascoe Prior Taversham

She closed the heavy volume with a thud. Now she knew who Pascoe was and why he was so mysterious about his past. Did Duncan know his friend was Viscount Denham? He must do, surely. She felt a spurt of anger, swiftly quelled. He would not break his word if he had promised Pascoe he would keep his secret, and it should make no difference to Sophie who Nicholas was, provided the man her steward had found her was effective and honest.

No wonder she had felt a familiarity about the Earl. He and Nicholas did not much resemble each other facially, but there was a likeness in build and colouring—or would have been before the older man's hair had turned iron-grey—and it was easy to discern a relationship once one was looking for it.

Now what did she do?

It all depended, she supposed, on the Earl's intentions. If he was courting her then that was decidedly... No, she would put an end to that swiftly. Not that she would ever consider marrying a man so much older a second time.

If he was simply offering to help her buy a horse because he was interested in good animals and wanted to help a lady, then she would accept and be grateful. Although it might create a degree of acquaintance that would be difficult to maintain without revealing that she knew Nicholas.

It would all depend on the next day's visit.

Chapter Twelve

Sophie paced slowly up and down the gravelled paths between the shrubs that filled the private garden in the middle of the square.

The Earl of Chalfont had been obliging, very helpful, and coolly formal in a way that had reminded her painfully of her early encounters with Nicholas. If he was intending a courtship then he was going about it in a very strange manner—unless he was playing a long game and intended to establish himself as an old acquaintance first.

He had arrived at three o'clock, had gravely accepted tea, and had produced a notebook into which he'd written her answers to a detailed list of questions.

What height of horse had she in mind? Fourteen and a half hands? Oh, fifteen? Certainly. Temperament—lively or placid? Colour? Did she want a town hack only or one suited for country work as well? Did she hunt? No? Did she like to jump obstacles when she was out hacking? Mare or gelding? Any particular breed?

Sophie had done her best, although she'd become quite cross-eyed by the time he had tapped his pencil on the book, frowned in thought and then suggested a price necessary to buy a horse meeting her requirements.

Truthfully, Sophie had had no idea whether it was realistic and reasonable, an amazing bargain or expensive. She'd wished Duncan was in London, to sit in on the discussion, but he was still in Norfolk. On the other hand an earl was hardly likely to be attempting to make a profit out of buying a horse for her.

In the end she'd said, 'That will be perfectly satisfactory, with a small margin either way.'

'Excellent.' He'd slipped the notebook into a pocket. 'Thank you—more tea would be most welcome. The weather is unseasonably warm, is it not? Or perhaps you are used to our stuffy London streets already?'

They'd made more small talk—the kind that Sophie could manage without giving it a thought. Wandering from the state of the new plantings in Hyde Park through to the latest worries about the King's health and the problems of obtaining suitable domestic staff.

'I am very fortunate,' Sophie had told him. 'My staff here only require the addition of two of the footmen and two of the maids from Vine Mount House—and my woman and the nursery staff and my secretary, of course. They have all been with me for an age. And

Mr Grant, my steward, travels between here and Vine Mount House as required.'

'And he has been with you for some time?'

'I have known him since childhood. He came to the estate when he left the army.'

'Cavalryman?' the Earl had enquired casually.

'The Eleventh Light Dragoons,' Sophie had said.

Something in the Earl's manner had changed then, although she could not have said what it was. A sharpening of his attention, perhaps. Then she'd realised what had happened. He had led her to talk about her staff, had checked that her steward was not his errant son, and then pounced on the piece of information he wanted. If Duncan had served with the Eleventh, then so had Nicholas. His father knew it, and now he had made the connection between herself and Pascoe that he had presumably suspected.

'I am aware of your direction,' he had said in the park.

If he was not courting her, when making a point of knowing her address would have been logical, then why had he known it?

No, it was not courtship. He was on the track of Nicholas, for whatever reason, and he had seen something or heard something that linked them. Now he was making a cautious approach to discover what he could.

Years of rigorous training had kept the smile on

her lips and her hostess manners impeccable, but as soon as the door had closed on the Earl of Chalfont she had gone to put on her bonnet and find the key to the garden.

It was intolerable to be spied upon and investigated simply because of who she employed. And under her irritation there was a thread of worry for Nicholas. If he wanted to be reconciled with his father then he would make the effort: she did not like to think of him being stalked like this. She should warn him. If only she knew where he was.

'The Earl has put you in a temper, I see.'

The lazily amused voice made her almost jump out of her shoes, and she spun around to glare at a laurel bush which shook slightly, then parted to reveal Nicholas, hatless.

'How did you get in here?' she demanded.

'Picked the lock.' He strolled out of the undergrowth. 'Shall we sit on that bench? Or are you still needing to pace? He does have that effect on people.'

'So do you,' she said, tight-lipped. 'I can see the family resemblance.'

She had tried to put him out of her mind. The fact that she had been entirely unsuccessful in no way lessened her agitation at seeing him now.

'Ah.' Nicholas flipped a handkerchief over the garden bench and waited to her to sit, then leant on an urn next to the path and looked at her ruefully. 'You know who I am, then?'

'I do. Quite by chance. The Earl spoke to me in Hyde Park yesterday and I felt I knew him from some-where…he seemed familiar.'

'I am not certain I am flattered.'

Sophie shot him a quelling look, which apparently failed to penetrate. 'Then he was startled to see someone in the crowd, and when I followed his gaze I thought I recognised your black mare. After he had ridden off the friend I was with told me the story of his two sons and I put the pieces together. The *Peerage* completed the picture.'

'Are you likely to encourage his courtship?' Nicholas enquired, almost, but not quite, managing to sound indifferent to her answer.

'There is no courtship. I thought you were skilled at reading these riddles. He has connected us, you and I, and he has set out to find you through me. He danced with me once, he has conversed with me in the park, and now he has offered to help me buy a new horse. If that adds up to courtship in your book, my lord, I pity your future wife.'

'What did you call me?'

'My lord. You are Viscount Denham, are you not?'

'I do not use the title.'

He straightened up from his casual pose and stared

at her, every inch the future Earl, she thought, with a flash of somewhat desperate amusement.

'I presume many of your male acquaintance know who you are—know your story and play along with your deception because in your guise as Pascoe you are useful to them? But you will have to shed that mask one day, even if neither you nor your father want it. Or I suppose you could allow this ridiculous feud to continue past his death and let the estates fall into rack and ruin.'

'Ridiculous?'

Now Sophie saw real anger in Nicholas's expression, in the tension in his body and in the cutting edge of his voice.

'My brother George was a kind soul, a gentle man. Not an intellectual—not very clever at all, to be honest. But he was just that—honest. He would have made a solid country gentleman one day, devoted to his dogs and game birds, good to his tenants, careful of the land, amiable to his wife. He would not have planned to marry to extend the landholdings or for political influence or power. He just wanted a contented, dull life.'

'And your father could not accept that?'

'No. You could argue with him until you were blue in the face, but if he decided that it was not raining, the fact that you were shouting at each other while drenched to the skin and standing in a puddle would not sway his opinion one inch. He decreed that George must be the ideal Earl, made in his image, and I should become a clergyman, take on the living in his gift, and support my brother.'

'I have to confess that I find it almost impossible to picture you as a man of the cloth,' Sophie said, and despite her mixed feelings at being alone with him again she could not repress a smile. His dark brows drew together in a frown and she added, 'Although I imagine that the image of Lucifer, the fallen angel, in cassock and bands, preaching hellfire from the pulpit, would be quite effective.'

'Lucifer?' he growled.

'Dark and deadly.'

The frown became a scowl, and then Nicholas's sense of humour caught up with him and he laughed. 'Conducting the choir with a poker and twitching my forked tail out of sight when the bishop approached?'

She looked up at him, so amused and very male against the background of green shrubbery, and felt something in her chest give a painful twist.

'Exactly. Don't let's scratch at each other, Nicholas. You startled me, that's all. And I was thinking about you.'

'You were?' He sat down beside her. 'Kindly, I trust?'

'I was thinking that the only reason the Earl has for paying me any attention is that he has somehow discovered that you and I know each other and he hopes to find you through me.'

'And you fear for my safety?' He sounded less amused now.

'I am sure his intentions are purely good, but I do not like to think he is…tracking you down and you do not know of it.'

'It occurred to Brough to wonder whether he was seeking a new wife in the hope of an heir, should something happen to me, but I acquit him of wanting to murder me. However exasperated he became with George, he never raised a finger to him. And our mother, although unhappy and disregarded, was never afraid of him. He is not a violent or unscrupulous man. He just expects to have his own way in everything.'

'Perhaps he is reconciled to the idea of you as his heir and he wishes you would come home? Take some of his duties from him?'

'He is fifty-two years of age—hardly in his dotage. I would have to prise his cold dead hands from the keys and seals if I wanted to take any responsibility now.'

Nicholas laid his hand over hers where it lay on the bench between them. After a moment Sophie turned it and let her fingers entwine with his.

'I have missed you. Perhaps he misses you too, and worries about you. No, do *not* snort at me like that, you cynical man.'

'You have missed me?' He lifted her hand and

kissed her knuckles, then let their joined hands rest on his thigh.

Sophie could feel his hard muscles under the cloth, his warmth. The touch of his lips lingered on her skin.

'Yes, I have missed you,' she admitted. 'We had become friends, had we not?'

Nicholas shifted on the seat to look at her. 'Men and women do not become friends. You employed me as your agent and then we discovered that we wanted something else. And that was not wise. How does that make us friends?'

Sophie gave an exasperated huff. *Men.* 'Do you like me? And I do not mean desire me.'

'Yes,' he said warily, as though being asked to sign a contract he had not first read.

'And you have confided your thoughts and feelings about your family to me, have you not?'

'Yes…'

'And you trust me? We find some of the same things amusing? I feel the same—I like and trust you, and you make me smile more often than you make me want to upend a vase of flowers over your head. I think we are friends, Nicholas.'

'I want to bed you,' he said bluntly.

'That does complicate matters, I agree—especially as I desire the same thing. But clearly we must not yield to that,' she said primly.

That surprised a gasp of laughter from him. 'Are you certain we must not?'

'Nicholas!'

'I'm a man. We do tend to dwell on the subject. Explain all the reasons why again.'

'You know them perfectly well,' she said severely, suspecting he was teasing her. 'But the one that overrides all of them is my son. I would not have him growing up hearing that his mother is less than chaste, discovering that she has a lover.'

'Very well. I give in. I might be a man, but I am not a rutting beast. I suppose I can manage to keep from kissing you if I try very hard.'

He lifted her hand to his lips again, the tip of his tongue flickering across her knuckles.

'Do so,' Sophie said repressively, in her best duchess voice. 'You will visit, will you not? I would like Duncan to know he can see his friend without having to hide the fact from me. He does not know why we…disagreed, of course, but he is aware that we did not part well.'

Inside she felt a warmth, a glow that was just touched by a tiny prickle of apprehension. She was asking Nicholas to behave with restraint when she was not at all certain how easy she would find it when faced with temptation. And deep inside was an even more worrying prickle: the suspicion that this man was becoming altogether too important to her.

'You are not leaving London, then?'

'No. I have been asked to detach a young gentleman from his latest very dear friend, who just happens to be a most accomplished card sharp, highly skilled at luring foolish youngsters into deep play. A leg, in other words.'

'A leg?' she asked, confused.

'Usually a gentleman-born, come on hard times, using his knowledge of the *ton* to lure pigeons into his net. By definition they are harder to wean their victims away from than some dubious Captain Sharp, because they appear to be "one of us"—well-dressed, well-spoken, with an edge of glamour to them. It will take me a few weeks to prise my young gentleman out of his clutches, so I have no doubt you and I will meet at all the very best parties. Will you dance with me, Duchess?'

'I will. And will you seek out your father and end this foolish game of hide and seek between you?'

'That would be best, I admit, but I do not want him announcing to all and sundry that I am his son and the Viscount Denham. That would end my career. And with it my income.'

'Surely there would be an allowance for you?'

'I'll not be a kept man.'

There was all the pride of generations of Tavershams in that instant response. Yes, one day he would take up the role of Earl and fit it well, she was certain.

Sophie did not voice the thought, but instead shrugged in a way she knew would be provocative. 'Then earn it. There must be something you can do to assist him and merit an allowance.'

'You, Duchess, sound like my tutor. He too was a great believer in duty and hard work.'

She thought that sometimes her own life seemed nothing but duty and hard work, and the flare of resentment at that startled her. Was she steering Nicholas towards reform whilst he was goading her to rebellion?

Another of her mother's pronouncements came back to her: *There is nothing more dangerous than a rake, because a woman believes she can reform him, but it is he who will change her.'*

She watched Nicholas from under her lashes. He seemed quite comfortable, sitting silently beside her. Was he a rake? There were certainly no tales of wild behaviour with women, spurned mistresses, ruined maidens or abandoned infants. If there had been she would be doing more than mildly lecturing him.

Yes, he was an undutiful and unforgiving son. Yes, he was secretive, and apparently quite unscrupulous when he went about his assignments. But he had never, in her limited knowledge of him, done anything shameful, his acts of larceny had been in a good cause, and Duncan trusted him.

A rogue, then, but an honourable one.

He flirted with her, kissed her, tempted her—but he took no for an answer.

'I am not attempting to reform you,' she said, partly in answer to his last teasing comment, and partly in answer to her own thoughts.

He shifted to look at her, and something dangerously like a challenge lurked in those dark eyes. 'No?'

'No. I have no right. And besides, it would be a great impertinence to try and change anyone,' Sophie said firmly. 'And now I must go home. I will let you out, so you have no need of your lock-picks. I shudder to think what the neighbours would say if they knew I was encouraging a man with your skills,' she added as she locked the garden gate behind them.

'But then you are *not* encouraging me, are you, Sophie?'

Nicholas tipped his hat to her and strolled off, leaving her torn between laughter and annoyance.

Maddening man.

She found she was watching his back as he neared the corner and turned away from the square and down one of the smaller streets. She told herself it was nothing to do with the fact that he was a well-made man who was a pleasure to look at.

Another man appeared—one who must have been walking along the edge of the railings at the far end of the square. He waited a moment at the kerb, although there was no traffic, and then took the same street that Nicholas had.

Sophie narrowed her eyes, uneasy suddenly. But he was respectably dressed—like a clerk, perhaps, or a shopkeeper—and was certainly not some footpad. Just coincidence…or someone unsure of their way. Or perhaps the Earl of Chalfont had located his son and was having him followed. But, however much Nicholas might resent it, that would do him no harm, surely?

She shook her head, which seemed to have far too many thoughts and emotions circulating inside it, and went up the steps to go and play with Freddie. There was nothing like a small child for simplifying one's world.

Chapter Thirteen

Nick scooped his winnings towards himself and stood up. 'Thank you for the game, gentleman. Now I must go and do my duty on the dance floor.'

The three men still seated greeted that with good-natured banter and he strolled away, taking a looping path through the card room. It had been an amiable game, with no great losses to anyone, and it had allowed him to keep an eye on the young baronet who was the subject of his latest commission, seated at a table a few feet away.

Sir Peter Tracy—eighteen, fat of pocket, green as grass and desperate to appear a man about town—was frowning over the cards fanned out in his hand. There was not much paper or coin in front of him, and considerably more in front of the three men he was playing with. With him signalling the contents of his hand the way he was, it was not surprising he was losing—even without any trickery on the part of his opponents.

Nick drifted past the table, coming to a halt behind

Captain Howard. These gull-catchers so often presented themselves as one-time military men that it seemed to Nick as though they ought to be wearing a badge reading *Sharper*. But there was never any shortage of gullible victims for them.

He waited until Sir Peter glanced up and saw him, then let his gaze drop to the Captain's cards, looked up again and raised one eyebrow. Then he smiled wryly, shook his head very slightly, and wandered casually away.

He heard the snap of some cards being played, then a youthful voice. 'Oh, these confounded cards. I have not had a decent hand all evening, I swear.'

Nick glanced back. The baronet saw him looking and frowned, apparently confused. It was a tiny thing, but he was now uneasy about that last hand. It was going to take considerably more before he was ready to accept that his smart new friend was out to fleece him, but he did not want the young man to see he was in Nick's sights as well as the Captain's.

Lady Oldstead's ball was proving as much of a success as her entertainments usually did. A lavish hand with the refreshments and wine, first-class musicians and novel decorations—that evening the guests were to imagine themselves in Venice—all resulted in a vast crowd with a great deal of noise and heat that came like a blow after the hush of the card room.

And there, promenading down the line in a country

dance, were Sophie and his father, who was manging to make the measure look more like a minuet than a frolic.

Should he make a move?

Was she right and this was time to end it?

Nick dug a coin from a pocket and flipped it.

Heads, I approach him.

Heads it was. He found a position close to the set of dancers and waited for the music to end in a flurry of bows and curtsies. It was a risk. If his father made a scene, or even said his name loudly enough to be overheard, then his old life would be at an end before he'd had the opportunity to negotiate the new.

Couples began to come off the floor and he saw Sophie look at him. He nodded, so she changed direction slightly and walked up to him, her hand still on his father's arm.

'Duchess, you look ravishing tonight.' He met the Earl's narrowed gaze and bowed slightly. 'Sir. It has been a long time.'

'It has. Too long.' The voice was as he remembered it—precise, chilly, lacking in emotion. 'I hardly recognised you.'

No? You cannot often look in the mirror in that case.

Nick found himself equally surprised. He had seen the Earl at a distance, but it was still a shock to discover just how much he had grown to resemble the older man. This was what he would look like at the same age. It was disconcerting.

'This is such a crush,' Sophie observed, making both of them turn to her. 'I am sure you have a great deal to discuss, and quiet and a neutral space might help. I would welcome you both to tea on Friday afternoon, but I fear I will have to leave you to your own devices almost immediately. Shall we say three o'clock, gentlemen?'

'That would be most kind, Duchess.'

He waited, wondering at the tightness in his muscles, and then realised this was how he had felt when he had faced his one and only duel—a piece of nonsense over a young lady in Spain that had suddenly become deadly serious. Fortunately his opponent had lost his nerve when sober, and with it his aim, and Nick had developed as he had always intended.

The Earl was his opponent now, and what was at stake was not his life, but the way he lived it.

'Indeed. A most sensible suggestion. In three days' time, as you say. Good evening, Your Grace…'

There was a pause, and Nick realised his father did not know how to address him.

'Jerrard…'

'It is Nicholas, sir.'

But the older man had already turned away and was walking towards the doors out of the ballroom.

'Goodness,' Sophie said. 'Are you suffering from

frostbite too?' She smiled when he nodded. 'I hope you do not think me interfering, but otherwise I suspect the pair of you would have stood here all evening, like a pair of fighting cocks eying each other before a bout.'

'I was thinking of a duel,' Nick confessed as the music began again. 'Are you promised for this dance?'

'I had intended to sit it out, but...'

He could see her swaying slightly in time to the music. 'Then let us waltz.'

Having Sophie in his arms was a delight, as he remembered. She was the right height, the right shape, the right woman. They moved together without him having to think what his feet were doing or worrying about her skill, and she smiled up at him happily.

'You have fought duels?' she asked.

'Just the one.'

'Over a lady?'

'It was. A foolish argument when drink had been taken and the Spanish sun was too hot. Tempers cooled rapidly in the dawn light and with a hangover. No blood was spilt.'

'And were you serious about the lady in question?'

Nick shook his head. He was never serious about women because that was the way to become entangled, and he liked his freedom. One day he would have to marry, or see the title and estates go to a cousin, but he was in no hurry. Marriage, as far as he had observed, was a cool affair of negotiation and the balancing of mutual gains. His own parents' match had been like that, and he could not see that it made for a comfortable home-life.

'I was not.'

'Was she your mistress?' Sophie asked without a blush.

'She was not,' he said.

'And do you have one now?'

'Sophie!' he said, shocked to find himself...well, shocked. 'I did have. But I do not go around kissing duchesses and at the same time keeping a mistress. Very bad form,' he added, making a joke of it.

'But you aren't kissing duchesses any more, are you?' she pointed out.

More's the pity.

'The lady in question is now otherwise engaged and I have no time for dalliance—not with a foolish young sprig to detach from Captain Sharp.'

'So you are not tempted to go to Mrs Sweeting?' she said.

'I am not. That, of course, will make her highly suspicious when she comes to think calmly about what happened to the diaries, but she cannot prove anything, after all.'

He sensed the change in Sophie simply from the way she felt in his arms, although he could not have described just how.

'I think she could be dangerous,' she said slowly.

'How?' Nick whirled her around and around again, sending her cream and bronze silk skirts flying and provoking a gasp that made him smile. 'She has no power, no influence. Or do you expect her to hire a footpad with a knife?'

'Don't,' she said sharply, and her hand tightened convulsively on his shoulder. 'Do not even think about it. I saw her in the park the other day—the day your father saw you. She looked at me in such a fashion it made me shiver. And I think someone was following you the day we met in the garden. It might have been a coincidence,' she said doubtfully, her teeth closing over her lower lip in a way that made him recall all too vividly the feel of her mouth under his in the mews.

'Don't you go biting your lip like that—it is too pretty. What was this sinister follower like, then?'

'A respectable clerk,' she said, with a rueful laugh and the hint of a blush for his flattery. 'I expect I was simply imagining things or it was someone set on by the Earl to track you down. After all, what can she do to us?'

'Nothing—although speak of the devil… here she is over there with Lord Philbey. I think I will stroll past and greet her when this is done. Just to confuse matters.'

He rather thought that Sophie muttered something about poking wasps' nests, but they did not speak of Mrs Sweeting again, nor of anything else for that matter. He did not know what Sophie was thinking about, but he was having a great deal of trouble making his body behave in a fitting manner for a ballroom. It was all very well for a lady to assert airily that she wanted to be friends and nothing else, but females did not have inconvenient bits of anatomy that had their own mind about the matter.

Nicholas left her with a group of female acquaintances and walked away, drifting with apparent casualness towards Mrs Sweeting.

'Well worth watching, my dear,' Lady Grace Doughty remarked, and Sophie realised she had been staring after him.

'He is a very good dancer,' she said casually, deploying her fan on cheeks that were suddenly heated.

It was all very well for Nicolas to stay cool and collected when she was in his arms—he had agreed readily enough that such things as kisses must cease—but she was finding it decidedly difficult to discipline her body. It got hot and bothered, and it ached in the worst places when he was near. And, as if that were not bad enough, she found herself wanting to touch him all the time.

'I imagine he moves well in any situation,' Grace remarked, her voice heavy with meaning, and the little group of ladies around them all laughed.

Somehow Sophie managed to join in. She was feeling possessive about Nicholas, she realised. He was her friend, and she did not like women whom she had always regarded as friends too ogling him as though he was someone they could amuse themselves with, simply because they thought him of lower status than they were themselves.

She turned a little, joining in the chatter, watching Nicholas as he 'accidentally' encountered Amanda Sweeting and Lord Philbey. The woman clearly intended to pretend she had not seen him—which proved, Sophie thought, that she was deeply suspicious of him. But her companion spoke to Nicholas and he stopped to talk, giving the lady a bow that must have set her teeth on edge. However, if she was attempting to lure the exceedingly wealthy Baron into an arrangement she could hardly indulge herself by saying what she clearly wished to say to Nicholas.

Suddenly Sophie felt vaguely nauseous. The room was too hot, the guests too loud, the mingled scents of perfume and hot bodies and flowers stifling. This was a cattle market, she thought with revulsion. Over there a group of hopeful mothers were watching their daughters like hawks, to see which of them were attracting the most eligible of the young men. In front of her Amanda Sweeting was negotiating the sale of herself to the wealthiest, most indulgent man she could find, and her married friends, bored with their pampered lives, were eying good-looking men and thinking about taking a lover.

She was no better. She was here to establish her place in society again and to collect useful acquaintances. And she had begun like those young women over there, their pale gowns signalling their virginity, waiting to be judged as acceptable by the circling men.

It was irrational. She knew that with the part of her mind that could ignore the gathering headache and the anger that watching Amanda Sweeting's hand curl around Lord Philbey's arm stirred. This was how society worked, and this was how the great houses passed from generation to generation, gathering power and wealth. But she could not bear it any longer that evening.

'Excuse me,' she said abruptly, cutting Lady Grace off in mid-sentence. 'I have a headache.'

She was almost running by the time she reached the row of French doors that stood open onto the terrace. The air they let in was tinged with the smells of London—soot and waste mingling with the aromas of the garden that lay beyond in deep shadow. Like many gardens attached to fine houses in the fashionable quarters it was not a large enough pleasure ground to make it worth lighting its paths with lanterns, and those guests who had stepped out for air were keeping to the terrace.

Sophie went straight across the flagstones to the balustrade and rested her hands on it, leaning forward to ease her breathing, uncaring about the lichen on her white satin gloves. Slowly the nausea ebbed away, and with it the worst of the headache, leaving her clear-headed enough to realise why she was so upset.

This game—this elaborate dance that she had been trained to perform to perfection—was nothing to her any more. All she wanted was her son and one man. The one who was so unsuitable.

Or was he? If Nicholas reconciled with his father he would be restored to society, the heir to an earldom…

Her spinning thoughts steadied. There were two ways she could be with Nicholas. She could marry him or she could become his lover.

What man in the prime of life, having to take on his responsibilities as heir to a great estate, would want to become a young duke's stepfather, with all that entailed? A less than scrupulous man would see the advantages to himself—at the expense of the baby Duke—but Nicholas was not that man. And besides, he too needed an heir—and not one who would be brought up in the shadow of his stepbrother's title.

Anyway, he never mentioned marriage, did he? said the cold voice of common sense. *He would have become your lover if you hadn't sent him away, but marriage…? No. He knows who he is, and that one day he will step forward as heir to the earldom. If he had wanted to marry you he would have told you the truth about himself.*

And why was she thinking about marriage all of a sudden? She was not in love—whatever that was—but she desired Nicholas with all the passion of a grown woman who had never experienced those feelings before.

A group came out from the ballroom, laughing, glasses clinking, and made their way towards the balustrade—presumably to sit on it, as all the stone benches were occupied. Sophie fled down the shallow sweep of steps on to the gravel path beneath and into the shadows of the shrubbery.

It was dark amongst the bushes, but there were spills of light from the moon and from the flambeaux on the terrace. She found a bench in a little arbour and sat down, soothed a little by the tinkle of water from an unseen fountain close by.

It was simply a matter of self-discipline, Sophie told herself. This would pass. Probably it was a reaction to the long year of mourning and then her alarm over the loss of the diaries. Her ordered life had been turned upside down, but all she had to do was set it to rights again.

'All…?' she murmured aloud.

'Sophie? What is wrong?'

She had not heard him approach, despite the gravel underfoot, but no doubt rogues who carried lock-picks and climbed into houses in the dead of night learned to move like ghosts as well.

That is what Nicholas is, she reminded herself, rather desperately. *A viscount, but also a rogue and an adventurer.*

'But he is my rogue,' she whispered, answering herself.

'Sophie?' Nicholas said again, and then she saw him.

The moonlight struck his face as he came around the edge of the arbour, bleaching him into the stark elegance of a carving in ivory.

'How did you find me?' she asked from the shadows.

'I saw you leave and it seemed…precipitous. I watched you on the terrace, in case you were unwell. You appeared better for a moment, so I thought it best not to be seen with you out here, but then you came down into the dark and that worried me.'

'All of a sudden I found the noise and the crowds too much,' she said.

Out here it felt as though the pounding of her heart was louder even than the music and laughter that reached them from the ballroom.

'Do you feel recovered now?'

Nicholas had moved out of the moonlight and she could no longer see his face.

'Yes. No. I have realised I am unhappy,' Sophie said, before she could stop herself.

'Why, Sophie?'

It did not seem she could say less than the truth. 'Because I lied to you when I said I wanted friendship only between us.'

'You wish we were lovers?'

'Yes.' She swallowed hard. 'But I know it is impossible.'

'I do not see why it should be,' Nicholas said, and sat down beside her.

Chapter Fourteen

'It is impossible for us to be lovers because I dread a scandal that would tarnish Frederick's name. And I fear getting with child,' Sophie admitted, with a burst of frankness.

'Then we would be exceptionally discreet. It is my business to take precautions. There are those who have been spying on us—we know that now—so we are forewarned for the future. And as for your other fear… we do nothing that might lead to conception,' Nicolas said.

He shifted a little and she sensed that he was just within touching distance now. Every nerve seemed to stretch towards him, trembling, but she made herself sit still.

'I know there are methods and I know they are not reliable,' she said.

One of her friends had told her about it, bewailing the fact that she might be presenting her black-haired husband with a red-haired offspring who would resemble his valet all too closely.

'Tell me, Sophie, did your husband ever come to your bed for mutual pleasure and dalliance or was it always to plant his seed in you?'

In the darkness he would not be able to see her burning cheeks. 'Dalliance? No. It was always—' she broke off, lost for words.

'Businesslike?' Nicholas supplied, his voice dry.

'Yes, exactly.'

'Then allow me to assure you that it is perfectly possible to have very fulfilling lovemaking without the slightest risk of unwanted consequences.'

'Oh.'

How? Sophie realised that she was exceedingly ignorant. But it must have a lot to do with how she felt when Nicholas kissed her, held her close, and her body flamed into life.

'Besides, I do not expect that you will want to become involved, even for a short time, and—'

Nicholas kissed her until she gave up trying to speak, let alone think, and then he took her hand and placed it firmly on the thin knitted black silk of his evening breeches.

'Now tell me that I do not wish "to become involved", as you put it.'

Sophie found she had no words to say anything. Her fingers had closed over the rigid length that proved his desire beyond question—the first time she had ever touched a man so intimately, despite the fact that he was clothed. She curled her other hand around Nicholas's neck and found his mouth, bumping his nose a little in the darkness.

'Mpmh...' he said against her lips.

It made her giggle, and suddenly everything was all right.

It was fortunate that one of them had some experience, she thought hazily when Nicholas finally sat back, leaving her reaching for him in the darkness.

'Not here, and not now. Duchess, you have to go back to the ballroom without a hair out of place and complain to all your acquaintance how hot it is, and how even a turn on the terrace has not quelled your headache. And I must appear in a secluded corner of the card room, having been waiting for a promised partner for at least half an hour. Come into the moonlight so I can see you.'

He helped her to her feet and stepped out of the arbour, bringing her with him to stand in a splash of silvery light beside the little fountain.

'The goddess of the glade,' he said, his voice curiously husky. 'You are so beautiful it takes my breath.'

If she was the goddess then he was the spirit of the place: black and silver, lithe lines drawn in pen and ink by a master.

She found herself too shy to say anything except, 'Am I fit to be seen?'

'Yes, perfect. No…your hair at the back. I will just catch this one lock.' He moved around her, kissed her nape as she felt the pins slide into place. 'There—the model of decorum, Duchess. I will walk you as far as the foot of the steps.'

They stood looking up at the figures walking past on the terrace until Nicholas whispered, 'Now,' with his hand in the small of her back.

She walked up, schooling her expression into one of calm. As she reached the terrace she thought she heard a laugh—a faint, mocking trill of amusement from below and to one side—but when she glanced back all was still. Imagination, Sophie told herself. They would have heard if anyone else had been in the garden.

'Oh, Lady Marchmont… Miss Marchmont… I see you too are attempting to find some air,' she said, approaching two promenading ladies from behind, so they could not tell she had been below in the darkness. 'A delightful ball, but such a crush.'

She accompanied them as they returned to the ballroom, and found herself looking at the scene before her with completely new eyes.

All these people…all these separate, secret, private lives. And now she had her own secret. She would have a lover, and she had already met him clandestinely in the darkness. It made her feel powerful in a way she had never felt before. She had dared speak of her feelings, her needs, to a man and he had responded.

Nicholas, my lover, she thought, as she caught a glimpse of a pair of very familiar shoulders disappearing into the card room.

'You are in great beauty tonight, Your Grace. Dare I hope you have this set free?'

She turned and smiled at the French *emigré* the Comte de Falaise. 'After such outrageous flattery, *mon cher comte*, how can I possibly refuse?'

Sophie ordered her open carriage for a drive the next morning, too keyed up after the ball to sleep in, despite the late hour of her return.

As she came down the front steps a young lad ran up. 'You the Duchess?'

'Here, lad, be off with you.' Her groom stepped forward protectively.

'No, he means no harm. Yes, I am the Duchess.'

'Got a note for you.' He held out a folded and sealed note, rather the worse for being clutched in his grubby hand.

'Thank you.' Sophie found him a sixpence and he ran off.

The note read simply:

Green Park, eleven, if you can. P

When they entered the park she was not surprised
to find her path intersecting with that of a rider—a
familiar figure on a black mare.

'Pull over, James,' she called. 'What a coincidence,
Pascoe,' she said for the coachman's benefit, as Nicholas brought his horse alongside the carriage.

'Will you walk with me a little?'

When she nodded he swung down from the horse
and helped her alight. They strolled alongside the carriage track, his mare following obediently without
being led. Their elbows bumped companionably and
she felt a little frisson of secret pleasure at every touch.

'I have to be out and about this evening, keeping
track of my young innocent as he blunders deeper into
the snares that lure him, but I wanted to be certain that
you meant what you said last night.'

'Oh, yes,' Sophie said.

'In that case I have a suggestion about how we might
meet and discuss it further.'

'I had not thought that much discussion would be
needed,' she retorted, shocking herself with her own
impatience.

'I was attempting to spare your blushes, but if you
will have it in plain words: we need a place where I
can remove all your clothing, lay you on a bed and
make love to you until your scream. Was that what
you had in mind, Duchess?'

Sophie felt her cheeks flame. 'Yes, that is exactly what I had in mind.'

It was a lie—she had no idea that anything or anyone might make her scream with pleasure. But if anyone could, it was this man.

'Excellent. Then I suggest that after luncheon you order your carriage to take you to your modiste. Which do you patronise?'

'Several, but shall we say Mrs Bell?'

'I know it. Tell your driver that you will return with a friend and not to wait. Make some trivial enquiry in the shop and then, when you are ready to leave, look out through the door and tell the assistant that you have seen someone on the street you particularly wish to avoid. As if you might use their rear entrance? They will agree, of course. You will find a closed carriage waiting for you a short distance along the alleyway. Wear something unremarkable and have a veil on your bonnet.'

'You appear to be very used to this kind of intrigue.'

'Not involving other women, I promise you,' he said, clearly hearing the undertone in her comment. 'But this is how I live, Sophie, and I am not careless. Not with my life and not with those very few things that are precious to me.'

The lump in her throat made it difficult to speak, but she managed somehow. 'If...if I change my mind?'

'I will understand. If you are not at the carriage by three o'clock, then it will leave.'

He turned, and they strolled back to where her pair of bays fidgeted in their traces, stamping impatiently.

'I'll not keep your horses standing, Duchess.'

He helped her into the carriage, swung up onto the black mare and tipped his hat when she looked back.

I must be certain, Sophie told herself before luncheon.

She climbed the stairs to the nursery and was rewarded by Freddie letting go of the chair he had used to haul himself up and propelling himself towards her. He sat down after two steps, looking surprised at what had just happened, but crowed with delight when both she and Nanny applauded and heaped praises on him.

'Oh, my clever boy! Let's do that again, shall we?'

Sophie knelt down close to his starting point and Nanny carried him back to the chair.

'Come to Mama.'

She held out her arms and he rushed into them, landing with a thump that almost knocked her backwards.

'That'll do the trick, Your Grace,' said Nanny. 'He'll be running about all over the place before much longer, and then we'll have our hands full and no mistake.'

Her son was growing up, she thought with pride. He was no longer a tiny baby, dependent on her, a part of her. If she could have her own life, be herself, without harming him, then she should.

I'll not dwindle away until one day he brings home his bride and I am the Dowager Duchess of St Edmunds, my youth behind me.

'Oh, bother!' Sophie said from the doorway, just loudly enough to bring the assistant hastening to her side.

'Your Grace?'

'I have just seen Lady— That is, someone I have no wish to encounter this afternoon…not without spending an hour at least listening to gossip,' she confided. 'Is there by any chance a back door I can use?'

'Oh, yes, Your Grace. It is a very clean, respectable area at the rear, and you will just have to turn to the right and right again and you are in Old Bond Street, ma'am. I could come with you if you wish?'

'Thank you, but I am sure it will be fine—provided there is no rubbish underfoot?'

'Oh, no, Your Grace.' The young woman led Sophie through the showroom, lined with bales of fabric, though a lobby and unbolted the back door. She looked out. 'There is no one about, Your Grace. Oh, thank you, Your Grace.' Her fingers closed around the coin.

Sophie lowered her veil as the door closed behind her and followed Nicholas's directions. And there was a small black carriage, facing out towards Bond Street, its blinds drawn down just as Nicholas had promised, a groom standing beside it.

He opened the door and handed her in, then closed it, leaving her in semi-gloom. She lifted her veil and a pair of hands caught her as the carriage jerked forward and she tumbled into a familiar embrace.

'Nicholas!'

'Who were you expecting?'

'Oh, any handsome gentleman with a shiny carriage would have done—'

Her nervous, teasing words were cut short by his mouth on hers as he gathered her against himself.

'Sophie, are you certain?'

She blinked as she opened her eyes in the gloom, staring up into his face, so close that she could see the faint frown of concern between his brows.

'Yes, of course.'

That did not earn a reply in words, only his mouth on hers again, and his hands caressing down over every curve of her body they could reach, holding her secure against the jolting of the carriage even as they built fires that flickered under her skin.

The carriage stopped.

'We are here,' Nicholas said, and lowered her veil again. 'It is a quiet street, but best to be careful.'

She'd expected to be hurried inside, and was worried that Nicholas appeared so casual—speaking to the driver, walking slowly up the front steps of a neat little terraced house. Then she realised that haste attracted attention, whereas acting as though one had the perfect right to be where one was, doing whatever one was doing—that just looked perfectly normal.

'Where are we?' she asked as he unlocked the door and they stepped inside. The house felt empty.

'Bloomsbury. This is where I live when I am in London. A maid comes in the morning, to keep it in order, and in the evening to cook if I order that. My valet and groom have rooms in the mews and come when I send for them. We will not be disturbed.'

Sophie heard the lock snick behind her and said, all of a rush, 'I feel ridiculously nervous about this. I asked you…and now I think I will disappoint you because I have no idea how to…'

'Make love?' Nicholas asked.

He stood behind her, his hands on her shoulders, as she stared rather desperately down the hall, wondering if she ought to run and find the back door and escape now, before she made a complete fool of herself.

'We can work that out together. It isn't like French grammar, you know, with one right answer—more a question of finding the accent that suits us. And standing here talking about it does not help, I suspect.'

Before she could reply Nicholas scooped her up in his arms and strode towards the stairs.

Sophie gasped. 'Put me down! I'm too heavy! You will drop me.'

'Now, that,' Nicholas said as he reached the landing, sounding only very slightly out of breath, 'is wrong. The correct response should be, *Oh, darling, you are so strong!*'

Sophie found a giggle escaping her. She rarely giggled. 'Sorry. Oh, darling, I could swoon…you are so strong and manly. Your muscles are *astounding*. Is that better?'

Nicholas gave a snort. 'Stop it, woman. I'll drop you if you make me laugh. It was a trifle overdone, but I am prepared to accept the compliment. However, you do need to save some exclamations of amazement for later, you know.'

It had never occurred to Sophie that the sexual act might involve laughter and teasing. She had so much more to learn than she had realised, she thought, as Nicholas shouldered open a door. And then she lost all desire to laugh as she saw the bed.

It was large, it dominated the space, and it made her nervous all over again.

And it was broad daylight.

She looked at the window as they passed it—the curtains were drawn back, and at least there were no windows opposite. But even so…

Nicholas set her on her feet beside the bed. 'Speak to me.'

'What about?'

'Why you have suddenly become stiff and nervous again. Is it the bed? Or the light?'

'Both.'

The bed is very comfortable, and no one can see in.'

'But *we* can see,' she said rather desperately. 'And I've never seen a man with no clothes on before. Or taken all mine off in front of one.'

The Duke had always come to her bed at night, in his nightshirt, and their congress had taken place under the sheets.

'Shall I take mine off first?'

She nodded. She could always close her eyes. Although her nerves were beginning to give way to a curiosity that was causing tingles in the most intimate places.

'In the absence of a valet, you will have to help,' he said.

He sat, pulled off his boots and stockings, then stood, his back turned, for her to help with his coat. He unbuttoned his waistcoat and untied his neckcloth with a flick of the wrist. He pulled his shirt free of his breeches, bent over, and in a somewhat muffled voice invited her to pull.

Sophie was left with an armful of white linen and confronting a naked torso. Intriguing muscles…even more intriguing hair and nipples. His shape was very like the Classical statues she had admired cautiously from a distance—a lady would not stare. But this lady wanted very much to touch.

Nicholas would say if he did not like it, she decided, and reached out her right hand, laid it flat against his breastbone, and smiled at the feel of crisp curls against her palm.

Nicholas made a sound remarkably like a purr and, emboldened, she touched him with her other hand, running her fingers over his chest. One fingertip touched his right nipple and he caught his breath. She had liked it when his caresses had brushed against her breasts—perhaps men liked that too.

Apparently they did.

'Enough.' He said it abruptly and stepped back, but she did not fear she had displeased him.

Nicholas managed to get out of his breeches and smallclothes faster than she could shed a petticoat.

'Oh.'

Now, *that* was not something to be disguised by a fig leaf, and it explained a lot about procreation that she had not quite grasped before, with all that sight-less fumbling under the bedclothes. In fact, *grasp* was probably the right word.

Greatly daring, Sophie stepped close and curled her fingers around the evidence that Nicholas was very much looking forward to what was to come.

He closed his eyes. 'Sophie…'

'Yes?'

'Keep very, very still and then let go.'

When she did so he exhaled, like a man coming

up from near drowning. 'I confess I had not realised just how much I want you. May I undress you now?'

Sophie nodded, confident at least that she was not disappointing Nicholas, and that her wish that they were lovers was mutual.

He proved as quick and efficient as any lady's maid, and she suppressed the thought that his dexterity betrayed considerable experience in undressing women.

He turned her gently to untie her stay laces, and she closed her eyes as they fell away and he turned her back. It was foolish. He could see her perfectly well, whether she had her eyes open or closed, but she kept them tightly shut none the less, as the last of her garments fell to the floor.

'Oh, Duchess...'

She opened her eyes a little. Nicholas was staring as though transfixed. She thought of the silvery lines that had appeared after Freddie had been born, of the fact that her stomach was not as flat as it once had been. She wasn't perfect—not that she had ever been that. But it had never mattered before.

Part of her flinched internally, but a small voice of rebellion—the one that had compelled her to tell him how she felt—murmured, *You are who you are. He doesn't want you because he wants perfection, and you wouldn't want him if he did, would you?*

And then she looked again, and all she could see in his eyes was desire, and the hand that stroked gently over her was tender and almost tentative, as though he touched something fragile and precious.

'I won't break,' she whispered.

Nicholas lifted his head and looked at her. 'But I might.'

Nicholas lifted her on to the bed and followed, leaning on one elbow beside her as he stroked down her body from temple to navel with one hand almost casually, leaving ribbons of fire on her skin. Then he stooped and followed the same path with his mouth, licking and kissing, and when he reached her breasts, gently teasing with his teeth.

When she moaned and twisted and reached for him he murmured encouragement, shifting and responding to her touch until they were twined together on the bed and Sophie was no longer certain where she began and he ended.

How long ago had she ceased to care that his touch was intimate? That her body was hot and wet and she was making desperate sounds? All that no longer mattered, and all that was left was the fact that something inside her was twisting and tightening, climbing towards a peak she could surely never—

And then she shattered, arching against his hand, and then she was gathered in close to his body, and the tidal wave took her as he pressed tight against her belly and thrust, and she felt warmth on her flesh, and heard his cry as he followed her into the darkness...

Chapter Fifteen

Nick surfaced to find the light fading and Sophie asleep, sprawled across his chest. Three times, he thought, with what he considered perfectly justifiable male smugness. It would be a wonder if either of them could stand.

He had dreamt about making love to his duchess, but he had not expected it to be like that. She was so passionate, so innocently demanding and giving, that it was hard to remember that she was not a virgin… that she had borne a child. Her husband must have been obsessed with his mistress to have come to his wife's bed simply to impregnate her with his son and then leave without even kissing her, without looking at her, wanting to caress her.

'Sophie?' he whispered, pushing back her hair to find an ear.

'Mmm…?' She wriggled without opening her eyes and kissed his chest.

'No. No more. We must bathe and dress and I must

get you home, before your household is out scouring the streets for you.'

She opened her eyes at that and looked at him, the green depths of her gaze full of mysteries and questions and unspoken thoughts. Then she smiled, and something inside him tightened painfully. It was almost like fear, but he had faced that down often enough to know it well. This was something else entirely.

He saw the moment when reality hit her.

Sophie sat bolt upright. 'Freddie's bath time!'

Nicholas absorbed the fact that he was most definitely not the most important man in her life and sat up too. 'Our bath time first. It will have to be in the scullery, which is where the only hot water is.'

Sophie looked down at their sticky, heated bodies. 'Oh, my goodness, yes.'

She was in too much of a hurry to get back to her son for them to indulge in any of the games that Nicholas had thought of, involving warm water and soap, but she stood in the shallow tin bath soaping herself while he scooped warm water from the washhouse copper over her shoulders. Then they changed places before hurrying back upstairs, dripping, to dry themselves and dress.

'Nicholas?' Sophie sat on the edge of the bed to put on her shoes.

'I am delighted that you recall who I am,' he said from the armchair, where he was tugging on his boots.

Sophie coloured. 'Of course I do. And I have just realised that I am rushing off and I haven't said—'

'Yes, you have.' He stood up and reached for his coat. 'We made love, and we said everything we needed to whilst we were doing so. And now I must get you home. Before a certain small duke gets very indignant.'

'But how?' Sophie put on her bonnet and frowned at him. 'I should have thought of that… I cannot arrive at the back door of Mrs Bell's establishment.'

'Take this.' He held out a Kashmir shawl from where it had been draped across a chair-back, giving a splash of peacock colours to the room. 'I will drop you at Hatchard's bookshop. You will go in wearing the shawl, and with your veil down, then slip behind the shelves in a quiet area, remove the veil, fold the shawl and put it in your reticule. Then you will buy a book and have the doorman hail you a hackney.'

'That is a good idea,' she agreed, swathing the thin shawl around her to cover the details of the bodice of her pelisse.

The look she gave him was half admiring and half suspicious, as though she assumed he was always arranging the tactful disposal of lovers after an hour or two of dalliance. Nicholas decided that protesting his innocence would only emphasise the point.

He scanned the room to make certain nothing of Sophie's remained, and then took her downstairs. A whistle at the back door sent a small boy running to the mews, and the carriage came around in only ten minutes.

When they were sitting in the shadowy interior he reached for her hand. 'It is not often that dreams come true. Making love with you has been a dream of mine for quite some time.'

'How long?' she asked, and he saw the tilt of her head as she studied what she could see of him.

'Since approximately ten minutes after I first met you. For the first few minutes I was busy feeling indignant that Grant had not warned me.'

'Warned you? About what, pray?'

'That you were intelligent, determined, beautiful and liable to leave my heart in shreds under your feet.'

He'd put just enough over-emphasis on the flattery to make her laugh, and Sophie did—a little chuckle of amusement. Nicholas swallowed. That had been a little too close to revealing just how much she was coming to mean to him. And wanting made a man vulnerable.

The carriage stopped in front of Hatchard's in Piccadilly and the doorman ran to the carriage before the groom could even descend to let down the step. Sophie was gone, with a fleeting touch of the hand. The door closed, and he was halfway to Green Park before he pulled himself together enough to raise the blind, drop the window and direct the coachman to take him home.

His body felt so relaxed he could hardly sit up straight. His mind felt like warm porridge, and he knew that somehow he had to get himself alert and ready for an evening of smoky gambling hells and his next step in extricating young Sir Peter Tracy from the sticky trap he had mired himself in.

Somehow Nicholas's usual self-discipline was just not working. He felt too good, too content. He lay back and watched the streets of London roll past, and only gradually did reality began to seep back under the warm blanket their lovemaking had laid over him.

The innocent baronet was not the only one who was in the mire. This *affaire* with Sophie couldn't last. Wouldn't last. She would realise that what she really wanted a nice, conventional life with no risk of scandal. He understood why she was wary of marriage, but as she became used to her independent life, and had the opportunity to know and assess the gentlemen around her, she would find that society was full of perfectly decent aristocratic bachelors who would give her what her elderly husband had not—appreciation, their full attention, and a satisfying time in the bedchamber. One day she would find one she could trust, and there would be no parental authority pushing her into a decision. Sophie would make her own judgment.

He might as well accept it now and face facts. And stop sitting daydreaming like a love-struck youth after his first kiss.

The carriage stopped. He was home in plenty of time to remove any trace that a woman had been in the house before the maids appeared. He knew his valet was as inclined to gossip as a clam, but he wanted no speculation amongst the other servants.

He was standing in the bedchamber, his face buried in the towel Sophie had wrapped around her hair to save it from their makeshift bath, inhaling her scent, before he realised just how much danger he was in.

He had best watch himself, before he found himself in love with her. He had never been in love—was not at all sure he would recognise it if he were. He had passed through all the usual agonies of adolescence, of course, but even at the time some part of him had known it was calf love, or a pretty cover for lust.

The estranged heirs to earldoms did not aspire to be anything but the occasional lover of a duchess who had declared herself opposed to marriage—even if, sooner or later, he was certain she would change her mind about that. When she did it would be to make a carefully considered, prudent match, as much for her son's sake as her own.

Nicholas tossed the damp towel into a heap, well-buried in his own laundry, and started to plan for the evening—and for the day after next, when he would confront his father.

His work and his family—those were reality.

'Lord Chalfont.' Sophie stood up from behind the tea table, where she was awaiting her two guests, and held out her hand.

'Your Grace.' The Earl bowed over it and took the seat she indicated as she sank back onto the sofa.

'May I pour tea for you? Such a warm afternoon again, is it not?'

'Indeed it is…and a cup of tea would be most welcome.'

They managed fifteen minutes of excruciatingly banal small talk before the butler announced, 'Mr Pascoe, Your Grace.'

'Please show him in, Padwick.' Sophie poured tea the way she knew Nicholas liked it, and stood up again as he came into the room. 'Mr Pascoe. I have left your tea here. Do help yourselves to biscuits, gentlemen. I fear you must excuse me…my son has a slight fever.'

She left without looking directly at Nicholas. She was not at all certain that she could do so without revealing too much to the Earl, but her hand brushed his as she passed.

'Padwick, the gentlemen are not to be disturbed under any circumstances. I rely upon you to make certain that they may have their meeting quite without risk of being overheard. Is that clear?'

'Perfectly, Your Grace. I will ensure that personally.'

Sophie walked slowly upstairs to the nursery, where Fredrick did, indeed, have a slight fever, having screamed himself into a tantrum after Nanny had removed the kitchen cat from the room.

She made herself think about her son, and not what might be occurring in her drawing room, and most certainly she would not dwell upon what had happened in a certain Bloomsbury town house two days before.

The flowers that had arrived the next morning had had a card she could quite openly display.

Your Grace: with much appreciation for your visit to Hatchard's on my behalf. I am delighted with the results and trust that your own expectations were fulfilled.

Sophie sighed. Her expectations had indeed been fulfilled. In fact they had fallen so far short of reality that she still could not quite believe it. The problem was, she now wanted more, and had no idea how to proceed. How could she indicate that she wished this to continue without it appearing as a demand, or, equally, as begging for Nicholas's favours? For all she knew he might feel hesitant about initiating another meeting because of her rank.

No, she thought as she opened the nursery door. *Considerations of rank do not trouble Nicholas.*

A pink-faced, rather tear-streaked little duke fell into her arms at the end of a rapid toddle, and she quite forgot to think about anything except soothing his upset and placating a very weary Nanny.

Frederick, she feared, was going to be as imperious as his papa had been if left unchecked. It was up to her to teach him that he could not have everything he demanded.

And that applies to me too, she thought, when sunny smiles had been restored and Nanny was settled with a nice pot of strong tea and assurances that she had done quite the right thing in removing the big ginger tom cat, who would be no respecter of dukes if his tail was pulled. *However much I want to be with Nicholas, I must show self-control.*

It was a pity that she could not be as firm with her dreams.

'Your Grace, I am in your debt.'

Lord Chalfont was drawing on his gloves as Sophie, alerted by a footman to his departure, came downstairs.

'You have had a useful discussion?' she asked, after a glance assured her that the hall was empty of staff.

'My... Viscount Denham and I have come to an understanding, I believe.'

Sophie managed not to let a smile escape her. The stiff-backed old devil was finding it difficult to say the word *son*, but surely he'd manage it eventually.

'I am so glad for you both. I do hope you will call again.'

She opened the front door for him herself, which caused him to raise an eyebrow and look alarmingly like Nicholas.

'I will have my groom bring the two mounts I have selected for your assessment tomorrow, if that is convenient? I think them both suitable, but they are very different in temperament, so it will be a matter of your personal preference. Of course, if neither is to your liking, you only have to let me know.'

'Thank you very much,' she said warmly.

It was, indeed, kind of him, when he must have so much else on his mind.

'My pleasure, Your Grace.' He raised his hat and was gone.

She found Nicholas in the drawing room, one arm propped on the mantel shelf. He was studying the untouched plate of biscuits as though they held the answer to the meaning of life.

'All is well?' she asked as he looked up and stood away from the hearth.

'I think so. It was interesting to have a conversation as adults and from a position of power.'

'Power?'

'I could walk away very easily, and he knew it. He wants the future of the title and the estates secured.'

'And you held that over him?'

That did not seem like the action of the man she thought she knew.

'No. I surprised myself. I had thought I wanted a reckoning for the way he bullied my brother, for the unhappiness he put my mother through, but it would have been petty and would do them no good now. He wants me to take one of the smaller estates as my own.'

'He must hope you will marry soon and settle down there…learn to be a landowner.'

It was ideal. So why did the thought of it make her feel hollow inside?

'The land-owning seems attractive. I suppose it is in the blood. But the marriage… I had thought to put that off until I found the right woman.'

'And you have not? Not yet?' Of course not, or Nicholas would not be trysting with her—she was certain of that.

'The "right" woman is not always the suitable or available woman,' he said, with a twist of his lips and a shrug.

What did he mean by that? Had there been someone in the past? Someone unsuitable because she was not of the right status for the heir to an earldom?

A sensation she realised was hurt gripped her, and

she had to control her voice with an effort. 'It will happen in time, I am sure.'

Uncertain what to say next, Sophie shut the door, then stayed in front of it, watching him. She wanted to ask whether they would meet again in that little house, but discovered that she did not have the vocabulary.

What an innocent you are, she chided herself. *A innocent widow and mother. A duchess should have more sophistication in worldly matters.*

'We have agreed that nothing will be said publicly about my identity until I have completed my current commission,' he said. 'I believe I am almost at that point. And I must thank you for what you have just done. There are not many people who could effect a reconciliation so tactfully.'

He came towards her, his head cocked a little to one side as he studied her face.

'What is it?'

'I was trying to find the words to ask a question,' she admitted.

'Mmm...?'

The interrogative murmur sent a hot shiver down her spine.

Coward. Just ask.

'Are we to meet again, as we did before?' She knew she was blushing.

'I very much hope so.' Nicholas moved even closer, until the toes of his boots brushed the hem of her skirts. 'Although it does not have to be exactly as before. The place may be different, for example.'

'Really?'

'Yes, really.'

She'd expected him to move even closer and to kiss her, as a promise of what was to come before he revealed their new meeting place. Instead Nicholas knelt, rested his head against her stomach, and began to lift her skirts.

'What are you—?'

'Shh…'

The skirts were all the way up now, petticoats and all, baring her to the waist, and he held them, one hand on either side of her hips. Some ladies were trying the daring new fashion for pantalettes, but Sophie was not too sure about them and had so far resisted Foskett's suggestion that she try them. It seemed that this decision met with Nicholas's full approval.

'What are you *doing?*' she asked again, but this time in a whisper.

'Kissing you,' he said, and did so.

Sophie gave a startled cry, then slapped her own hand over her mouth. This was indecent, surely? She should push him away… She should hit him over the head… She should…

She leaned back against the unyielding panels of the door and went limp with pleasure, held up by Nicholas's firm grip, her mind a confusion of sensation, shock and delight. She knew where he was taking her now, and her body responded eagerly, whilst all she could do was moan against her own palm and surrender.

When she came to herself Nicholas was still kneeling, possibly because her free hand was locked in his hair. Her skirts were around her ankles again, but they were the only orderly thing about her, she thought rather wildly as she looked around the room.

'Oh,' she managed, and fell silent.

She was in her own drawing room, in broad daylight, and the curtains were wide open. Admittedly the house had a semi-basement, so that nobody outside on the street could stare in, but even so she could see out.

'What if someone had ridden by or gone past in a carriage?'

'You cannot see in. I have tried,' he admitted, his voice muffled. 'You might be able to if the candles were lit, but then the curtains would be closed.'

'You planned this?' Sophie tugged at the thick black lock of hair twined in her fingers and Nicholas stood, his hands still firm on her waist.

'No. I rode past the other day and looked, that is all. I would never risk your reputation otherwise.'

'Risk? What if one of the servants had come in?'

'They would have been unable to open the door.' He tipped up her chin so that he could look down into her face. 'Was it so awful?'

'It was outrageous. Indecent.' She bit her lip. 'Wonderful… And don't smile like that. Smugness is never attractive. Let me go.'

Nicholas released his grip and her knees sagged. She straightened them, and her back, and walked to the sofa, where she collapsed inelegantly against the cushions. The wretched man was still looking pleased with himself.

'What you just did…can a woman do that to a man?' The image in her mind was vivid and quite shocking. And very compelling.

'She can. Although it is not considered something one should ask a respectable lady to do.'

He had stopped looking smug and she realised that he was seeing the same picture that was in her mind.

'Sophie—'

There was a light scratch on the door panels and Padwick came in. 'The afternoon post has arrived, Your Grace. And a delivery from the toy shop.'

'Thank you, Padwick. Mr Pascoe is just leaving.'

There was a frown between his brows as Nicholas looked at her. She could hardly expect him to understand the wave of guilt that had swept over her. She had been performing a positively indecent act with a man, and discussing one that apparently no respectable lady would contemplate, only two floors beneath her innocent child's nursery, even as new toys were being delivered to her door.

Do not think about doors.

'May I take you driving tomorrow afternoon, Duchess?'

'Yes, certainly. That would be delightful.'

And it would give her a day to try and decide whether she could bear to continue like this any longer. Or bear to stop.

Chapter Sixteen

⁓⁓⁓

That had been a very satisfactory night's work, Nick thought as he strolled back through the still, dark streets of Mayfair.

It was almost four o'clock—the dead hour in fashionable London. Balls and parties had disgorged their most persistent guests into waiting carriages and weary coachmen and their teams had plodded home. The gamesters were slumped on their beds or snoring under the tables in the clubs, and the ladies of the night had seen their last clients and returned to wherever they laid their heads. Even the criminals had given up, aware that very soon households would be awakening and sleepy scullery maids would be poking kitchen ranges back into life.

Nick yawned hugely, but kept going. It was foolishly sentimental of him, but a slight detour would take him past Sophie's house. He would lean against the railings and look up at where he thought her bedchamber would be while he dwelt happily on the expression on Captain Howard's face when Sir Peter Tracy had looked across the card table at him and the ace that Nick had just shaken from the sleeve of his coat.

The young Baronet had thrown the contents of his brandy glass into the sharper's face and stormed out. Nick had followed him at a distance, leaving the other players at that table to reckon up their losses and deal with the Captain.

Sir Peter had managed to find a hackney, and Nick had turned for home as he saw him drive safely away. *That should do it*, he thought. There had been no mistaking what had happened, nor the cries of accusation from the other players.

Almost there. He paused as he turned a corner, then quickened his pace a little. Had he imagined the footfall behind him? Possibly…it was quiet now. But the prickle at the nape of his neck that had warned him of French snipers and Covent Garden pickpockets was insistent.

He reached the square and stood in deep shadow, with the railings to guard his back. No, nothing. Imagination? Or more likely some footpad making his own weary way home.

The house was dark, and he settled himself against the railings to indulge in five minutes of thinking about Sophie. Of the taste of her and the scent of her. Of the feel of satin skin and soft curves under his hands. He remembered the sounds she'd made as he brought her to her peak, the look in those lovely eyes, so wide and lost in—

The snap of a twig in the garden on the other side of the railings gave him just enough warning to begin to straighten up—and that probably saved his life. Instead of plunging straight inside his collarbone, the knife hit the top of his shoulder and slashed down his left arm.

Nick turned with a roar and grabbed at the knife. Inside the railings his attacker took to his heels, and as he gathered himself to give chase Nick felt his knees begin to give way. Then the pain hit, and he grasped at the railings to stay upright. He could hardly see, but he could tell he had lost too much blood already. He could lie down and die there, on the pavement, or he could make it across the street, up those steps, and hammer like hell on Sophie's front door.

She won't be best pleased at the bloodstains, he thought vaguely as he reeled across the cobbles, tripped on the kerb and crawled up the steps.

At least the front door was heavily moulded, which gave him something to hang on to as he hauled himself upright and began to pound with the great brass knocker.

'Pas?' a small voice enquired from the level of his ear.

Nick opened one eye and turned his head. It appeared to be on something soft, but moving sent a stabbing pain down his arm and across his back.

When he saw who the owner of the voice was, he bit back the word he was about to utter. 'Hello. You're walking.'

The little Duke nodded enthusiastically and toddled out of sight. Then the bedclothes started to move. There was the sound of a small boy grunting with effort, and then something landed with a thump on Nick's feet.

''lo, Pas,' the Duke announced, crawling up the length of Nick's body and finally sitting on his chest. Big blue eyes stared at him. 'Get up, sleep-head.'

'What time is it?'

'Tea!'

That provoked bouncing, which was painful.

'Frederick! Stop that this minute! Poor Mr Pascoe is not well.' Sophie swept into the room, with a plump woman he recognised as Nanny Green at her heels. 'I told you not to disturb him. Thank goodness you are awake,' she added.

'I am now,' he said, and managed a grin in case she thought he was complaining.

Nanny swooped upon the Duke, scooped him up and carried him away.

A faint cry of 'Horse!' floated back.

'He wants to show you his hobby horse,' Sophie said 'It is too big, really, but I couldn't resist buying it and he drags it about everywhere. Oh, Nicholas, I am so cross with you.'

'I'm sorry. I know I bled on your nice steps.'

'Idiot. They are scrubbed clean. So is the hall floor and the stair carpet. What on earth were you doing to get yourself stabbed?'

'I didn't ask to be,' he said plaintively. It was becoming difficult to keep his eyes open. 'That's what comes of crossing a professional card sharp.'

Even as he said it something felt wrong about the statement, but the room was blurring and so was Sophie's face. That must be why he imagined she was weeping…

After that first awakening Nicholas slept until the next morning. Sophie sent for his valet, Sitwell, to look after him, and firmly resisted the doctor's offer to bleed him on the grounds that he had already lost enough to fill a bucket, judging by the state of the front steps. Then she set Monsieur Guiscard to making beef tea, which he denounced in ringing terms as 'an English abomination'.

Sitwell came down at ten, to inform her that his master was awake and had taken breakfast, refusing the beef tea. From the man's expression, Nicholas's opinion of it matched that of Monsieur Guiscard.

Sophie told herself that now was not the time to indulge in the tears she had been fighting back for most of the night. If Nicholas was awake, and swearing at his valet, then it seemed likely that he would live. She would go up mid-morning, with more beef tea, in the hope that he would not swear at her, and that would appear in the eyes of her household that she was not desperate to rush to his side.

When the door opened and he walked in, ten minutes after she had made that resolution and was listlessly turning the pages of *La Belle Assemblée*, the shock brought her to her feet. But instead of tears her shredded nerves unleashed her temper.

'What do you think you are doing? Get back to bed this instant! Isn't it bad enough that you get yourself stabbed? That you bleed all over my house and terrify me? Do you have to make yourself even sicker? I thought you were *dead*, you wretched man!'

Nicholas was shockingly pale, and his left hand was tucked between the buttons of his waistcoat. He visibly swayed at the force of her anger.

'I am sorry that I frightened you, and for the blood,' he said. 'But I did not think I was capable of getting anywhere else before I passed out.'

'Where were you when it happened? Who was it?'

'I was leaning against the railings opposite this house, pausing as I strolled back from a gaming hell in St James's.' He frowned and swayed again slightly. 'I had not thought that Captain Howard was the sort of take revenge like this. The sharps normally fade quietly away when they are exposed.'

'Oh, sit down, for goodness' sake.' Sophie almost ran across the room and took his good arm. 'Look, here—before you fall down.'

Nicholas moved, obedient to her tugging hand, but he was still frowning, and was not paying her any attention as he sat.

'But it cannot have been him... There was no one he could have sent after me that quickly, and I doubt he could have extricated himself from a room full of angry gamesters to have followed me himself.'

'It must have been a footpad.' Sophie made herself sit down and not fuss over him.

'They rarely use knives, and they usually work in pairs. And why did he climb over the railings into the garden in order to stab me through the bars in the middle of a respectable street? He could have caught up with me in any number of alleyways.'

'I thought someone was following you the other day,' Sophie said. 'Nicholas—what if this is Mrs Sweeting taking revenge? She must have realised it was you who took the diaries.'

He lay back in the chair, eyes narrowed in thought. 'It seems possible, yes...'

'It seems probable,' she retorted. 'She is not going to get away with this. I shall tell Lord Philbey just who he is getting into bed with and warn him to lock up his valuables.'

'Sophie, no.' Nicholas sat bolt upright. 'You are prodding at a wasps' nest.'

'I let her escape unpunished after stealing from me. I listened when you talked about her need for security, her fear of being penniless. But I will not let her get away with attacking you. If you had not found help so quickly you would have bled to death. That is murder.'

She could have killed you. And I love you.

'Sophie…' Nicholas propelled himself out of the chair to kneel at her feet. 'Sophie, you have gone stark white. Put your head down or you will faint.'

She fought against the pressure of his hand, twining herself around him as best she could without hurting him. 'Kiss me.'

The touch of his lips was tender, careful, not at all what she wanted, but it gave her a moment to compose herself and think rationally about the devastating realisation that had struck her. Then she pushed it back into a chamber in her mind, slammed the door on it, locked it away.

She could not deal with that now.

'If we let this go unpunished there is no knowing what she might do next. What if she wants you dead? Or Frederick?' Sophie felt sick.

He sat back on his heels. 'No, believe me, she is not such a fool as to attack a duke and a duchess—the risk to her is too great. But a man of no account, so far as she is aware, an adventurer…someone who she tried to get into her bed and who resisted? I deceived her and she fell for it, and she is not the kind of woman who forgives easily. And Philbey is an unknown quantity. I have no idea whether he would believe you, or whether he would be unable to resist such a piece of gossip. All the harm that you have hoped to avoid by recovering the diaries would be undone.'

'Then I shall write to her. Tell I that I know what she has done and that if you have so much as a splinter in your finger in the next ten years I will hold her to account.' Another idea struck her. 'I will threaten to set every lawyer I can employ on proving that she has taken more than my husband's will allowed. Perhaps they might even find evidence that the will had been tampered with. I will have her house repossessed and that will just be the start of it.'

'You wanted to avoid talk…' Nicholas said.

'I wanted to avoid my husband's diaries being released or used for extortion. There will be no reflection on Frederick if his father's mistress is found to be a thief and a forger. It will all have died down years before he will be old enough to understand—and after all, half the gentlemen of England keep a mistress.'

'Be careful what you do, Sophie.'

Nicholas stood up and went back to his chair, leaving her feeling cold and alone.

'You would let her get away with this?' she asked.

'There is no proof,' he said, sounding weary.

'Nicholas, you should be resting—not arguing with me. Go back to bed.'

'I will go home. I should not be staying here…we risk talk.'

I risk a broken heart, she thought, but nodded.

Nicholas knew his own limits, and he was not such a stubborn male as to kill himself over this.

'Go, then.'

She waited until she was confident that he would have reached the upper floor, then went in search of Grant.

'Duncan, I want someone reliable and discreet to watch over Nicholas,' she said as she closed his office door behind her. 'He insists on returning home now, and I believe that Mrs Sweeting is behind that attack on him.'

'So do I. I will put someone on it—although if Pascoe spots them they'll doubtless end up with a boot in the backside. This is a mess, Sophie.'

'I know, but I will write to that woman and threaten her with contesting the will if she does anything else. I doubt she would risk that.'

'I agree, but that is not what I meant. Pascoe is my friend, but he is too dangerous for you, my dear. The man's not tame.'

She snorted. 'I know that. I am not planning to keep him as a lapdog.'

'Then what *are* you planning? You have reconciled him with his father and you are lovers, are you not?'

'How dare you? I am not going to be lectured by—'

'By an old friend who loves you dearly? You need to marry, Sophie. To marry a man of status and wealth who will see Frederick as neither a threat nor a source of income. There are some perfectly good candidates out there who will take the burden from you. And Pascoe, if he is to accept that he is Chalfont's heir, needs a wife who is devoted to him and him alone, and to concentrate on establishing himself in society and learning to be a landowner.'

'You are, of course, perfectly correct,' Sophie said, with as much dignity as she could summon in the face of a lecture by Duncan and the ache in her heart.

'It will be hard enough when word gets out of who he is. Members of society have used his services... have entrusted their darkest secrets to him to make safe. They will be wary of him once he is revealed as one of them, and the gossips will soon be out at work on his reputation—can you imagine what they will say if he marries the widow of a duke?'

'That I am a means for him to achieve respectability, at best, or that he is bent on using his dark skills to enrich himself at Freddie's expense,' she said bitterly.

'Quite.'

'But it would be ideal, would it not, for him to live to find this suitable bride?' She spoke tartly, in an attempt to hide her pain. 'And another thing—why did you not tell me who he really was? You must have known.'

'He did not want it known. I do not betray my friends, Sophie.'

'Then make sure that poisonous witch doesn't have him killed,' she snapped, and flung open the door before he could reach it.

She felt better when she had written her letter to Amanda Sweeting. It was, she thought, a masterpiece of careful wording that contained no overt threats and no outright accusations. But the other woman was no fool—she would read what Sophie had intended.

The satisfaction lasted just as long as it took to put the letter into the hands of a footman and send it on its way.

She had fallen in love with Nicholas Pascoe, she thought bitterly. Or the Viscount Denham, as if that made things any better.

They could continue as lovers, she supposed, until such time as his sense of duty told him he must court and win a bride. But she suspected that every hour spent in his arms would only make parting that much more difficult. And Duncan, as always, was correct—she was the wrong wife for him and he was the wrong husband for her. So even if he felt more than affection and desire for her—and he certainly had not said he did—marriage was out of the question.

No. Not out of the question. *Imprudent* was probably the right word. And she was not prepared to do anything imprudent when it came to Frederick's upbringing. If she married again, her son's stepfather would be of a rank close to his and in a position to devote his attention to the ducal estates and his stepson, she told herself firmly.

I would risk that. I trust him. Nicholas could manage that difficult balancing act between his inheritance and Freddie's. But he doesn't love me so I must not ask it of him.

Sophie went out into the small garden at the back of the house and paced along the gravel paths, hardly noticing the flowers she brushed against. Duty. It was the touchstone by which she had been raised and had lived. To give Nicholas the slightest hint that her feelings for him had changed—had deepened into something that would, she knew, last for her lifetime—would be wrong. Wrong for him, even if so right for her. It would be undutiful, and careless of her obligations as the Duchess of St Edmunds.

And one day he would come to resent his position, she thought.

Their *affaire* must end almost as soon as it had begun, Sophie resolved. She must not meet him again alone—or at all if she could help it. And she must not let anyone see that her heart was breaking…because surely that was what this pain in her chest was.

Chapter Seventeen

Nick spent the rest of that day in bed, and half the next strolling through Green Park until he felt confident he was not going to fall flat on his face if he had to exert himself. And then, his arm in a black silk sling, he went to report to the anxious trustees of Sir Peter Tracy.

They assumed his injury had been incurred in the course of rescuing the baronet, as he'd intended. They were exceedingly grateful that the young man had taken himself off to his Kent estates, swearing never to set foot in the cesspit that was London again, and they told Nick so, at length.

'Not that he means it…but in another year or so he'll have grown up a little,' said the elderly lawyer who had first approached Nick. 'Now, do you have your account? We will settle immediately. And if you are considering another commission at this time, there is a young lady who is causing a client of mine some anxiety. An unsuitable young man, you understand…'

'Perfectly.' Nick folded the bank draft and slipped it into his pocket book. 'However, I am now retiring. I have come into some property.'

There—he had done it, he thought, as he emerged from the lawyer's offices on to Ludgate Hill, with the great dome of St Paul's looming above. A decision and a commitment. Now all he had to do was keep an eye on what Amanda Sweeting was up to.

He had been honest when he'd told Sophie he did not think the woman would try any direct attack on her, or the young Duke, but he was a firm believer in the old adage about keeping your enemies close.

'She's gorn,' said the small urchin who had sidled up to Nick as he stood looking at the smart little house. 'Left yesterday in a right 'andsome carriage, wiv a crest on the door an' all.'

The windows were shuttered, the knocker was off, and a young man who looked like a clerk was turning the key in the front door.

'Good day, sir,' he said when he saw Nick. He raised his hat. 'This very desirable residence has just come on the market. If you care to apply to Wilkins and Son, they can give you full particulars.' He offered a card.

'Thank you, but I am familiar with the property.'

He took the card, however. It was a very good property, and would be a sensible investment, but he baulked at the idea of putting money into Mrs Sweeting's grasping hand.

'The owner has left town, I assume?'

'Indeed she has.' The man smirked slightly. 'Gone to Ireland, I understand. Good day to you, sir.'

Nick turned to the urchin. 'There might be a sow's baby for a bright lad who remembers things. But only if he remembers rightly. And I'll know if you are making it up.'

The lad screwed up his grimy face. 'Wot you want to know, guv'nor?'

'What was the crest on the carriage door?'

That provoked deep thought, signalled by some energetic scratching, a tongue thrust into the corner of the lad's mouth and much frowning. 'A bird. White one. Like an 'eron, sort of. And it had got an eel, I fink.'

A white stork with a snake, Nick guessed. The new Earl of Longferry had been in London for a while, settling affairs after his grandfather's death. It looked as though he was returning to Ireland with rather more than parchments from the College of Heralds and a fashionable new wardrobe.

He gave the boy a shilling, not the promised sixpence, and strode off with shrill thanks echoing in his ears. That was good news. It even made the nagging ache in his shoulder and arm feel better. The woman had taken her revenge and now had not just left London, but English shores. Unlike many Irish peers, Longferry was plump in the pocket—with any luck he'd be able to keep Mrs Sweeting at his side for years to come.

It would set Sophie's mind at rest.

He smiled as he walked, anticipating the meeting.

'The first post, Your Grace.'

The footman proffered a silver salver and Sophie took the half-dozen letters from it. She rifled through them and stopped at one addressed in an unfamiliar hand.

It felt very thin between her fingers as she broke the seal. There was no salutation, no signature.

You do not learn, do you, Your Grace? I kept your husband for years—and I do not give up what is mine easily. Your lover may regain the use of his arm in time—but you will not find it so easy to retrieve your reputation. Remember that it was you that caused this, with your threats. Still the little innocent, so pure that you could not imagine I had more than one string to my bow. I shall enjoy reading of your disgrace in the Irish news sheets.

What on earth did Amanda Sweeting mean? For it could only be she who had written this…

'Lady Trent is here, Your Grace.'

Dorothea swept into the drawing room, her arms full of newsprint, and cast the papers on the table. 'Sophie, darling, what *have* you been doing? Or rather, I know what you've been *doing*, but how could you be so indiscreet?'

Sophie dropped the poisonous little note and stared at her friend. 'Whatever are you talking about?'

'You and that Pascoe man—your *affaire*.'

'My what?'

She had been half on her feet, but she sat down again with an inelegant thump, scattering the contents of her sewing box.

'Your liaison with Pascoe. He isn't a footman or a groom, but he might as well be your secretary or your steward. The man's an adventurer. A complete rogue, if the gossip is to be believed.'

Dorothea sat down on the nearest chair and fanned herself with what Sophie recognised as a scandal sheet.

'I mean, my dear, no one could blame you for a discreet arrangement with someone of rank, who knows how to keep things quiet—but this is all over the gossip columns. And the talk! I was in Madame Rousseau's for the final fitting for my new court dress and the place was abuzz. They used to call you the Dutiful Duchess, but the most repeatable name I heard today was the Dark Horse Duchess! I can quite see the attraction, of course. Any woman with a pulse could…'

Dorothea rattled on while Sophie's head spun.

She reached out and took one of the newspapers. The evidence of her disgrace was not hard to find.

Much surprise has been caused by the news that the D— of St E— has found consolation for her lonely state in the arms of a certain gentleman of fortune at a time when Her Grace's recent reappearance in Polite Society was expected to bring forth news of a betrothal to some fortunate nobleman.

It seems that N— P— has been trespassing amongst the strawberries on the ducal estates!

'They think it is amusing,' she said, throwing the paper down with a shaking hand. 'They even make jokes about the strawberry leaves in the ducal coronet. So beastly...'

'Is it true?' asked Dorothea.

Sophie nodded. There was no point denying it now.

'But how did it get out?' Dorothea sat back, one hand resting over her swelling stomach. 'Oh, all this excitement has disturbed The Heir.' She puffed out a breath. 'That's better. I cannot believe you would flaunt a lover, Sophie.'

'I wouldn't and I haven't. And Nicholas has been exceedingly careful. He— Yes, Padwick, what is it?'

'Mr Pascoe has called, Your Grace.'

'Show him in, please.'

Nicholas came in, smiling. The humour faded from

his eyes as he looked at her, at the litter of newspapers, and at Dorothea fanning herself with a crumpled handkerchief.

'Soph— Duchess, what is wrong?'

Dorothea stood up. 'I had best go and let you discuss this, Sophie darling.' She shot Nicholas a poisonous glance. 'If you need any help, do let me know. Trent has some admirable shotguns.'

'What the devil was that about?' he asked.

Sophie pointed to the newspaper at her feet. 'Apparently it is all over town that we are lovers. I am the gossip in the *modistes'* and a scandal in the salons.'

He went down on one knee, swearing under his breath as he read half a dozen of the poisonous little paragraphs. 'You have said nothing to anyone?'

'No, of course not. And you have not?'

'No. And I refuse to believe that we were careless, or that this is someone making a very tenuous link from the fact that you employed me.' He sat back on his heels, his face grim. 'We have been followed, and I think I know who has paid for it. This is the last sting in the tail from La Doucette. Mrs Sweeting has left London for Ireland, in the company of the Earl of Longferry, and her house is up for sale.'

Sophie took a deep breath. 'The woman is clever. I will give her that. Very well. I will deny it. I will be quite brazen and indignant and lie in my teeth. Dorothea is right—I used to be known as the Dutiful Duchess, and this is completely out of character. I will be believed.'

'That won't do, Sophie. It doesn't matter whether you are believed or not. This is the juiciest bit of scandal in months.'

'Nonsense. You will deny everything too. There has been nothing for anyone except for that woman's spies to see. It will be unpleasant for a while, and then it will die down. Thank heavens Freddie is too young to understand any of this.'

'Sophie—you have got guts, and you are a fighter, but this touches your reputation. There is only one thing to be done, and that is to—'

'Oh, Your Grace!' Foskett rushed into the room, her bonnet askew, bobbed a curtsy, gave Nicholas a filthy look, and then thrust a handful of printed pages at Sophie. 'Look what is in the print shops, Your Grace.'

Sophie dropped them on the low table. The topmost one showed a scantily clad woman with honey-coloured hair sprawled in a strawberry patch, her decencies only just covered by leaves and large, juicy red strawberries. A blackbird with glossy plumage and a very human expression in its beady eye was pecking at the fruit between the woman's breasts.

The title was *The Strawberry Thief.*

'Enough.' Nicholas scooped the newspapers and the prints into a bundle and thrust it at Foskett. 'Burn this lot now, and stay with the fire until you are sure it has all been consumed.' He gave the abigail a push towards the door. *'Now.'*

He turned back to Sophie.

'This is what we are going to do. Firstly, I shall inform my father of the fact that he had best start acknowledging me publicly. Then I will go to Brook's, and all the other clubs my father had me made a member of before he sent me off to Cambridge, and I will tell anyone who will listen that I am the Viscount Denham and that my longstanding estrangement from my father is over. And finally I shall let it be known the length and breadth of this town that I am going to marry the Duchess of St Edmunds, much to the gratification of my esteemed parent.'

'But even if we were to marry that would not stop the gossip about our *affaire*,' she protested.

'Oh, yes it would. The talk will all be of the reconciliation between my father and his long-lost heir. The reconciliation that *you* brought about. You negotiated the peace between us, and any amount of contact between us that might have been noticed can be explained by the need for caution and diplomacy whilst both he and I were persuaded that our reconciling was the right thing. As a result, you and I have realised we should be together and there we are—a perfectly respectable marriage, and anyone who says differently must be ashamed of themselves for their dirty minds.'

'But I do not want to marry you,' Sophie said.

And it was the truth. She did not want to marry a man who did not love her—a man who was being forced into marriage to save her reputation. A man who ought to be focused on nothing but his new standing in society and his new responsibilities.

'This is not about what you want, Sophie.'

Nicholas's face was hard, and he looked every inch as dangerous as she had thought him when they had first met.

'No. It has never been about what I want,' she said bitterly. 'Not who I married, not how I lived my life, not what I would have chosen when I was widowed.'

'You would walk over broken glass for your son, and do not try and tell me otherwise,' Nicholas said.

'Of course I would. I would love my son as I do whether he was a pauper or a prince. That does not mean I would choose to be the mother of a duke if I had the choice.'

She felt sick and desperate. The right thing to do for the man she loved was to reject him. Freddie was very young—this scandal would be ancient history before he was old enough to hear of it and understand it, if he ever did.

'Sophie, we have a friendship, do we not? We worked together well in a dangerous situation. And we have passion—do not tell me I do not know what we shared when you were in my arms. Is it my rank?

Is it that you will not stoop to marry the heir to a mere earldom?'

He was angry, although his self-control meant that it showed only in the tightness of his jaw, in the clipped speech and the tension with which he paced the room.

'No,' she said wearily. 'It is not that.'

It was no longer anything to do with that, or with the risk of gossip about Nicholas bettering himself by marriage to her. It was all about entrapping the man she loved into marriage.

'Very well. You will not do it for yourself, and you will not do it for your son. Will you do it for me?'

'For you?'

Sophie found she was on her feet. Was this a declaration? Was Nicholas telling her he wanted her to marry him because he loved her?

'For my good name. For my honour. To spare my father the knowledge that his heir has dishonoured a duchess and is apparently unable to make things right,' he said harshly.

Now there was absolutely no mistaking the anger he was reining in.

Of course, she thought. The blood drained away from her head so that she had to sit down again. Fainting at Nicholas's feet would really be too melodramatic for words, she found herself thinking. *He doesn't love me, but he will do the honourable thing, and if I pre-*

vent that then I am wounding something fundamental in him.

Sophie almost shrugged as disappointment flooded through her. For one second she had expected a declaration, fool that she was. But she had been trained to hide her feelings, so she supposed that she could somehow not reveal that she loved this man who did not want anything but her body in his bed and his honour intact.

'Very well. It appears that I have no choice.'

For all her training she could not inject any pleasure into her voice.

'Thank you, Duchess,' Nick replied, with about as much conviction as his betrothed had just shown. 'If you will excuse me? I have a great deal to do. I will return later.'

'Of course. Thank you. There is much to decide upon and to arrange,' Sophie said flatly.

She extended her hand and he took it, kissed the air an inch above her knuckles, and left.

She would not marry him for her own reputation, and she could even overlook a smear on her son's good name, but apparently she could not bring herself to threaten his honour. Never before in his life had he found himself the subject of pity—and that must be what it was. Or perhaps obligation? Yes, that was it. In just the same way as she had expected to pay for the clothing he had damaged when he'd protected her from the camping mob, she would pay the price now they were compromised.

He had thought there was something between them. Something he could not pin down or put a name to. Something more than the comradeship of shared danger or the heat of mutual passion. Well, that was gone, whatever it had been. And to live up to his own expectations of himself he had to swallow his pride and behave as though he could not believe his good fortune.

Just how foul a mood that had put him in he discovered as he walked into Brooks' Club on St James's Street.

'Good morning, sir. May I assist you?' The hall porter, all striped waistcoat and shining brass buttons, came forward.

'I am a member here.'

'Sir? I am afraid that I do not know you...'

The porter had the air of a man who was ready to lay down his life to prevent anyone but a member crossing the sacred threshold.

'In that case I suggest you consult your membership records,' Nick said, with enough edge in his voice to make it clear that leaving dead porters on the front step was an option. 'You will find Jerrard Nicholas Pascoe Prior Taversham entered ten years ago. In August, I believe. I was not Viscount Denham at that date, of course.'

The hall porters at the gentlemen's clubs were as familiar with the *Peerage* as any duchess. The man paled at the prospect of having failed to identify not just a viscount, but one who was a member.

'My lord—'

'No doubt it was before your time. Under-porter then, were you, Jenkins?'

He had made it his business to know a great deal about the exclusive clubs of Mayfair in the course of his work, and that included the names of the hall porters.

Jenkins went a shade paler. 'Yes, my lord.'

'We will say no more about it.'

Nick strolled over to the register, signed his name, and glanced at who else was present. Yes, that would do nicely—two men who knew him as Pascoe, and who had used his services in the past.

When he walked into the library Ludovic Farquerson, younger son of the Viscount Hurlington, dropped his newspaper. 'Pascoe?'

'Shh!'

Mr Farquerson ignored the irritable hiss from one of the newspaper-shrouded figures. 'I say, old man, aren't you—? And all the scandal sheets—'

'Didn't you know, *old man*? I am Viscount Denham, and I have been a member here for years,' Pascoe said, dropping into the armchair next to Farquerson, whose ex-mistress's blackmailing husband he had discouraged the previous year.

He had not spoken loudly, but half a dozen newspapers crackled as they were dropped into laps.

'Denham?' The Marquess of Westermount raised a quizzing glass and studied him. 'I thought you'd gone abroad… Fell out with your father, what?'

'I did indeed find myself estranged from him,' Nick said evenly. 'But now, thanks to the good offices of the Duchess of St Edmunds, we are reconciled.'

'But it is all over town!' another voice broke in. 'You and the Duchess. They're calling you The Strawberry Thief.'

'They will soon be calling me the man who killed whoever repeats that,' Nick said. 'You are speaking of my affianced wife.'

He had them then, all of them, and they listened avidly to the tale of the Duchess's kindness in bringing together father and son and the injustice of the scandal it had exposed her to.

'My father is advising the Duchess on the purchase of a new riding horse, which is how it all came about. Our mutual affection has been an unexpected gift. Naturally, meetings were covert at first, in case the Earl and I could not find common ground, and that has led to these unpleasant rumours.'

Nick left feeling queasy, and crossed the road to White's. He could stand one more club, he thought, but with any luck that would be enough.

It was. He encountered no resistance at the door,

and had the good fortune to meet Percival Gates, who was possibly the worst gossip in London, although a very good-natured one for all that.

He satisfied the rampant curiosity of those he encountered, dashed off an order to a stationer for new calling cards, and then set out for Grosvenor Square and the family town house. His anger was under control by the time he was shown into the Earl's study, although the feeling in his gut had settled into a cold lump of misery.

'There you are! I sent for you two hours ago. Now, I have been making notes on how we will deal with this. I shall instruct my solicitors—'

'It is taken care of.' Nick took the chair on the other side of the desk, reflecting that this was the first time he had ever taken a seat in that room without a direct order. 'It is now known around town who I am, and that the Duchess has brought about our reconciliation. The necessary secrecy surrounding that had laid her open to these foul rumours, but as in the course of her efforts she and I developed a mutual affection, everyone will be delighted to hear that we are to wed.'

His father stared at him, all his habitual cool composure gone. It was a day of firsts, it seemed.

'You are *marrying* the Duchess of St Edmunds?' he managed eventually.

'Yes, sir.'

'Good God,' the Earl said reverently. 'You know what this means?'

'It means that I shall not be able to give the affairs of estate that you have kindly given me the attention they deserve for some time.'

'It is well enough now,' his father said, with a wave of his hand. 'It means you are marrying the daughter of a marquess. It means that your sons will grow up alongside a duke, with all the benefits that will bring them. Your daughters will make magnificent marriages…'

His voice trailed away as he contemplated the glorious prospect.

Another first, Nick reflected wryly. He had pleased his father.

'I shall see to it that all those scurrilous prints are removed from circulation,' the Earl said, and waved a hand towards the door. 'Go and start work, Denham. There is much to do! Have you agreed a date yet? Where is the ceremony to be?'

'No, and it shall be as the Duchess wishes.'

He was beyond caring, he told himself as he left. Whatever it took to set this mess to rights he would do, because that was better than contemplating what would come after—marriage to a woman for whom he was just one of a long list of things her sense of duty compelled her to attend to.

Chapter Eighteen

'Pas!' Frederick launched himself across the room and flung his arms around Nicholas at knee height, then tipped his head back. 'Up!'

Sophie watched with a lump in her throat as the tall man stooped, picked up her son and tossed him into the air. Freddie shrieked with delight as he was caught and tossed again. Nicholas was a natural with children, it seemed.

'Your shoulder!' she protested.

'Quite healed. Exercise does it good.'

''Gain, Pas. 'Gain.'

Nicholas caught the boy around the knees and dangled him upside down. 'Please?' he suggested.

'Please...'

Freddie was rewarded with one more throw, then set on his feet. 'We are keeping your mama waiting. Good morning, Duchess.'

'Good morning. Freddie, go with Nanny now.'

'Pas—'

'Frederick…' He went.

'He cannot keep calling you Pas,' she said, worrying out loud. 'It isn't fitting.'

'I have no objection. It is better than Step-Papa.'

'But that is what you will be.'

'I am many things, and he can call me what makes him comfortable. He is going to have to learn to share his mama, and the smoother we can make it for him, the better, I would have thought.'

'But it is not respectful.' This was not what she wanted to be doing…bickering over details.

'Respect has nothing to do with what one is called. You respected plain Pascoe enough to trust me with retrieving those diaries, did you not?'

'Yes. Of course. As you wish. Shall we take tea? I expect there is much we should be discussing. I received your note. Thank you for telling me how well the story has been received. It is a great relief. Lord Chalfont has also written, most kindly. He is calling this afternoon. It would be good to have some plans made to tell him about.'

She tugged the bell-pull and took her place on the sofa, aware that she was gabbling. She took a deep breath.

'He sent me two lovely horses to choose from and I have taken the bay mare.'

'Coffee, thank you.'

Nicholas sat down opposite her with the easy grace

that had become familiar and the elegance of muscles and long legs that stirred the heat deep in her belly.

'Good, I am glad you found something that suits. I agree—there are decisions to be made. Date, place and title to begin with.'

'Title?' Sophie blinked at him.

'You are the daughter of a marquess marrying a man of lower rank. It is your choice whether you call yourself Lady Sophia Denham or Lady Denham.'

'Lady Denham, of course.' She did not have to think about it.

'Very well. Special licence, I assume?'

She nodded.

'So where? Here?'

'That would be appropriate. It will be our London home, after all.'

He might as well have been discussing the arrangements for a dinner party, she thought resentfully. Didn't he find it the slightest bit awkward to be marrying a duchess in the splendour of a ducal mansion? Didn't he resent not being able to take her to his own London home?

'In three weeks' time?' she suggested, keeping her slight smile firmly in place as a footman entered. 'Oh, Peter… Coffee for His Lordship and tea for me, please.'

'If that is not too rushed for you that would be perfect,' Nicholas said politely. 'Have you any particular wishes for after the wedding?'

Her wishes were so vivid that she could only pray she had not blushed crimson. 'Er…no.'

'Then would you object to spending a few weeks at Prior Marten—my estate? It came into the family on the marriage of Lucinda Prior to an ancestor in the seventeenth century.'

'Which is why the family uses the name? I see. Yes, of course. Where is it?'

'Devon. Just north of Axminster. In the Blackdown Hills. They are not high, but they are lush and green, as I recall.'

'I will look forward to it. I have never been to Devon.'

How stilted she sounded to her own ears. But there was something else they had to discuss, and she should do it now so there was time to prepare.

The footman brought in the tea and coffee and they managed to deal with the issues of who was to perform the ceremony—a cousin of Sophie's who was a bishop, assisted by Nicholas's cousin, a rural dean—and the guest list. Nicholas said he would send his list to her secretary, who would deal with the invitations.

When he put down his coffee cup she stood up. 'There is something I would like your decision on,' she told him. 'If you can spare the time to come upstairs.'

She led the way and gestured towards the paired

doors at the front of the first floor. 'The ducal suite. Frederick will have his father's rooms when he is old enough, and they have been redecorated in a less imposing style. I would like your opinion on our rooms.'

'I assume you already have a bedchamber?'

'Not one for which I have much fondness. It is rather like being inside an icicle.' She opened one of the doors with its carved over-mantel. 'You see? Apparently the plasterwork is so very fine that it would be an outrage to redecorate. Also, it is at the front overlooking the square.' She closed the door firmly and led the way past the head of the stairs and towards the rear of the big house. 'I would prefer a garden view. What do you think of these rooms? We can redecorate and refurnish, of course, as you like.'

It had not occurred to her until he stepped into the right-hand bedchamber that there might be any awkwardness in discussing sleeping arrangements with Nicholas. She had been painfully aware that the last thing he would want was to find himself in the late Duke's monstrous half-tester bed—stepping into the man's slippers, as it were. And it would be years before Freddie would be old enough for the splendours of the ducal suite, but it was a good enough excuse to move to the back of the house.

Now Nicholas stood in the middle of the room and looked around him, and she felt a frisson of awareness as he looked at the bed—the only piece of furniture not draped in dust cloths—then at the connecting door to the other chamber. The one that would be hers.

'This will do very well. I will send my own men over to furnish and decorate it.'

There was no doubt that he would take no argument over that and she nodded.

'The dressing room is a good one, as well—and the valet's room is, of course, vacant.'

Forgetting herself in her eagerness to demonstrate the merits of the chamber, she moved right inside the room and found herself standing beside Nicholas. And the bed.

'Sophie.'

She turned, stumbling as she trod on the trailing edge of the coverlet, and Nicholas caught her in his arms.

'Are you frightened of me?'

'No. No, of course not,' she told the black onyx of his tie pin.

'You are trembling.'

'Nerves,' she mumbled, fighting the desire to burrow close against him, to feel that lean, muscled body pressed to hers, have those clever hands caress her, lay herself open and vulnerable and let him see that she loved him.

He would not be unkind about it. Nicholas was not unkind. He was a gentleman, and he would carry the burden of her love with the same gallantry as he had shown throwing his body between hers and the mob, or risking his neck and his liberty in housebreaking for her.

He put one finger under her chin and lifted it so he could look down into her face. 'Nerves?'

'It is very…stressful, getting married.'

'We have had *some* practice,' he said, and kissed her.

It was the kiss that had haunted her dreams and her waking memories: Nicholas's mouth on hers, the taste and heat of him, the subtle, nerve-shaking tenderness mingled with demand that sent a message that said, *Yield…* straight to the base of her spine.

And yet under it she could sense something else… could taste anger. For all her resistance she had trapped him into this marriage, because she was a woman and he would go to any lengths to protect her.

They had shifted a little as they'd kissed…as her hands had tangled into his hair and her body had swayed into his. Now the bed was behind her legs, pressing, ready to catch her when she fell.

And when they did they would make love—fully— and there would be no going back.

Part of her—the sensible, dutiful, rational part— knew there was no going back, whatever happened in this room now. The invitations had gone out, the gossip had been squashed, and their 'love story' was causing a flutter in every romantic breast.

But the part of her that was foolish, that yearned to hear words of love and wanted the fairy story to come true—that part still hoped for a happy ending. Although what that might be, she had no idea. Perhaps Nicholas falling to his knees and professing his undying love for her?

'Sophie…' he said, his voice a sensual rasp. 'Let me—'

'No.' She opened her hands, sat down on the mattress, pushed him away. 'We are going to be married. Properly. In the eyes of the church. I want—' *You… now.* 'I want to wait. To do this properly.'

No, Nicholas did not love her. For he would have said so, surely? He liked her, and desired her—of both of those she was certain. But love? No. To give herself to him now, with only desire between them, seemed impossible without breaking down and telling him how she felt.

On their wedding night it would be different, she thought distractedly. She knew how to hide her feelings then, after all.

'You have such fond memories of your first wedding night, have you?' Nicholas asked, stepping back from the bed.

He was very aroused—she could see.

Sophie sat on her hands to stop herself from reaching out.

'You are yearning to repeat the experience?' He

sighed, closed his eyes. 'I apologise. That was uncalled-for and unkind. Your memories must be very…difficult. This room will be perfect and you are thoughtful to suggest it. I will see you tomorrow, no doubt.'

He closed the door carefully behind himself and the expensive carpets muffled the sound of his retreating footsteps.

'Nicholas…' Sophie said into the emptiness. 'Oh, what have I done?'

Three weeks had passed at a snail's pace and yet like a lightning flash, Sophie thought distractedly the day before the ceremony. There had hardly seemed time to do everything that was necessary, even though she'd had all the help she could need and it had not been necessary to shop for an extensive trousseau. And yet the nights had passed so slowly that she might have screamed, lying awake in the darkness, unable to imagine what life would be like married to Nicholas.

At least his swift action had put a stop to the foul 'Strawberry Thief' gossip, and the prints had vanished from circulation. Friends and acquaintances had hurried to congratulate her, and to hint—subtly—that they had naturally never paid any attention to gossip, all without mentioning which juicy titbit they meant.

Sophie had decided that to snub everyone who had gossiped about her would result in her shunning most of polite society, but the humiliation still stung. After a lifetime of care and duty she had indulged herself once—and had been punished for it out of all proportion to the fault. And so had Nicholas.

In the small hours she found things to worry about in every detail. And then, when she did wake, after a few hours' troubled sleep, she could not even recall what had been fretting at her. She had lost weight, gained dark circles under her eyes, and was being lectured by Foskett, by her mother and by Monsieur Guiscard.

Nicholas had not commented—presumably because the distance between them had widened into a gulf after that scene in his new bedchamber. He was not angry because she had refused his advances, she was sure, because he was always there, unfailingly pleasant, when she wanted to consult him about something. And yet the connection she had sensed between them from the first time she saw him had gone. It was as though he had raised a drawbridge and retreated behind its defences.

Now she stood patiently, revolving on a chair, while the seamstresses put the finishing touches to her gown—after taking it in for a second time. Her mother fussed over Foskett's choice of silk stockings.

When the women had finished, and she was free of the gown, she stepped down and slipped on a robe. 'Thank you, Foskett, that will be all for the moment.'

'Yes, Your Grace.'

The maid closed the door behind her—which, as Sophie should have predicted, was the cue for her mother to wring her hands and peer at Sophie's complexion.

'It is too late now to change your mind,' she said. 'After today you will not be *Your Grace* any longer, but you must simply reconcile yourself to it. At least Denham appears to be a competent and honest young man, and Frederick will be in safe hands with him. Oh, dear... I do wish you had waited a little. I had such great hopes of Lord Lillington on his return from the West Indies.'

'He might be the heir to a marquess, Mama, but he is a most argumentative and pompous man. I could not think of marrying someone with his temperament. And I am not regretting my decision in any way,' she lied. 'It is simply that there is so much to be done and to be thought of.'

'And he is so plain, too,' her mother said with a sigh, clearly not having listened to a word she had said. 'That is one thing to be said for Denham—such a handsome man. Your children will be charming.'

'Yes, Mama,' Sophie said.

Children. Nicholas's children.

She had not really given them much thought, but now she could visualise them vividly. Dark hair, dark eyes, and tall. Or perhaps his dark hair and her green eyes. Or fair hair and dark eyes. The thought cheered her—until she remembered that to be with child there were inevitable preliminaries, and somehow she had to learn how to lie with Nicholas without betraying herself.

'Rice powder under the eyes with a little Cuisse de Nymphe rouge,' Lady Radley was murmuring, regarding Sophie through narrowed eyes. 'And cucumber compresses this afternoon, will help.'

'Yes, Mama,' Sophie said obediently. It was the line of least resistance.

Nick stood in front of the white-draped table that the Bishop had arranged as a temporary altar and wondered whether all bridegrooms felt quite as helpless as he did. His fate was in the hands of the woman about to descend that sweeping staircase and walk the length of the great drawing room between the packed seats of guests.

Heaven or hell?

Marriage was for life, and he had no intention of carelessly falling downstairs as Sophie's first husband had. So, Providence willing, they had decades ahead of them. He had every intention of making this marriage work—even if heaven was perhaps a bit much to hope for—but did Sophie feel the same? Something had changed quite suddenly, and now he felt a barrier between them. It was like watching her through a pane of glass: he could almost touch her and yet he did not think she felt him…not as she had before.

Perhaps it was nerves, he told himself, as he had done repeatedly over the past weeks. It was a big step for her to take—especially after the objections to re-marriage she had given him. And it was a loss of status for her. Would that matter to Sophie? He thought not.

He thought of the way she had climbed into that house to warn him…of the way she had lain trust-ingly in his arms through those long hours before they could make their escape. Surely once this wedding day was over they would find their way back to that relationship. But he still felt as though someone had hollowed out his gut.

There was a rustle and a murmur from the guests.

Duncan Grant at his side gave him an unobtrusive nudge in the ribs. 'Wake up—here comes the bride.'

Nick turned and saw a slender figure in cream and gold walking towards him. She was veiled, and he could not see her face, but the truth hit him like a blow to the jaw.

Sophie was coming to him. She would be his. And—

'I am in love with her.'

'What did you say?' Grant whispered.

'Nothing. Thinking aloud.'

Nick wiped the dumbfounded expression off his face, replaced it with what he hoped was a reassur-ing smile, and swallowed hard as Sophie arrived at his side on her father's arm.

They turned to face her cousin William, the bishop.
'Dearly beloved, we are gathered together here—'

Nick had recovered his composure by the time the
ring was on Sophie's finger and they were walking
down what he could not help thinking of as the aisle.
He'd almost lost it again when she'd looked up at him,
full in the face and unveiled for the first time.

She had lost weight, and there were shadows under
her eyes, skilfully dusted with a powder that did not
quite conceal them.

Why hadn't he seen this happening?

Because he hadn't looked, he told himself savagely.
He had been too busy pretending that everything was
all right…that Sophie would be happier if he kept out
of her way unless she asked for him. Too busy making
sure he was not tempted to take her in his arms again.

'You have made me a very happy man, Lady Sophia,' he said, and felt a disproportionate sense of relief when she smiled.

'Lady Denham. I know I am entitled to use my own
title, but I do not want to. I am your wife now.'

Nanny was waiting with Frederick, who was wide-
eyed with excitement and confusion. He and Sophie
had not tried to explain about stepfathers and wed-
dings, but his new mother-in-law had, and had suc-
ceeded in baffling the young Duke, who had scowled
at her and said, 'Pas.'

Nick scooped him up in his free arm. 'Come along and help us. You are never too young to learn how to manage a receiving line, Freddie. You just smile at everyone.'

The young Duke was very good—charming all the starchier matrons, making the young ladies coo, and even most of the men gruffly announced that he was a fine little fellow.

By the time everyone had filed past, kissed the bride, congratulated the bridegroom and been treated to a gummy smile from Freddie, Nick's arm was ready to drop off, but he would have stood there for another two hours, just to see how happy it made Sophie.

'He had best go up with Nanny now—and I must take off my veil,' Sophie said. 'It went well, don't you think?'

'It went very well. Now all we have to do is survive the breakfast and the speeches and then escape.'

And I can finally get you to myself, my love.

He still felt moonstruck as he watched Sophie hand Frederick over to Nanny and gather her skirts to climb the stairs, her mother hovering behind her with admonitions about her lace, her veil…

'Are you quite well?'

That was Grant, of course. A man who had fought alongside you was sensitive to whether or not you were present in the moment or had lost your focus.

'Yes. Fine. Just new husband shock, I expect,' he said vaguely. 'What am I expected to do now?'

'Mingle,' Grant said, with a grin and a jerk of his head towards the ballroom, which had been turned into a banqueting hall to accommodate two hundred guests.

Nick told himself that this was simply a commission to be carried out—that he had to concentrate, and that everything else could be thought about when they were finally seated in the carriage and driving away. Alone.

Chapter Nineteen

Sophie turned before she mounted the carriage steps and threw her bouquet, which sailed through the air into the arms of Cousin Maria—just as she had planned. Perhaps it would give her the confidence to smile at one of the men who had turned to look at her.

She settled into the seat, arranging the skirts of her new travelling dress, and Nicholas followed her, waving before he too sat down and the carriage rolled off southwards, towards Piccadilly.

'Who knows?' he asked as they turned a corner.

'Only Duncan and the staff,' Sophie said as they turned again.

The wheels rattled over rough cobbles and soon the carriage drew up.

'Do be careful, Your G— my lady,' said Felgate, the groom, as he opened the carriage door. 'We cleared up as best we could, but you know what horses are like.'

'Let me.' Nicholas jumped down, then swept her into his arms and walked through a gate in the wall and across the garden to the kitchen entrance. 'I suppose I should not be carrying you over the threshold of your own home, but I believe this is traditional.'

'It is *our* home,' Sophie said firmly. 'One of several, when you add them all up. Oh, thank you, everyone.'

All the staff who were not involved in seeing off their guests upstairs were pressed against the walls of the basement passageway.

'Everything went so well—thanks to all your hard work. We very much appreciate it,' she said, determined not to be deterred from showing her appreciation, even if she was blushing like a peony and in the arms of her new husband. There would be a gift for all of them when they sat down to dinner in the servants' hall that evening.

'We certainly do,' Nicholas added. 'Change is never easy, and my wife and I thank you for your support. And also for keeping our secret—setting out on a long road journey in November is no way to spend one's wedding night!'

There was genuine laughter at that, and then, to her vast relief, they were at the foot of the service stairs and the door was closed behind them.

Nicholas set her on her feet. 'I regret, but I do not think I can negotiate stairs this narrow with an armful of wife.'

That was the second time in a few minutes he had called her his wife. There had been the speeches, of course, but she had been too tense and dizzy with champagne and noise and heat to take those in.

She was Nicholas's wife. Or she would be by morning. And somehow she had to strike the right balance between happy bridal anticipation and love-struck yearning. Nicholas's life had been turned upside down by the need to protect her and she must not be a burden on him, she resolved fiercely.

'You could toss me over your shoulder and storm up like a pillaging Viking warrior,' she suggested lightly, trying for a humorous note. Then she remembered his stab wound. 'Oh, I never thought… You should not have lifted me at all with your shoulder hardly healed.'

'I managed—but I confess it did occur to me by the time we reached the kitchen door,' Nicholas admitted. 'But it is all right—nothing has reopened. We will walk up in a decorous manner, shall we? And save our breath for when we reach the top,' he added, so softly that she hardly caught the words.

Surely he did not intend them to go to bed immediately? It was still daylight. Of course they had made love in the daytime before, to a point—she gave a little shiver as her body reacted to the memory of that point—but this was somehow different.

To her relief, Foskett was waiting on the landing and opened the baize door, so they could step through from oilcloth to thick carpet.

'Your bath is ready, my lady.' Trust Foskett to get her new title right without hesitation. 'And your man is in your dressing room, my lord. I believe he also has hot water.'

'I see that hostilities have opened between valet and lady's maid,' Sophie observed when they were in her new dressing room.

The late Duke's valet had been a most superior specimen, and considerably older than Foskett. Technically they had been equals in the servants' hierarchy, but Foskett had had to fight every inch of the way to maintain her position.

She sniffed. 'Sitwell's not so bad, my lady, but I'll not have him taking liberties. Now, do you want the rose salts or the lavender in the bath, my lady?'

'Definitely the rose.' Lavender was too redolent of dowagers and decorum for her taste.

'And the sea-green ensemble?' Foskett asked as Sophie climbed into the tub.

She sat down with rather a splash. She had ordered the nightgown and negligée in a mad moment at Madame Cerise's shop, when she had been buying new undergarments and had seen the design drawing displayed alongside the fabric. When she had tried it on she had been startled by how fine the fabric was, but had consoled herself with the thought that the negligée, with its layers and ribbons, would cover her decently.

* * *

Sophie stood outside the door that led from her bed-chamber to the small sitting room between the two suites, trying to put into practice the advice her mother had given her when she'd been presented at court.

'Back straight, shoulders back, deep and slow breaths, smile,' she murmured as she turned the door handle and stepped inside.

Then she forgot to breathe.

Nicholas had bathed and changed and was wearing a heavy silk brocade robe in black and silver. On his feet were black Morocco slippers, and she suspected he was not wearing another stitch.

Her skin prickled with desire, and she felt her toes curl inside the satin and swansdown slippers. It hardly felt decent, the way that she wanted him, but he was her husband now and desiring him was perfectly right.

Nicholas seemed to misinterpret her hesitation.

'Sophie, you look delectable, but do not fear that I am about to leap upon you like one of your Viking warriors. I think we should give Foskett and Sitwell the opportunity to tidy up and leave, don't you?'

'Yes. Yes, of course.'

She came into the room, very conscious of his eyes on her. There was something in his expression she could not read. There was desire, certainly, but some-thing else... A tenderness, and—surely she was imagining it?—a pain. As though something he wanted very much was being withheld.

'After all, it is broad daylight,' she added, with a smile that felt woefully lop-sided.

Nicholas said nothing until she had sat down, and then, as if to reassure her, took a chair beyond arm's reach. 'Sophie, are you frightened?'

'No! Only a little shy, that is all.'

And how I can protest inhibition when I am wearing this negligée, I do not know.

'I understand. I suspect that I am also.'

'You?' She stared at him. 'But you have had many lovers—I mean, you have had more experience than I have.'

'You make me sound like Casanova.' Nicholas's smile was wry. 'I have had experience, yes. It does not mean that I am not very aware that this is no love affair. This is marriage. This is for life. And I want to begin it in the right way.'

No love affair. No, of course it is not.

For all her training, Sophie knew she had retained a romantic idea about marriage that even the reality had not completely stifled. For men of their class marriage was a business transaction first and foremost. Affection might blossom, even possibly love, but that was not the purpose of the transaction. Nicholas was fond of her, she was certain. And he was a considerate and skilled lover. Those things were a novelty, and she was being greedy to expect more.

'I have ordered a cold meal to be set up in here,' he said. 'You ate hardly anything at the breakfast. And I do not think you have been eating very well for the past few weeks, have you? Nor sleeping well, either.'

'I know. Mama says I look a fright.'

Nicholas surged to his feet, strode across the space between them and pulled her up against him. 'Sophia Louisa Andrea Taversham, I would find you desirable if you were as thin as a rake, afflicted with ringworm and had shaved your hair off. I hope you will not test me on that, but I will not tolerate you listening to such rubbish from your mother. If you have lost your appetite and cannot sleep then that is reason to nurture you—not lecture you on your looks, dammit.'

'Oh.' She looked up into his angry face, stood on tiptoe and kissed him full on the mouth. 'Jerrard Nicholas Pascoe Prior Taversham, that is the nicest thing anyone has ever said to me.'

'All I can say is that you have been woefully short of pleasant conversation in your life. Are you tired, Sophie?'

He was not asking whether she wanted an afternoon nap.

'Not in the slightest,' she said steadily.

'In that case, Duchess—your bedchamber or mine? I heard the landing doors close several minutes ago.'

'I'm not a duchess any more,' she protested. 'Um… mine? No. No, yours.'

All those years of lying waiting, of having no choice… She would choose now, and she chose to go to Nicholas.

'You are my duchess in my heart,' he said simply, taking her hand and leading her towards the door.

She did not know what she had expected as a setting for this dark lord who dressed in black and rode a black horse. But blues and greens, white muslin drapery and elegantly simple modern furniture was what greeted her in Nicholas's bedchamber. And the bed was a French sleigh bed, with no pillars or canopy or looming headboard. Fresh and elegant and yet unmistakably masculine.

'This is lovely!' She turned on the spot to take it all in, and laughed when she made herself dizzy and Nicholas caught her in his arms.

'And so are you. And this delightful garment has far too many ribbons,' he grumbled, working his way down the bows. 'I expect that is the point—to torture men.'

'I think so.'

Sophie gave an experimental tug to the end of the sash cinching his narrow waist. It parted immediately and the robe fell open. She had been quite correct. He was wearing nothing beneath it.

His body was beautiful, elegant, muscled. Already

she knew the feel of it, the taste of him, and she ached for him in a way that was purely physical. But what she wanted more than anything was to kiss him and caress him and tell him with her hands and voice and passion that she loved him.

Nicholas had controlled himself enough to tease open the last of the ribbons and now the soft folds fell around her feet like piles of sea foam, leaving her in only the nightgown, which she knew showed shadowed promises of what lay beneath it.

But Nicholas was backing away—one pace, two— his eyes never leaving her.

'What are you doing? What is wrong?'

'I was too close,' he said hoarsely. 'Too close to see.'

'But you have seen me with fewer clothes than this,' she protested.

'You look like a dream shrouded in mist,' Nicholas said. 'You are possibly the most erotic thing I have ever seen.'

'Nicholas…'

'Do you not want me to tell you how much I desire you?' He came close again.

I want you to tell me you love me. But desire must suffice.

And her treacherous body was telling her that all it wanted was to be skin to skin with him…telling her that desire would more than suffice.

Somehow, despite a kiss that had reduced her to

helplessly clinging to him, Nicholas managed the knots of ribbon at the shoulders of the gown and that too slid down, caught between their bodies until he scooped her up and laid her on the bed.

She opened her eyes to find him straddling her, a knee either side of her hips, his hands resting lightly at her waist.

What he saw in her face she had no idea, but it gave him pause. 'Sophie, it has been a long time for you. A year... If you are nervous, I understand. We can go as slowly as you wish.'

If he had but known it, had been almost two years since the last time her husband had lain with her. As soon as he had been certain she was pregnant his visits to her bedroom had ceased.

Something flared inside her. She was not going to be reduced to the state of a trembling maiden overawed by masculine virility. She wanted to enjoy every moment of this—lose herself in it.

A swift glance down reminded her that this was going to be considerably *more*, in every way, than what she had experienced before. Nicholas was...impressive.

'I am not nervous,' Sophie said, and reached out to touch him, to curl her fingers around him, stroke the hard need sheathed in the softest skin. 'Make me your wife, Nicholas.'

He came down over her and she opened to cradle

him between her thighs. He covered her, enveloped her, and she arched up to meet him as he took his weight on his elbows and kissed her.

This was different from when they had made love before, she realised. That had been almost playful—a joyous exploration, an exchange of caresses and kisses. This felt more profound. This was a joining in all senses of the word.

She shifted, restless beneath his weight and his hands, wanting all of him. And there he was. Sophie gave a sob of relief as Nicholas entered her slowly, possessing her until she thought he must reach her heart, and then he thrust and she shattered instantly, crying out as he strove above her, sending waves of pleasure through her that were almost too much to bear.

She was conscious of his voice, hoarse with a triumph that sounded like pain, and then of heat flooding inside her. His weight bore her down into the softness of the mattress and he buried his face against her neck.

Nick did not know what woke him. Perhaps the unfamiliar sounds of the house…perhaps the new bed. He lay spooned around Sophie's sleeping body, his hand under her cheek going numb, the other curled possessively over her waist.

He was going to have to extricate that hand before he lost all feeling in it, he thought, smiling into the darkness.

They had made love twice, the second time slowly, lingering over each touch, each kiss, each new discovery. Sophie had been passionate beyond his wildest hopes, giving and receiving without inhibition—except, perhaps, in what she said or did not say.

Sophie did not love him. He knew that. And he did not really know what he had expected she might say as they made love, but it had almost been as though she was biting back words. Perhaps she had become so used to meekly lying there while her husband did his duty that she did not know how to say what pleased her, what she felt. Or perhaps he was the inhibited one, not daring to let slip words of love in case she rejected them.

But whatever she felt there was trust. He knew that too. After they had come to themselves the second time she had curled up against him, snuggling into his body. He had slept deeply, and almost instantly, and judging by the soft breathing beside him so had she.

A clock chimed. So early? He had lost all sense of time as they had found each other, but they could not have been asleep more than half an hour, at most.

Nick began to slide his hand out from beneath Sophie's cheek. She muttered something in her sleep and shifted a little, but he managed to pull it clear without waking her.

Now he was fully conscious, his right hand tingling painfully with pins and needles. He shifted carefully

away, sat up against the pillows and began to mas-
sage the feeling back into his fingers. His hand was
damp—wet, even—in the lines of his palm.

It took him a few seconds to realise what it meant,
and then he slid from the bed, found a striker and lit
a candle. The soft light was not enough to wake her,
but it showed clearly the tear-tracks on her cheeks.

His bride had cried herself to sleep in his arms.

Chapter Twenty

They would take three days to journey to Prior Marten, Nicholas's new estate in Devon, he told Sophie the morning after the wedding. It was over one hundred and sixty miles. If they drove hard, changing horses as the mail coaches did every ten miles, they might manage it in one very long day if the weather permitted. But…

'But there is no need for haste,' Nicholas said, spreading marmalade lavishly on toast. 'It would be exhausting for you, and Frederick would be utterly miserable. I have written to secure rooms at The Crown in Basingstoke and The Red Lion in Shaftesbury.'

'That sounds a good plan,' she agreed, pouring them both more coffee. 'At what time do you want to set out?'

'The carriages will be ready for us at ten. I have sent our riding horses on ahead, in easy stages, and the heavy luggage.'

He went on to describe how they would be taking three carriages: one for themselves, one for Freddie, Nanny and the nursemaid, for when he was not with his mother, and one for Foskett and Sitwell and the rest of the luggage.

Sophie nodded and sipped and let it all wash over her. She was still feeling unsettled after the previous day. No, she corrected mentally, the previous evening. Making love with Nicholas had been everything she had dreamt of and more, but it had broken her heart not to be able to speak of her love. And she had sensed a reticence in her husband too.

Was he unable to let go of the thought that he had been trapped into this marriage? Into the mass of obligations it had laid upon him? A stepson and the guardianship of a great estate were no easy burdens to take up, and she dreaded the thought that he might come to resent them—and her.

Perhaps she was bringing trouble down by imagining it, she told herself. The last thing Nicholas needed on top of everything else was a brooding wife. Certainly she had woken to the drift of Nicholas's hands over her body, the press of his lips on her nape. And they had made love twice again, both times with an urgency that had thrilled her.

She smiled at him over the breakfast table and was rewarded with an answering smile that made her toes curl.

* * *

By the time they reached Bagshot, halfway to Basingstoke, Nanny had been reduced to using smelling salts and Sophie, who had rescued her from Freddie's violent objections to coach travel after two hours, was, she declared, quite ready to sell her darling child to the next female she saw silly enough to take him.

'Frederick,' Nicholas said, 'I think we should drive the carriage ourselves.'

Freddie stopped howling and stared at him. 'Pas?'

Nicholas jerked the check cord and when the carriage came to a halt got down and held out his hands for his stepson.

'Nicholas? I didn't mean… Will he be safe up there?'

'He will. And it isn't raining. I'll wrap him well.'

Nicholas, with Freddie clinging like a monkey around his neck, told the groom to take the rumble seat at the back of the vehicle, passed up the wide-eyed Duke to the coachman and swung up onto the box.

Sophie, hanging out of the window at a perilous angle, heard no cries of terror but instead a gurgle of laughter.

'Horsey, Pas! Fast!'

Well, so long as they didn't send James the coachman completely distracted, so that he drove off the road, she supposed it would be all right, she thought, settling back against the squabs in blissful silence.

Nicholas was going to make a wonderful father. She rested one hand on her stomach. She might already be carrying his child. The sooner the better, she thought. Freddie must learn to share both her and Nicholas. It would do him good and his half-siblings would grow up close in age to him—he was a strong-willed child, and having some healthy competition to rub his corners off would be no bad thing.

But she knew it was not the benefits to Freddie that were putting the smile on her lips—it was the thought of Nicholas's child. They would be a family, and she would be able to express the love that she kept hidden and he would not know it was as much for him as the child.

They arrived in Basingstoke just in time for Freddie's supper—although when Sophie stood looking up at the men on the box she wondered whether she would be able to wake him long enough to eat, let alone have his bath.

He was curled up in a blanket in Nicholas's arms, one chubby fist tight on the end of a rein. Nicholas handed him down to the groom and then climbed down himself.

'I doubt we are going to be able to keep him off the box from now on,' he said ruefully as they went into the inn. 'We may have an amateur stagecoach driver on our hands.'

Freddie woke up as they entered the private sitting room Nicholas had reserved.

'Mama, druv,' he announced, then beamed up at Nicholas and gave him a smacking kiss on the cheek.

'He loves you,' Sophie said as Nanny, recovered after a good nap in the coach, retrieved the little boy and bore him off for supper.

Nicholas shrugged. 'He associates me with treats, that is all.'

'No. Many people spoil him, but he doesn't react to them as he does to you. Right from the beginning it was Pas this and Pas that. He likes Duncan Grant, but he loves you.'

For some reason that made the colour come up over Nicholas's cheekbones. 'He's a loveable child,' he said gruffly.

'With good taste and sound judgement,' Sophie retorted, distracted by the maid coming in with a tea tray. 'Thank you—put it there, if you please. That will be all.'

When she turned back there was something in Nicholas's expression that caught her attention. Or perhaps it was his stillness.

'What is it?'

'Nothing.' He shook his head. 'He gets it from you, does he? His good taste and sound judgement?'

There was something there that she could not read—an undercurrent…almost a bitterness. 'Why, yes, of course,' Sophie said, laughing. 'Freddie owes all his best points, except his blue eyes, to his mother.'

Nick spent the whole of the next two days on the box of the carriage. Freddie was firmly held between his knees, convinced that he was driving with the ends of the reins in his hands. The coachman had found some whip points to tuck into a buttonhole in the little boy's smock dress, just like a real driver, and he stayed awake for hours at a time, chattering incomprehensibly to both Nick and the coachman.

Then he would suddenly fall asleep, and Nick would sit enjoying the solid weight in his arms and the view from the box over the wintry landscape.

Sophie was best left alone to rest, he told himself. He had found tear traces on her cheeks again that morning, but he'd pretended not to notice how rapidly she'd slipped from the bed to wash her face. If it had not been for that then he would have been the happiest of men, he thought as he dug out a handkerchief to blow Freddie's nose.

That almost made him laugh out loud. Here he was, Nick Pascoe, rogue and adventurer, undutiful son, occasional cat burglar and lock-picker, acting as nursemaid and nose-wiper to an imperious small boy and tying himself in knots because a woman did not love him.

It was pathetic, he thought, mentally flaying himself. The way he hoped…the way he watched her and listened to every change of tone in her voice, every change of expression in those lovely eyes.

They were spectacularly good in bed, they laughed at the same things, they could be silent together comfortably—what more did he want?

Everything.

When they finally rolled to a halt in front of Prior Marten House Sophie was weary of travelling, but grateful for Nicholas's consideration in planning their journey. She had never slept so much, she thought, putting her hand on his arm as he opened the carriage door for her.

'Welcome to Prior Marten, my lady.'

'But it is lovely!'

And it was. She was used to the overpowering grandeur of Vine Mount House, but this smaller house was refreshing. It was still large, with perhaps a dozen or more bedchambers, she guessed, but its scale was domestic, with two short curving wings either side of a central block, all built from a warm honey-coloured stone under a stone-tiled roof.

The wings looked as though they reached out welcoming arms to new arrivals, she thought, and as she thought it the front door opened and staff streamed out to line the steps.

'You look happy,' Nick said a week later, when he came upon Sophie strolling in the pale December sunshine on the wide south-facing terrace that looked out across the small parkland to the lake.

'I do love—' She broke off and sneezed. 'Do excuse me. The cold air always does that to me. I was saying I do love this house,' she said, turning to him with a wide smile. 'What is it, Nicholas?'

He recovered himself fast. 'You surprise me, that is all. I had not expected such a modest house to appeal to you after all the splendour you are used to.'

Fool. Do you expect her to breezily announce that she loves you?

'But that is just the point. It is homely and domestic. Large enough for entertaining, but comfortable for family life. I love this rolling countryside, and the woods will be wonderful in spring. And the staff are excellent, are they not?'

'Excellent,' Nick echoed as Sophie chattered on, happily extolling the virtues of all the things that she loved about Prior Marten.

He could not decide whether to tell her of his feelings or not. One moment he told himself he was a coward, dreading rejection, the next that it would place an intolerable burden on her—having to live with a man who loved her when, for her, this was a marriage of convenience. One that made her weep softly at night.

But now, seeing her so joyful, so relaxed and at

home, here with him, he caught her hand and tugged gently so that she pirouetted in to his arms.

'Nicholas! We're in the middle of the terrace in broad daylight.'

'May a man not kiss his wife on his own terrace at any hour?' he asked, and without waiting for an answer he did so.

He kissed her gently, but deeply, with every ounce of care and intensity in him, thinking over and over, *I love you, I love you,* as though she might hear him.

When he broke the kiss she stared up at him, lips parted, swollen from his passion, her eyes wide and sparkling green.

'Nicholas…?' She sounded breathless.

'Sophie, I have to tell you… I haven't found the words, and it is difficult to say, but—'

There was a shriek and a thump from inside, echoing through the open long windows of the garden room. Then came the high-pitched wail of a small child in distress.

'Freddie!' Sophie gathered up her skirts and ran.

'Damnation.' Nick followed her, cursing even as he worried.

He found Freddie in the hall, howling his head off at the bottom of the staircase, and Sophie leaning over him, trying to hold him still.

'Hush, darling. Let Mama see what is wrong. How

far did he fall?' she asked the nursemaid who was hovering beside them, twisting her hands into her apron.

'The last six steps, my lady. He turned around to say something to me and tripped over his own feet, I think. Oh, ma'am… I should have had him on his reins, but he hates them so.'

'It is not your fault, Madge,' Sophie soothed. 'Freddie, do try and lie still for me.'

She sent Nick an anguished look, and he recalled sharply that her husband had died in just such a fall.

'It was a short distance,' he said calmly. 'He is more shocked than hurt, I'll wager.' Nick knelt beside her, pinned the child to the floor with gentle hands on his shoulders and said firmly, 'Quiet, Freddie.' He hadn't much hope of being obeyed, but the boy gave a hiccup and stopped howling. 'There's a brave man. Now, let Mama see. I expect you've got some fine bruises to show James Coachman.'

The mention of his wonderful new friend—he of the multi-caped greatcoat, huge mother-of-pearl buttons and fascinating red nose—worked magic. The tears still flowed, but Freddie sniffed and lay still.

'Can you wiggle your fingers for me? And your toes? Good boy,' Nick said. 'What hurts most?'

'Bum,' said Freddie.

'Where did you get that dreadful word?' Sophie said, half scandalised, half laughing.

'The boot boy, my lady,' the nursemaid said. 'And

it's true. He tumbled and fell hard on his behind. I don't think he hit his head at all.'

'When I hurt myself and it is not bad enough to need a doctor I get my valet to patch me up,' Nick told Freddie. 'Shall we go and see Sitwell? Just us men together, eh?'

How much of that Freddie understood, Nick wasn't sure, but the offer of doing something that didn't involve nursemaids and females fussing seemed to appeal. He held up his arms and Nick picked him up.

'We shall have to stop feeding you, young Freddie,' he grumbled as he carried him upstairs. 'You weigh a ton.'

Had Freddie prevented him from making a major mistake or ruined a perfect moment? Probably the first, he thought, as Sitwell produced the full array of medical equipment that a gentleman's gentleman thought essential and solemnly dealt with the young Duke's bruised posterior and damaged dignity.

If he was going to make a declaration he needed to think it through…word it perfectly. It would be different falling in love with a woman one was courting. Then declarations could be made before any commitment was made, and if the lady felt the same, she could say so. If she did not, and did not feel she would develop sufficient fondness, then no harm had been done.

There were enough 'suitable' marriages made for the discovery that one was in love with one's wife to be commonplace, he supposed. But it was not a thing that any gentleman spoke about, even to his closest friends. There was not much hope of any help from that quarter.

But Sophie had been forced into this marriage and that made a difference. She might have liked him well enough beforehand, and she certainly desired him, but she had not expected to have to deal with his love, and the thought of her being kind and tactful about it turned his stomach.

He was not used to finding himself at a loss for words, or a way of expressing his feelings, but now it felt as though he could not catch hold of the right phrase, the right way to behave. It was making him angry. Not with Sophie—never that, he thought—but with himself.

What had Nicholas been about to say, out there on the terrace in the wake of that wonderful kiss?

Nothing good, she was certain.

Nicholas was a man who spoke his mind, and had no problem expressing himself. And yet he had seemed hesitant, stilted. Whatever it was, it had not been easy for him to think it, let alone say it, and the fact that he had not returned to the subject once Freddie's little drama was over only proved the point.

And why had it been preceded by that intense but gentle kiss? Almost as though he was apologising in advance for something?

* * *

Two days later, when he still had not said anything, but she had been brooding on it constantly, the idea came to her that he had guessed her feelings for him and had been trying to explain to her gently that theirs was not a love match and never could be.

She put down the brush that she had been drawing through her hair, ready for Foskett to pin it up again for dinner.

Since then Nicholas had been almost formal with her, she realised. He had kept his distance, seemed preoccupied, and had even excused himself from her bed last night—they had been taking turn and turn-about with bedchambers—pleading a headache.

'That should be my excuse,' she muttered now.

'My lady?'

'Nothing. The cream silk this evening, I think.'

It was not her grandest evening gown, but it was the one that she knew suited her best, and it was the one that had inspired Nicholas to quite glorious heights of passion a week ago.

'And the simplest arrangement of my hair.'

So simple that it would come down if just a few pins were removed.

If Nicholas would not tell her what was wrong, or what he had started to say on the terrace, then she would seduce it out of him.

The cream silk whispered around her legs as she

walked into the drawing room. The simple thin gold chain around her neck caressed her skin before vanishing into her cleavage, and the plain gold ear bobs swung against her neck, where she had sprayed the finest mist of the perfume Nicholas had given her.

The memory of Nicholas making love to her with his mouth and tongue and teeth as she'd gripped the drawing room door in an effort not to scream was one that haunted her. He had used the same technique again—although it had not seemed so wickedly daring when they were lying in bed. But she had never ventured to make love to him the same way.

Now, she thought as she watched his shadowed gaze on her, she would find the courage to do it. If it reduced him to anything like the state it had left her in, he would tell her anything.

'I am in the mood for champagne,' she said as she sat opposite him, taking the sofa so she could recline a little. She was going to need something to help her, because she never tried to seduce a man before.

'Peters—champagne. Well iced,' Nicholas said to the footman. 'You look very lovely tonight,' he added, when the man had left the room.

'Thank you.' She looked across at him from under her lashes, hoping she looked provocative and not as though she had something in her eye.

When the wine came she drank a glass, and then another. Dinner was announced and she gestured to Peters to bring the bottle through and to refill her glass.

She normally only drank one glass of wine with her food, and the effect of three glasses of champagne was miraculous. She felt beautiful, powerful, witty...

Nicholas was watching her like a hawk—she was obviously succeeding in riveting his attention. And when she made love to him in that provocative manner he would tell her anything, she was certain.

'I think that maybe you have had enough, my dear,' Nicholas said, when she waved a hand towards her glass.

'Oh, just one more...it is almost empty.' She nodded to Peters.

He filled it again with a glance at Nicholas, who shrugged and pushed his half-eaten dessert aside.

'Thank you, Peters, that will be all. We will ring when we need you.'

There—it had worked. He could not wait to be alone with her.

Sophie got to her feet, surprised to find the room shifting a little as she did so. Odd... Still, it gave what was surely a seductive sway to her walk as she went to where Nicholas stood at the head of the table.

'Sophie, what the blazes are you about?'

'I'm seducing you,' she said, twining her arms around him.

If he would just sit down, then she would kneel and—

'You are drunk,' he said. 'And since when have you

needed to seduce me? Or drink wine to give you the courage?'

She pouted. It shouldn't be this difficult, surely?

'Sophie, what is wrong with you?' Nicholas turned around and sat her down none too gently down on his chair. 'What the devil are you up to?'

Her head spun. It wasn't working, and Nicholas was angry with her. He would never love her, and now she probably disgusted him as well. A lady never became drunk—never even the slightest bit tipsy—and she, she realised hazily, was very drunk indeed. She should have eaten a proper dinner, but she had been too excited to do more than peck at her food.

'I couldn't bear it, you see...' she began to explain, stumbling over the words. 'So I thought...'

She lost her train of thought and looked up at him hopelessly.

'You couldn't bear the thought of making love with me?' he demanded harshly. 'You have given every indication of liking it well enough before now.'

'Oh, I do.' Sophie nodded emphatically, and then wished very much that she had not. 'It's not *that*. It's you...'

The words trailed away and the room swirled as she slithered helplessly to the floor.

Chapter Twenty-One

Her brothers had often complained of having no recollection of the evening before when they awoke with hangovers. Sophie found that she had only too vivid a memory of what had happened.

She had been drunk, she had made a fool of herself, she had disgusted Nicholas, she still had not the slightest idea of what it was that was troubling him, and she was utterly miserable.

Foskett, thin-lipped with a disapproval that she was unable to express, handed her a disgusting-looking mixture in a glass as she sat in bed, moaning as the light from the windows hit her.

'Drink that, my lady. Mr Sitwell says it is a certain cure.'

'What's in it?'

'I have no idea, my lady. He said to drink it down in one.'

Sophie did, and gagged. 'That is vile.'

'Then he said you must have half an hour outside in the fresh air and a good cooked breakfast.'

'Really?' Sophie queried faintly. 'I think I'm dying.'

'Mr Sitwell says they all say that.'

To her surprise, the cure worked, and she was feeling only a little fragile when Peters found her in the rose arbour.

'His Lordship's compliments, my lady, and would you be good enough to join him in his study?'

So she was summoned for a lecture, was she?

Sophie felt her temper rise, although she knew that it was mostly defensiveness. She had been in the wrong, but even so...

'You sent for me?'

Nicholas did not look as though he had passed a good night. 'I requested your company. Sophie, what the devil was that about last night?'

It was apparently a rhetorical question because he ploughed straight on.

'I know that neither of us wanted this marriage, that our hands were forced, but I would have thought you'd be able to tell me that you felt you had to take to drink before you could tolerate my company.'

He always seemed to be able to mask his feelings, but now she saw anger in the dark eyes and in the set of his jaw. And something ese... Not hurt, surely?

'But I—'

'I was surprised that you could have deceived me so effectively. I had believed that we were in a tolerable state together.'

Tolerable? No, he wasn't hurt—how could anyone be hurt over something that was merely 'tolerable'?

'I am very fond of Frederick…' Nicholas was still talking. 'And you and I have always got on well, or so I had thought. There is no need to be afraid of me, Sophie, surely?'

'Yes, but—'

'I realise that you have been used to having everything just as you like it, as you order, and that this must seem like a comedown. But I thought you had accepted that that would happen when we married. You are not the Duchess of St Edmunds any longer.'

Something snapped. 'But I *am* the mother of the Duke, the widow of the Duke, and the daughter of the Marquess of Radley. I am not diminished, whoever I marry. I am delighted that you find our marriage tolerable. No, do not interrupt me! I would like to get more than half a sentence said. I am going home for a few weeks and taking Freddie. We have been away too long.'

'Home? This is your home.' He was on his feet now.

Sophie tipped up her chin and did her best to look down her nose at him. 'It is one of them, yes.'

'It is not convenient for me to leave, Sophie. The land agent and the manager of the Home Farm and I are only halfway through a long list of the decisions we must make. If you still want to go in a few weeks' time I will take you then.'

'I do not require your escort, thank you, Nicholas. I can take grooms as outriders. I know the business of the duchy, and can manage that very well myself. I have not suddenly become feeble-minded upon marriage.'

'I never thought that you were!' he flung at her. 'I do not know what to think any more. What to feel. But you will not leave. I am your husband and I know what is best for you.'

'I see.' Sophie stood up, the headache that had been lurking behind her eyes suddenly emerging at full force. 'Well, it did not take many weeks of marriage for my worst fears about it to be proved right.'

The skin seemed to tighten over his face as though she had slapped him.

'I am sorry that is how you feel. I have an appointment with the land agent at the Home Farm now, perhaps that will allow tempers to cool.' He reached out one hand across the desk. 'Sophie.'

No, I will not be coaxed into submission.

She wanted to take his hand so much that it hurt, but she knew that if she did she would never manage to find a way to love him, to be true to herself, and somehow to make this marriage work. She needed time and space to think, to feel, without the fear of betraying her feelings.

'Then we will talk again when I return this afternoon,' Nicholas said, his voice flat.

She swept out without answering him and went directly upstairs to the nursery. 'Nanny, please pack the essentials for His Grace. We are travelling to Vine Mount House immediately. We are taking one carriage. I wish to leave within the hour.'

'The hour—? But, my lady...'

'The hour.'

Foskett was in the dressing room, rolling up stockings, when Sophie walked in.

'Pack at once, Foskett. We are leaving urgently for Vine Mount House. I have just spoke to James Coachman. The carriage will be at the door in an hour. Just the necessities—I have enough clothing at Vine Mount.'

They rattled away down the drive with an armed groom up on the box and two outriders. Sophie had no intention of putting Freddie at risk from the many dangers of the road, even if Nicholas appeared to think that marriage had dulled her wits.

It was about one hundred and thirty miles to Oxford, she calculated, staring at the road book. They would be there by midnight unless the weather broke and could spend the night. There were enough good inns there to be sure of finding accommodation, even for a very late arrival. Then another long day, or perhaps two, would see them home.

'Mama?'

'Yes, darling?'

'Pas?'

'He is busy, my love. We have to go home now.'

Freddie hadn't realised that Nicholas would not be with them, she realised. He was going to be very upset when he did. This was not going to be a pleasant journey for any of them.

She hoped the letter that she had left would explain matters. She had said in it that she felt it best they spent a little time apart. That she looked forward to welcoming Nicholas to Vine Mount House in a week or so, when his business at Prior Marten was complete.

Dignified, pleasant… Really, there was nothing in it he could object to. It was hardly as though he would be hurt. He did not love her, after all.

That unpleasant but true fact stilled Sophie's conscience as far as Yeovil, which they reached two hours later. She should be feeling better, she thought. Her temper had cooled, she no longer had to hide her emotions from Nicholas, and she had done nothing irrevocable. In a few weeks they could begin again afresh.

So why was she feeling so miserable?

Because I love him, she thought as she drank a hurried cup of tea at the Crown Inn and Freddie petted a kitten under Nanny's watchful eye.

'They are worth all the pain and the anxiety, aren't they, my lady?' Madge, the nursemaid, had followed the direction of her gaze. 'Oh, excuse me, my lady. I was thinking aloud.'

'That is perfectly all right, Madge. But what do you know about the pain and the anxiety?'

'I'm the oldest of six, my lady. I helped deliver the two youngest and I know Ma wouldn't be without any of us. She says you can't put a limit on love—it just keeps coming.'

No, love just came to you, Sophie thought. Whether it was for a child or for a man. And it wasn't all rose petals and doves and sweetness and light. It was worry and pain—physical and mental. It was a struggle, because loving someone didn't mean they were perfect, or that you were. Or that you were two halves of one whole, either. You had to be prepared to bridge gaps. Or perhaps it was like darning a hole in your stocking. Whatever it was, it needed work to make a whole out of two individuals.

It was as though being away from Nicholas had cleared a mist, allowed her to see clearly.

I haven't been honest with him. I should have told him, not kept secrets from him. He is no fool. He must have known I was hiding something. I must go back. Love is too important to lie about...to keep hidden.

She owed Nicholas an explanation. If they found it difficult to live together after she had told him—well, they would work something out. It couldn't be worse than this, with anger between them and secrets. What did her pride matter? It wasn't love if she couldn't trust, wouldn't give.

'We are going back,' she announced to the rest of the staff, who had gathered around a table by the door with their own refreshments. 'I have forgotten something very important. I am sorry to have inflicted an unnecessary journey on you.'

'Where are we, my lady?' Nanny asked.

Freddie had fallen asleep on her lap at last, placated by the promise that they were going back to Pas.

'Less than an hour from home now,' Sophie said as she studied the map.

Staring at it wouldn't make the miles go any further, she knew that, but she was counting off every milestone, every village in the darkness.

'I expect—' She broke off as the carriage came to a jolting halt.

'Oh, my Lord,' Nanny said, clutching Freddie to her. 'Highwaymen!'

Sophie dropped the window glass and leaned out, peering through the gloom. 'No, not highwaymen.' She swallowed. 'It is Lord Denham.'

She had counted the miles until she reached him.

Now she realised she had no idea what she was going to say to him.

He rode right up beside the window, his mare snorting and sidling on a tight rein.

'Sophie.'

He looked older, if that were possible in only a few hours. There were lines on his face she had never noticed before and the dark eyes were like onyx.

The lump in her throat was making it impossible to speak.

He swung down off the mare and opened the carriage door. 'Get down, Duchess. I will take you home.'

His tone was neutral, but he had called her *Duchess*, his pet name for her. Did he mean it affectionately, or was it a jibe?

Sophie mentally threaded her darning needle and stepped down. 'Thank you, James, you may drive on now.'

They stood in silence, watching the carriage vanish around a bend in the road.

'We will walk a little. I have ridden hard. How far did you get?'

'To Yeovil. We stopped to give Freddie a little break and I realised that I had to come back.'

She matched his even tone as they walked without touching along the muddy road.

'Why? I was angry with you, and spoke in a way that you might not be able to forgive. I had thought that I was losing you. I am sorry, Sophie. I should have been able to control my fears better and not allowed them to escape in anger.'

When she stopped walking and stared up at him he added, 'So why come back?'

His fears? He thought he was losing me?

'Had you forgotten something?' Nicholas prompted as she stumbled into motion again.

'Yes. Something very important.' This was easier while she was not looking at him. 'I realised that in being less than honest with you about my feelings I was doing us a great wrong. I would be taking a risk telling you the truth, of course, but it came to me that I could not always do the safe thing and that I was being a coward.'

Nicholas stopped walking too. 'You mean that you had decided that you could not live with me at all? Sophie, I never wanted to make you unhappy. You suffered enough with your first marriage. I thought this could be different, but I think I have become the man you always feared you'd remarry.'

'No!'

She turned and faced him, just far enough away that she could see his face, and also his body. His expression, always so carefully schooled, was betraying him now. Could she read pain and hurt? Surely not fear? It might be a trick of the poor light, but it gave her the courage to go on.

'I love you, Nicholas. I am very sorry if this is a…a burden for you, but I think you knew I was hiding something, didn't you?'

When he just stood there, eyes fathomless, lips parted as though on a sigh, she made herself go on.

'I quite understand that you were forced into this marriage. I do not expect you to pretend to love me.'

'Good.'

'Good…?' she faltered.

She had expected rejection or pity, but not this flat response.

'Because it is very hard pretending that I do not.'

'You…?'

What did he mean? Surely not that—?

'I love you, Duchess.' He dropped the reins and reached for her hands. 'I love you so much that I found it impossible to say the words because I did not think I could bear the pain of your rejection. You talk of cowardice, but I was worse. A viscount with a courtesy title, a man with one estate to his name and a history as an adventurer, a plausible rogue, ready to do whatever it took to earn his crust—and here I am married to a duchess. A clever, brave, beautiful, *perfect* duchess, who does not want to be married to me. I did not think for a moment that if I confessed that I loved you, you would be anything but kind about it.' His mouth twisted into a wry smile.

'Oh, that was what I feared too.' She clung to his

hands. 'That you would be kind about it and pity me. My wretched pride.'

'It is more than pride—deeper than pride. Sophie, I love you so much that I thought I could bear keeping silent rather than risk your rejection. It made me a coward and it made me angry with myself. I said some cruel things—things that must have hurt you, made you believe I did not understand the pain of your past, the sacrifices you made to marry me.'

His smile twisted with rueful self-mockery and she lifted both hands to cup his face. 'No coward. Simply human, my love.'

Nicholas caught her hands in his, kissed them. 'I never thought I would hear you say those words except in my dreams. Duchess, can you truly love me?'

'Oh, with all my heart.'

Sophie had no idea which of them moved, but she found herself in his arms, being kissed until she thought she might swoon for lack of air—and she found that she did not care.

This was a miracle. Nicholas loved her. He understood what she felt, why she had hidden the truth from him, because he felt it too.

They might have stood there in the middle of the highway until the cold finally roused them from their trance. Instead Sophie found herself staggering off-balance as the mare butted Nicholas in the back.

'I believe our chaperon is giving us a hint,' he said,

still keeping one arm around her. 'Might I suggest a bed?'

'How far is it?' She lifted her skirts to look at her kid boots, designed more for their looks than walking along a road in December.

'She can carry us both.' Nicholas mounted, then reached down for her. 'Hold up your arms.'

He lifted her, twisting her in mid-air so that she landed sitting sideways in front of him, and the mare began to walk, tossing her head a little—in protest, Sophie supposed, at the extra load.

She laid her head against Nicholas's chest and relaxed into the horse's rhythm. 'Why did you follow me?'

'I went to the Home Farm seething, but more at my own idiocy than at anything you'd said. By the time I got there I knew I had let my own frustrations and emotions get the better of me, and that I had no right to lose my temper with you when something was obviously wrong. So I resolved to go back after the meeting and apologise…try and discover what was behind your unhappiness. And when I did, I found your note. The meeting had lasted longer than I had expected, and then I wasted half an hour kicking the furniture.'

'Oh. Nothing is broken, I trust?' she asked, hoping to make him smile.

She heard it in his voice when he said, 'My big toe, I expect. And then, when I was sitting with my head in my hands, feeling sorry for myself, I started think-ing…letting myself feel. It was as though I could hear your voice, feel your touch.' His arm tightened around her. 'I thought, *What have I got to lose? At least I will have been honest with her.* So I set out to follow you. I told myself that if you didn't want me I would go back. And if you did— But I didn't allow myself to think that far…hope that much.'

'When did you realise that you loved me?'

She tipped her head and kissed the only bit of him she could reach—the edge of his jaw. It made him growl and twist to catch her lips with his.

'When I turned and saw you walking towards me on our wedding day. It was like someone drawing back the curtains on a darkened room. I could see clearly for the first time. And I began to realise that you were not the conventional lady that you strove so hard to portray. You were a creature of courage and independence and fierce loyalties. It made me love you more, even as I feared that it made you quite unobtainable. And you?'

'When you were stabbed,' she admitted.

'Is it illegal to be this happy?' she asked, after a while.

Perhaps she had slept, lulled by the beat of Nicholas's heart and the steady plod of the horse.

'Probably. Although this is damnably uncomfort-able. My toe hurts like the devil—I wasn't joking about kicking the furniture—and it looks as if it is going to rain, so we may be paying the fine for it already. At least we are too uncomfortable to be dreaming.'

'Oh, it is so good to laugh with you again. I thought we had lost that.'

Sophie felt the pressure of his cheek against the top of her head. 'We will find the laughter again…it only went into hiding,' Nicholas said. 'And look, there are the lights in the East Lodge. We'll go in there and cut across the park.'

'Freddie will be so pleased to see you.'

'It will be mutual. But that must wait until tomorrow.'

'Why?'

'Because I fully intend to take my duchess to bed, and to stay there until she has completely convinced me that her love for me is not my dream.'

'Mutual convincing is required,' Sophie said, suddenly very much awake.

'Oh, I intend to be very mutual indeed,' Nicholas said. 'And here is the rain.'

He urged the mare into a canter, scattering the little herd of fallow deer that had been asleep under the trees, and they went straight as an arrow for the house.

Chapter Twenty-Two

What the staff thought Sophie had no idea, and she never did find out. The two of them ran in through the side entrance from the stable yard, dripping wet, and made straight for the stairs.

'We are not to be disturbed,' Nicholas said as they passed Lubbock, the butler. 'Not for anything short of the house burning down or His Grace being in danger. Understood?'

'Yes, my lord. Absolutely, my lord. Food, my lord?'

'We'll ring.'

Nicholas tossed Sophie over his shoulder and began to climb the stairs.

'This should be introduced at Gentleman Jackson's boxing salon as part of his fitness regime—wife-toting.'

He sounded slightly out of breath, and Sophie suppressed a giggle. When they reached their suite he went to his own bedchamber, set her on her feet and went to lock the doors. Then he reeled towards the bed and collapsed on his back.

'Come and be a dutiful wife, Duchess, and pull off my boots.'

'As my lord commands.'

Sophie went and tugged at each boot in turn, stood them beside a chair, then took off her spencer, her gloves, her half-boots and began to undo her gown.

'I can do that.' Nicholas came up on his elbows.

'You stay there, my lord. It occurs to me that you have made love to me, and we have made love together, but I have never made love to you.'

The idea visibly appealed to him, Sophie thought with a surge of confidence. She wriggled and twisted and managed to undress herself right down to her corset and stockings—an ensemble that she knew always met with Nicholas's approval—and then she began to undress him.

That was much easier, and finally she stood at the foot of the bed, tossed aside his breeches and took a deep breath. Did she dare? What if she did it all wrong? It could not be as difficult as telling him she loved him, could it?

'Sophie? What are you doing?'

Nicholas was up on his elbows again, peering down the length of his body to where she had climbed on to the foot of the bed and was slowly crawling up from his feet.

'Lie back and relax,' she purred, reaching out to curl

her fingers around the hard length of him. 'I have told you that I love you—now I will demonstrate.'

'Relax?' Nicholas shot up into a sitting position.

Sophie reached out her free hand, placed it in the middle of his chest and pushed him flat. 'Tell me if I am not doing this right.'

And then she said nothing for quite some time.

Nick pulled his wife onto his chest and sighed deeply. They had made love three times and it was now past midnight. He had thought himself bone-weary after the day's turmoil and fears, the hard ride and the emotion of their reconciliation. Then they had ridden back in the dark and fallen into bed, and Sophie had demonstrated a natural talent for reducing a man to a melting puddle of desire that exceeded even their most passionate embraces before.

It should have finished him for the night, but instead he'd found the energy to make love to her again, after they had dozed in each other's arms for a while.

He felt decidedly strange, and he had to puzzle for a moment before he realised what it was.

He was happy. Purely, simply, honestly happy.

And hungry.

'Duchess?'

'Mmm...?'

'Are you hungry?'

She sat up, her glorious hair spilling over her naked

breasts. 'Yes, I am. My goodness, it is hours since we have eaten or drunk anything.'

'We will go and raid the kitchen—it is far too late to disturb the servants.'

Besides which, he wanted her all to himself for a few hours longer. Weeks would not be long enough to come to terms with this happiness…with the miracle of loving and being loved, of being able to express that feeling and hear his beloved's reply.

They found robes and slippers, took chamber sticks, and then, grinning at each other like naughty children in search of a midnight feast, crept down to the kitchen.

There was most of a roast chicken, a loaf and butter, a half-consumed apple pie and a jug of thick cream.

Sophie put it all on the table and cut the bread while Nick filled tankards with cider. As he did so she had the fleeting thought that they owed all this to Amanda Sweeting. If it had not been for her they would never have met, and 'Estelle Doucette' would never have prompted the scandal that had ensured their marriage.

But she said nothing; there was no need ever to think about the woman again.

'To my wife,' Nicholas said, standing at one end of the scrubbed pine table and raising his tankard. 'To the love of my life. My miracle. My Sophie. When I met her she was a dutiful, dignified duchess. Now she is my viscountess and—'

'Vivid? Vivacious?' Sophie suggested, laughing at him.

'Voracious?' Nick tossed back, making her blush. 'Oh, Sophie, you have taken a rogue with no future who had learnt to bury his feelings deep, and you have turned him into a man who cannot believe his good fortune and has everything to live for.'

Sophie thought she must be glowing with happiness, contentment, excitement. This man was hers to love, to raise children with, grow old with.

'To my husband,' she said, lifting her own tankard. 'I fell in love with a rogue and I would not want anyone else but that man by my side. I had believed my happiness lay in doing my duty. Now I realise that all I need to find it is to follow my heart—and that leads straight to you.'

* * * * *

Author Note

Although the game of camping, or campball, is often described as an early ancestor of football, it was more akin to rugby, with the ball thrown from player to player to reach a goal. It dates back to at least the fifteenth century, and was particularly popular in East Anglia.

Originally it was played from one end of a town or village to another, but by the nineteenth century it was usually confined to common land, or to a 'camping ground', and reached a peak of popularity in the eighteen-thirties, before football took over.

It could be a very brutal game, lasting at least three hours, and in one recorded contest lasted for fourteen. Rules hardly existed and were ignored, grudges were acted out, fights were common, and much drink was taken. A notorious match at Diss in Norfolk in the early nineteenth century left nine men dead.

I have taken the liberty of moving the game from the common into the town of Diss, where the building that was once the Dolphin Inn still stands.

COMING SOON!

We really hope you enjoyed reading this book. If you're looking for more romance be sure to head to the shops when new books are available on

Thursday 13th April

To see which titles are coming soon, please visit

millsandboon.co.uk/nextmonth

MILLS & BOON

MILLS & BOON ®

Coming next month

THE NIGHT SHE MET THE DUKE
Sarah Mallory

Pru was sitting opposite the stranger at the table, sipping at a glass of small beer, while her companion feasted on the cold meats and pickles she had provided. How prosaic she was. How ordinary. The heroine of her novel would have fainted off to find an intruder in her house. She would not have *fed* him.

"What do you find so amusing?" Her companion's voice cut through these wry thoughts. She looked up to find him watching her. He waved a knife in her direction. "You were smiling."

"Not intentionally."

"Perhaps not." He studied her. "I see now. Your mouth curves up naturally at the corners."

"Yes." She looked away. "It is a fault."

"It is as if you are always on the edge of laughter. How can that be a bad thing?"

"My mouth is too wide."

"I do not think so."

Pru realized this was not a proper conversation to be having with a strange man and did not reply.

"May I know to whom I am indebted for this supper?" he asked her presently.

"To my aunt, Mrs. Clifford. This is her house."

His eyes narrowed. "It is your name I wish to know."

"I am Miss Clifford."

He raised his brows and she firmly closed her lips, determined not to tell him her first name.

"And who are you, sir?"

"Garrick Chauntry. Duke of Hartland."

"So, you really are a nobleman."

Continue reading
THE NIGHT SHE MET THE DUKE
Amanda McCabe

Available next month
www.millsandboon.co.uk

LET'S TALK

Romance

For exclusive extracts, competitions and special offers, find us online:

f facebook.com/millsandboon

𝕏 @MillsandBoon

⃝ @MillsandBoonUK

♪ @MillsandBoonUK

Get in touch on 01413 063 232